The Mysterious Affair at Styled Magazine

C.A. Larmer is a journalist, editor, teacher and author of multiple crime series, stand-alone novels and a non-fiction book about pioneering surveyors in Papua New Guinea. Christina grew up in PNG, was educated in Australia, and spent many years working in Sydney, London, Los Angeles and New York. She now lives with her musician husband, boomerang sons and their very cheeky Bluey on the east coast of Australia.

Sign up for news, views and giveaways:
calarmer.com

ALSO BY C.A. LARMER

The Murder Mystery Book Club series:
The Murder Mystery Book Club (Book 1)
Danger On the SS Orient (Book 2)
Death Under the Stars (Book 3)
When There Were 9 (Book 4)
The Widow on the Honeymoon Cruise (Book 5)
Gone Guest (Book 6)
Peril on the Indian Pacific (Book 7)

The Ghostwriter Mystery series:
Killer Twist (Book 1)
A Plot to Die For (Book 2)
Last Writes (Book 3)
Dying Words (Book 4)
Words Can Kill (Book 5)
A Note Before Dying (Book 6)
Without a Word (Book 7)

The Posthumous Mystery series:
Do Not Go Gentle
Do Not Go Alone

The Sleuths of Last Resort:
Blind Men Don't Dial Zero
Smart Girls Don't Trust Strangers
Good Girls Don't Drink Vodka

PLUS
*After the Ferry: A Gripping
Psychological Novel*

An Island Lost

C.A. LARMER

The Mysterious Affair at Styled Magazine

The Murder Mystery Book Club

(Book 8)

LARMER MEDIA

Published by Larmer Media
Northern NSW, Australia
calarmer.com
ISBN: 978-0-6459449-5-2

Cover design by Nimo Pyle
Cover photography by Chiociolla, InspirationGP
Edited by D.A. Sarac, The Editing Pen
& Elaine Rivers, with thanks

To fans of this series who joined the Book Club
from the very beginning.
This one's for you.

CAST OF CHARACTERS

The Murder Mystery Book Club
Alicia Finlay (club founder/journalist)
Lynette Finlay (her sister/restaurant manager/chef)
Claire Hargreaves (vintage-store owner)
Missy Corner (librarian)
Perry Gordon (palaeontologist)
Veronica "Ronnie" Westera (wealthy philanthropist)
Queenie Dobson (executive assistant to Claire's husband)

Arial Publishing House
Ted Johnson (CEO)
Dionne Barnes (Ted's Executive Assistant)
Bob Chalmers (Chief Financial Officer)
Austin Smythe (Manager Sales & Circulation)
Arabella (Director of Human Resources)
Blake (Receptionist)

Styled Magazine
Saffron Toya-Jones (Editor)
Frances (Saffron's Editorial Assistant)
Tiani (Deputy Editor)
Kora (Fashion Director)
Pascal (Art Director)
Chloe (Beauty Editor)
Virginia "Ginny" DeRosso (Beauty Assistant)

Lout Magazine
Hamish Keener (Editor)
Mel (Hamish's Personal Assistant)

Others
Detective Inspector Liam Jackson (Alicia's husband)
Detective Inspector Indira Singh (Jackson's senior
partner)
Gail DeRosso (Ginny's mother)
Isla-Mae Cavendish (Ginny's flatmate)
Kirsten (Ginny's aunt)
Ebony Johnson (Ted's wife)

READING MATERIAL

The Mysterious Affair at Styles (Agatha Christie)
The Thursday Murder Club (Richard Osman)

PROLOGUE

Virginia DeRosso waited until the coast was clear, then slipped out of *Styled* magazine's office, past the unmanned reception desk and down the corridor towards the room marked ARIAL SPECIAL PROJECTS, a white tote bag wedged under one arm.

The room was empty, of course it was empty, and she was glad. She was on a mission and she needed complete privacy, or the whole thing would fall apart. And she couldn't have that. So much time and effort had been put in. It *had* to work.

But first!

Stepping inside and towards the shemozzle her colleague called a desk, Ginny's eyes rolled upwards, not surprised. The woman was a pig, no doubt about it. Still, it would work in her favour, provide some camouflage.

Make the game a little tougher.

Sniggering, she carefully nudged a few things to the side, pushing the keyboard closer to the desktop and the manila folders slightly to the right, then she glanced back towards the door before reaching into her tote.

Slowly, carefully, she pulled each item out and placed them strategically amongst the clutter, making a few changes, rearranging a few things, getting it just right.

Then she stood back and admired her work, her kohl-lined eyes twinkling, her gaze dancing across the desk:

The small thesaurus.

The wad of cash.

The statement T-shirt.

And *The Mysterious Affair at Styles*.

Manicured fingers to her glossy lips, she smothered a smile. That was the piece de resistance, the Agatha Christie book, and she couldn't be more delighted! She'd really nailed the brief there. Could not believe she'd found it! It was like the icing on the cake, the olive in the martini, the bait that would get the amateur detective hooked.

Not that there was anything amateur about Alicia Finlay, founder of the Murder Mystery Book Club, of course. That girl could solve a murder in her sleep. In fact, she had, only recently, while on a luxury train across the Nullarbor Plain…

Still. Ginny did wonder whether she ought to leave a note, give her a few more clues. Then she shook her head. Where was the fun in that? Wouldn't want to make it *too* easy.

Or too obvious, she thought now, sneaking another furtive glance towards the door.

This was supposed to be a secret after all. Wasn't keen to ruffle any feathers, and there were plenty of them to ruffle. Jesus, half the company behaved like peacocks, the other half like chickens! Well, not her. Not anymore.

It was time to get the truth out.

Enough with all the lies!

Smile slipping like her crimson bra strap, she wondered briefly if she was overstepping. Poking the peacock, so to speak? Then she shook her honey-highlighted locks and scoffed at herself for being *so* dramatic.

"Chill, babes," she told herself. "This is a harmless little mystery."

Not life-and-death stuff!

And that's what she believed—truly, deeply believed— as she hoicked her strap back into place, slung the tote across her shoulder again and slipped out and into the elevator, down to the ground floor. There she noticed the winter rain was still bucketing down, so she pulled out her coat and slipped into it, then out onto the street, then strode swiftly towards Town Hall station, heading for home.

Except she wasn't going home tonight. Would never make it home again.

She would be dead in eighteen minutes.

A little later if there was the usual delay at Central.

CHAPTER 1
The Honeymoon is Over, Baby

Alicia Finlay tried to swallow back her tears as she made her way home from her honeymoon. Alone. Did not want to make things any more uncomfortable for the taxi driver, who had been shooting her worried glances in his rear-vision mirror since he collected her, red-eyed and sniffling, from the airport just fifteen minutes earlier. But she was utterly bereft, completely confused.

How had it come to this? How could it all end so tragically?

When she got to her former Woolloomooloo address, Alicia's sister, Lynette, was standing at the open doorway, her own worried frown etched to her face, long, tanned arms wrapped around herself. Within minutes they were around Alicia, and she was hugging her as hard as she could. And they stood like that for several minutes, until Alicia realised she still had to pay the poor driver who was politely waiting by the car, her suitcase at his feet.

She apologised profusely, overpaid him unnecessarily, then waved him off with a rallying smile before returning to her sister's embrace.

Eventually Lynette said, "I'm so sorry, honey." Alicia sniffed and nodded into her chest. "It was so unexpected though, right? How're you faring?" Now Alicia shrugged. "And Jackson?"

Lynette was referring to Alicia's husband of four days, Liam Jackson, and now Alicia was stiffening. She pulled away. Tried for that rallying smile but landed something closer to a grimace. Then her eyes puddled up again.

"Come on," said Lynette, "let's get you inside. I've got coffee on the boil."

That's not all that was bubbling away. The moment Max

caught sight of Alicia, the black Labrador threw himself upon her, tumbling her over her wheelie bag, slobbering her with kisses, and she laughed for a moment as Lynette caught her and helped her to their spongy couch, demanding she sit.

Max promptly did as instructed, and now they both laughed and Lynette said, "I was talking to Alicia, you dill!" She gave the pooch's head a ruffle, then told her sister, "I'm making your old favourite, Lucky Duck. It's guaranteed to cheer you up."

But as the professional chef got to work marinating the duck and rinsing the fresh broccoli, putting the jasmine rice on to boil, Alicia wasn't sure anything could cheer her up today. And the sight of *Styled* magazine on the coffee table certainly wasn't helping. She ignored it for a bit, sat back and closed her eyes, but then they snapped open and she found herself scooping it up and flicking through, as if she wanted to torture herself.

And it did feel like torture when she got to the beauty section and spotted the face she was dreading—all sparkly and smiley and far too pretty for her own good.

Virginia DeRosso.

Ginny.

Her best pal at work. The woman she bantered with in the tearoom, scoffed at as she flirted with every courier who stepped through the elevator doors, and laughed with over cocktails as she revealed her outrageous antics from the evening before.

But Alicia wasn't laughing now.

"Damn you, Ginny!" she said. "You stupid, stupid girl!"

Then she hurled the magazine across the room and fell into herself, finally letting the tears flow with abandon.

~

Detective Inspector Liam Jackson shifted the sheet to one side and stared at Ginny's face. My God she really was beautiful. He wondered if she knew it. Deep down.

He thought of his new wife then. Of Alicia's desolation

last night when he'd broken the news while holidaying in Vanuatu. How stunned she was, then sad, then—and this was so normal—angry. She was so bloody angry and not just with Ginny. With herself. Like if she had been around more this would not have happened.

He tried to tell her it was probably inevitable. A cliché, sure, but often true. Any case, the honeymoon had imploded, and here he was, standing beside Ginny when he should've been with his wife.

"Not the nicest way to end your honeymoon," came a familiar voice, and he turned to see his senior partner Detective Inspector Indira Singh at the door, black hair pulled back in a tight ponytail, her smile equally as tight.

"Hey, Singho," he said. Then he turned and stared hard at Ginny again. "Yeah, trust Ginny to steal the limelight."

"You knew her well? Before?"

He waggled a hand in the air. "Not *well* well. She was a colleague of Alicia's. That's why I'm back."

"Wondered about that. I could've handled it you know. Probably still should. If you're close—"

"Weren't close. Just met her a few times. When I visited Alicia at the magazine. Ginny worked reception, or she used to. Moved on to some posh woman's mag—"

"*Styled.*"

"Yeah, that's right. Alicia dragged me to some event they hosted a few weeks ago at the Opera House."

"That is posh."

He nodded. "And she was at our wedding, of course. Not sure I swapped more than a g'day."

Singh nodded along. She'd been at the wedding too. Told Jackson how she'd noticed the young woman there, dressed to the nines, falling out of that dress, far too much makeup on, but then all the young girls did these days. They hadn't even got as far as g'day.

"Figured I'd never set eyes on her again. And yet here we are." She glanced from Ginny to Jackson. Arched one eyebrow. "There is no story here, right? I mean, it's early days, but it looks open and shut to me."

This wasn't really directed at Jackson. She was hoping he'd pass the message along.

He offered her a weary smile. Nodded. Then he thought of Ginny at his wedding, too, how she practically camped out on the dance floor, screaming out the words to every song, one hand clutching her champagne, the other raised in a fist to the sky, big goofy smile upon her face. There wasn't a tune Ginny couldn't find a groove to.

"She was a lot of fun," he said.

"I noticed," said Singh. "Not so much fun anymore though."

Then they both stared down at Ginny's beautiful face. Now void of makeup. Now void of life.

~

"I don't understand why she'd do it," Alicia said for the umpteenth time, and Lynette looked up and across to her barely touched bowl and sighed. Didn't bother answering. There were no answers, at least none that didn't sound trite.

"I can't believe she'd… she'd *kill herself*. I just can't."

Lynette sighed again. "Can't or don't want to?"

"Both! It's so… *pessimistic*. Ginny was the opposite of that. She was happy and positive and…"

"…spontaneous and a little loopy? I didn't know her as well as you, but she was flighty, I remember that. And the way she did it… Well."

They both shuddered thinking of that. Of Ginny falling. Of the north-bound train screeching to a halt. Of the poor driver, probably traumatised for life, not to mention the many onlookers, just ordinary folk going about their lives. It was the kind of image that often circled Alicia's mind as she stood on a station platform, watching as a train whooshed towards her. But it was always herself she imagined, never Ginny. She was too full of life.

"And she was *kind*," Alicia added, thinking again of the poor onlookers.

"But clearly depressed," said Lynette. "When people get

to that point, they're not really thinking clearly."

But what got her to that point? Alicia wondered now. What would make her carefree, happy-go-lucky colleague do something so *final*? "I don't understand any of it," she said again, and once again Lynette sighed.

"But how well did you really know her though? I'm sorry, sis, but no one really knows how people are feeling, deep down."

"Except I did know! Ginny was a sharer; she spoke her mind. Hell, she gave me every icky detail of her last pap smear but not a word about being sad or depressed? It makes no sense."

"Some people are good at hiding it," said Lynette, scooping up their bowls. "Sometimes you just don't know."

Alicia nodded finally. Of course. It wasn't always so simple. She got that. And yet she'd always thought of Ginny as simple but in a good way. She wasn't shallow so much as uncomplicated. What you saw was what you got when it came to Ginny. She could be a drama queen though, that was true, and she'd certainly made a drama of her life now— or her death to be precise. Alicia's mind turned to what she did, how she did it, and she felt her tears well up again.

Lynette and Max were saved from a fresh round of crying by the sound of the front door opening.

"Permission to take my new bride home," Jackson called out as he made his way in.

He didn't bother asking how Alicia was, and she didn't bother saying, because they both knew this would take some getting used to.

"Of course," said Lynette. "I'm just sorry your honeymoon got cut short."

"Well, there's worse things, right? One of us could be lying under a sheet in a morgue."

"You make a good point," she replied, hugging him tight and then, ten minutes later, hugging them both again before waving them out.

Back at Jackson's inner-city apartment (now Alicia's too,

of course), the newlyweds fell into bed exhausted. It had been a mammoth seventeen hours.

They had been polishing off a delicious coconut pudding in the resort's poolside restaurant when the news came through. Jackson had ignored Singh's first call—"Poor Singho. Can't live without me"—but by the second call, he knew to pick up. By the time he'd ended the call, Alicia was as white as the dessert. She'd only caught scraps of the conversation, but they were the important scraps—Virginia DeRosso, train incident, deceased.

She'd rushed straight to their room to try to rebook their flights home from the Pacific nation. Like that was somehow going to turn back the clock. Jackson tried to stall her. Make her see sense. Abandoning their holiday was not going to change a goddamn thing—Ginny was dead, wasn't getting any deader (*not* that he'd used those precise words). But eventually he realised things had already changed. Irrevocably. There would be no more beach-combing and sunset cocktails and creamy coconut desserts. At least not for Alicia.

The honeymoon was over. She needed to get home.

And so he ordered her a comforting mint tea through room service and took charge, booking the first-available flight home, the next afternoon as it happened. And upon landing back in Sydney, he'd headed straight to work to "get the intel", and she'd headed straight to her sister for more comfort.

And now here they were, four days into their two-week honeymoon, and Alicia felt flat and miserable, and Jackson's "intel" wasn't helping. Everything pointed to suicide, he told her, that or misadventure. There were no signs of foul play—"Because I know that's what you're thinking, so does Singho." It was just a terrible, senseless tragedy.

Ginny had left work as usual on Monday, right on the dot of five o'clock. Never one to do a minute's unpaid overtime. She had walked to the busy inner-city train station where she walked every weekday, then waited on the packed platform until the train approached. As it did so, she casually stepped out and in front of it.

Singh had spoken with every witness they could find, and there were *a lot*, he told her. Ginny might not have uttered a word, certainly nothing audible, but she did not go quietly into the night. There was a lot of screaming—just not from Ginny.

Singh had also trawled through plenty of CCTV footage, watching the incident from several different angles thanks to the public platform's ample coverage, and they all supported the theory that Ginny stepped out and into the path of the oncoming train. It was as simple and unequivocal and horrific as that. So either Ginny was massively distracted and didn't realise what she was doing, or she did it deliberately.

"Either way, it's unfathomable," Jackson told Alicia as he switched off his bedside lamp. "Her family must be gutted, and I know you're hurting too. The best thing you can do now is cherish the memories you had with your old colleague. Keep them in your thoughts, not the way she went out."

But as her new husband drifted off to sleep beside her, Alicia felt more awake than ever, her mind galloping in all directions, and it was *because* of her memories. They were haunting her now.

Ginny was so much more than a colleague to Alicia. She was the first person to befriend her when she started at Arial Publishing a decade earlier. Despite being several years younger and out on the reception desk, Ginny had taken Alicia under her wing, fetching her much-needed cups of coffee and dragging her to lunch so she could give her "all the goss", mostly about who to hook up with and who to avoid like the plague, all said with a twinkle in her eyes. Ginny was the one she laughed with as they heated up leftovers for lunch and gossiped with over after-work drinks and the one who first introduced her to the Monday Night Book Club.

That was a seminal moment in Alicia's life.

If it wasn't for Ginny, she would never have joined a literary book club she loathed so much that she had created her own—one totally devoted to murder mysteries. She might never have met her lifelong friends—Missy the librarian, Claire the vintage queen and Perry the "Queen of Surry Hills"—and begun poking her nose in unexpected real-life mysteries. And she definitely would not have met Jackson and married him in a haze of champagne and rose petals the previous Friday.

And that's what made her feel so unbearably sad. She owed so much of her life to Ginny, and now Ginny's life was over.

Alicia's chest hollowed out. *Oh God.* Had she ever thanked Ginny for all that? Had she ever repaid her? Had she even spent any quality time with her recently?

She shook the questions away. Couldn't face them tonight…

So she turned over in bed and tried to sob softly so she wouldn't wake Jackson. But he heard her anyway and pulled her towards him, squeezing her tight.

And for some reason his kindness made her feel even sadder.

CHAPTER 2
Arial Publishing

The first thing you noticed when you stepped out and on to the editorial floor of Arial Publishing's glamorous inner-city headquarters was not the lavish reception and its plush furnishings, the magazine covers blown up and framed on every available wall, but the symphony of busyness that streamed out from the offices beyond—the shrilling of phones and hubbub of chatter, the clatter of keyboards and photocopiers and clashing music streams.

It used to excite Alicia, give her a buzz. Today it just sounded like noise.

"You're not due back for weeks," said the smartly dressed man on the front desk, and Alicia offered Blake a slim smile.

"Yeah, well… Wasn't going to be much fun… you know?"

He nodded. He knew. They were all bereft. Ginny could be the proverbial pain with her gossiping and distracting and frankly inappropriate flirting, but she was also beloved.

How could you not love Ginny?

As Alicia made her way down the corridor, she didn't stop at her office to dump her things or even in at *Styled* magazine to offer her condolences. She headed straight for the one person she knew would be as distraught as she was. Hamish Keener. The gruff and misogynistic editor of lads' magazine *Lout*.

Hamish was middle-aged, short and stocky, with the remnants of a cockney accent and what looked like a poor attempt to grow a mullet, his grey hair now dyed an obvious shade of black. That, the skinny jeans, the baggy hoodie and the neck-to-toe tattoos all suggested a midlife crisis in the making, but he'd always dressed and acted like one of his readers—brash, juvenile, unapologetic.

Today he just looked diminished, his shoulders slumped, his arms wrapped around himself as he stared out the window of his private office. But when he turned around, he looked ready to unload—he'd told his assistant no interruptions!—until he realised it was Alicia, and his eyes turned soggy.

"Stupid sod," he said, and she knew he wasn't referring to her.

She nodded. "I'd kill her myself if she hadn't already beaten me to it."

He barked out a laugh, then his face crumpled and she stepped towards him and pulled him into a hug.

It was the first time Alicia had ever hugged Hamish. First time she'd ever even touched him that she recalled. And if you'd told her even two days ago she'd be here, holding on to him like a life raft, she would have scoffed, and Ginny would have sniggered right beside her. "As if! Urgh!" Hamish was on Ginny's "avoid like the plague" list even though she'd infected herself willingly, many times over.

"I loved her, you know," he said as he pulled back and waved her into a chair.

"I know you did," she said. "You were fooling nobody."

Because they sure did put on a strange act, Hamish and Ginny—regularly sniping at each other, teasing and taunting at every opportunity. An outsider would presume they loathed one another. But the opposite was true.

Despite their age difference—fifteen years at least— they'd been secret lovers on and off for more than a decade, not that Ginny kept that secret from Alicia. She told her every gory detail, that was how Ginny rolled. So Alicia knew Hamish was shattered each time they broke up, because it was always at Ginny's behest; she simply wasn't the commitment type. And he'd laugh it off, like it didn't matter. But Alicia knew it did, and she wondered now how he was coping.

"Why'd she do it?" he said, slumping into his chair.

"Just don't understand."

She shrugged. Her turn now to play Lynette. "Maybe we never will. How's Saffron?"

Saffron Toya-Jones was the editor of *Styled* magazine where Ginny had worked.

He turned his frown into a scowl. "Probably dancing around in her effing kitten heels. She hated Ginny."

"Well, Ginny would've been a hard employee to wrangle."

"She was the best thing about that load of bollocks she calls a magazine. Can't believe it still sells."

Alicia half chuckled. She wasn't much of a fan of the vacuous title either, even though she liked women's magazines as a rule. But *Styled* was different, as shallow as Saffron, not even bothering with the odd worthy article to give it some depth. And yet it was the highest-selling women's lifestyle title in the country. And growing in circulation every day.

Go figure.

"She's crying up a storm though," said Hamish. "Acting like she cared, the hypocrite. Has probably already measured Ginny's chair for her replacement." He frowned again. "Aren't you supposed to be shaggin' some copper in the Pacific right now?"

She smiled. No longer shocked by his crassness. She shrugged.

He nodded. He got it too. "How was the wedding?"

Now Alicia was cringing, embarrassed she'd deliberately left him off the guest list.

Hamish was grinning, enjoying her discomfort. "Ginny showed me the pix. You looked good. Like a bloody princess."

"Don't sound so surprised!"

He chuckled. His smile plummeted. "Ginny looked good too." It was almost a whisper. Then louder, harder— "What was she doing with that gobshite on her arm?"

He was referring to Ginny's current beau, Austin Smythe. He worked on the executive floor at Arial, in the Sales and

Circulation department. Alicia shrugged again, hoping he'd give it up. He did not.

"They weren't… you know?"

"Serious? Nah!" Alicia added a fake puff of air to that, but the truth was they seemed pretty tight at her reception, barely leaving each other's side. Alicia had been surprised by that and not just because Ginny was a commitment-phobe. Austin was a player too, according to the tearoom gossip. Yet that night they only had eyes for each other. That made Ginny's suicide seem even more unfathomable. Perhaps she was on the cusp of something real. If only she'd hung around to find out.

Hamish stared hard at Alicia like he wanted to press her on the matter, but she was saved by a face at the door.

"Hamish—"

"What'd I tell you, Mel?" he barked. "I'm busy!"

"Sorry," came the dull tones of his long-suffering personal assistant who did not sound in the least bit sorry. "Just letting you know Ted's switched the meeting back an hour. Dionne said to go straight into Chalmers, he'll see you in there."

"Oh right. Okay. Thanks."

He offered the PA an apologetic smile, and she shook her head at him as she closed the door behind her.

"Top Dog's in town?" asked Alicia, referring to Ted Johnson, Arial's CEO. He spent most of his time at the company's London headquarters. "That was fast."

"Already here. Launching that new digital mag. He's playing the victim card too. Shitting himself the truth will come out and damage our reputation or something. Says we're to call it a tragic accident. Suicide is not 'on brand', apparently." There was so much contempt in his tone.

"Yeah, well, they can dress it up how they like, but Jackson seems pretty convinced. Says the CCTV footage is pretty convincing too."

"Except it all feels like bollocks to me," he said. "The Ginny I knew wouldn't have done it that way—so ugly, so violent. Wasn't her style."

Alicia agreed. And it wasn't just ugly. It was *ordinary*. Too ordinary for Ginny. Drowning herself in a bath full of champagne? *That* she could see. Throwing herself off a superyacht? Absolutely. But falling under the wheels of the 17:18 City to Berowra via North Sydney?

Bollocks indeed.

Still, she pulled out another Lynetticism and told him, "I guess we never really knew her."

That was bollocks too. If these two didn't know Ginny, who the hell did?

~

Ted Johnson dropped his mobile phone from his enormous paw and turned back to offer his tiny wife a big fat smile. It was a facade. Bit like this stupid brunch. Ebony had been getting suspicious of late, and he had to play his cards right, so he'd spent the morning with her, pretending that sipping Mimosas on a workday was perfectly acceptable behaviour for the CEO of a busy media organisation. It was all very well for a slacker like Ebs. That's all she ever did. Brunching and lunching and spending his money, like it was a job in itself. And if it was, gee she'd earned herself a couple of promotions, she was that good at it. And so he went along to smooth things over.

Besides, he wasn't in any great hurry to meet with that bigheaded Hamish Keener. Talk about *lout*. If it wasn't for the fact his lads' mag was helping prop up half the company, he'd have booted him out years ago.

But he needed Hamish and Hamish knew it. So they played a little dance. Ted was dancing with Virginia DeRosso too. Only recently. He thought of her then, of the things she whispered in his ear, and how his smile evaporated.

If anyone knew…

He glanced at his wife, and she was still watching him. Closely. Another of her occupations.

"All good, sweetie?" she said, her cosmetically tattooed

eyebrows wedged together, her lips still swollen from the last procedure that cost him a bomb.

"'Course," he told her, even though he wasn't convinced.

Ginny might be gone, but it wasn't over yet.

There was still some cleaning up to do.

CHAPTER 3
Styled Magazine

If Arial Publishing was the Royal household, thought Saffron Toya-Jones, then *Styled* magazine was its Buckingham Palace and she was the elegant, eloquent monarch. *And not King Charles, heaven forbid! He was so common compared to Elizabeth, such a drably dressed grouch. Lizzie was poised, unflappable, could really rock a Norman Hartnell skirt suit. Had all the grace of a—*

"Jesus, Frances! Are you trying to give me third-degree burns?"

The young assistant snatched the almond milk latté back from the *Styled* editor and blushed. "I'm so sorry, Saffron. It's just—"

"Just fix it. Please. Oh, and tell Pascal I want those layouts sent through. He can't faff around forever!"

Frances nodded and scuttled back out as Saffron yanked her black-rimmed Chanel spectacles off and chewed on one temple, gazing out her enormous picture windows. Dark rain clouds were threatening to break again, but it didn't diminish the stunning view across Sydney Harbour. Best view in the house.

Well, apart from the executives up on level seven of course. "Seventh Heaven" they called it, the smug prats. She might be the hardworking monarch, but they were like gods, that lot, lounging idle above, half of them based in the UK, the other half out to golf or brunch or wherever the hell it was the CEO's assistant, Dionne, just told Saffron he was at.

Honestly, why Ted Johnson stayed married to that waste-of-space Ebony, she did not know.

"You get the CVs I sent through?"

This was Arial's head of Human Resources, Arabella,

lingering at the door, nibbling on a pastry full of calories and cholesterol.

"All rubbish," Saffron said, swirling around, her recently coiffed locks swirling with her. "What else you got?"

"Really? One or two were pretty good—"

"*Good?* We are the top magazine in this country, Arabella. I don't want *good*. I want great! Need I remind you of our motto?"

"'While others fall, you fly'. Yes, yes, I appreciate you're one of the few magazines soaring in this market—"

"So find me someone with wings. Advertise if you have to."

Arabella frowned, which she was prone to do. Saffron hoped she had some decent anti-wrinkle cream in her boudoir or enough cash for injectables. She'd find out soon enough—it all catches up with you. Just like those pastries were now catching up with her thighs.

"It has just been a day or so. Do you want to maybe wait a bit?"

"Why would I do that?"

"Because, frankly, it feels a bit insensitive. Inauthentic. We're supposed to be sad, Saffron. The optics aren't great if we replace her too quickly. I mean Ginny only just passed—"

"Ginny killed herself. She *chose* to leave us, yes? What are the optics like on that? I have every right to replace her. We're the ones left in the lurch."

Arabella gave her a look. Saffron knew what that look meant. She dropped her head to the side and softened her tone. Millennials were such snowflakes.

"We *are* sad, Arabella. I've been telling everyone how sad I am. But we have to finish the September issue, and the beauty pages aren't going to write themselves, are they? Or are you offering to come in and do them?"

Arabella held out her palms. "I'll put something online."

She smiled. "You do that."

Then she swivelled back and returned to staring out at the Sydney Opera House, a splash of white on the surly horizon.

Saffron remembered the last time they were all there.

The *Styled* team. At the Opera Bar, sipping champagne and pretending they were excited by the recent sales figures. And she was excited at first. Until Ginny made some off-the-cuff comment that left her reeling.

She'd laughed her off, muttering something dismissive, then strolled to the women's toilets where she locked herself in a cubicle, scrambled through her bag, whipped out her stainless-steel water bottle and took a good long swig from it, her nerves calming with every drop.

How did Ginny *know?* What was she trying to *say?* And why did she say it with such a sneaky, snaky grin, the little bitch? She had been nothing but trouble from the start, that Ginny, and now Saffron was supposed to waste time in mourning?

Talk about *inauthentic.*

"This should be better," said Frances, reappearing with a fresh latté, and Saffron took it tentatively, sipped, then offered her a smile. An authentic one this time.

She continued smiling as she placed the glass down, popped her glasses back on, and returned to her monitor, scanning the fresh advertisements that had come in for the latest issue, including six sparkling pages from Apple. Six! And that was all thanks to Saffron. No one else.

While others fall, we fly, she thought. And I am the queen of—

"You can't just walk in!" came an ugly squawk from the door, and she glanced up to see Alicia Finlay striding through, Frances hot on her heels, screeching like an ugly fishwife.

"I'm so sorry, Saffron! I couldn't stop her."

"You never can," Saffron replied with a withering snarl, which she redirected to Alicia.

Urgh. Alicia Finlay.

There was something about her fellow editor that got under Saffron's skin. No, amend that. There were *lots* of things. Like the careless way she dressed, as though she'd reached for the first thing in her wardrobe—or floor, judging by today's crumpled number. And how she'd had the same shaggy haircut since *forever*. Even Queen Lizzie had more imagination than that. And, most annoyingly, how she had such little regard for Saffron she thought she could swan in whenever she damn well pleased, helping herself to a chair, utterly uninvited.

"I'm so sorry," Frances stammered again, clinging onto the door like that would save her.

Saffron shooed her away, then pulled her glasses back off and snapped, "What do you want, Alicia? Unlike you, I do have a real magazine to run."

Alicia ignored her slight—another annoying trait!—and said, "Just wanted to say I'm sorry about Ginny."

"Oh. Yes. Well, as are we all. Thank you."

Saffron hadn't meant to sound so stiff. She had to be careful here. Alicia and Ginny were thick. She'd caught them multiple times, sniggering by the espresso machine, gobbling back their gossip as she strode past. She knew they were bitching about her. Didn't normally give a jot. But there was something about Alicia...

Despite Saffron's loathing, she had to confess she also, quietly, admired her. They were a small cohort, these magazine editors, fifteen in all, and Alicia seemed to get along with every single one of them. Even that hideous dinosaur at *Lout*.

Worse, she seemed to know everybody's business, helped along no doubt by gossipy Ginny. Hopefully that was now over. Alicia was not the kind of person you wanted snooping about. Now more so than ever.

"If that's all..." Saffron began, returning her gaze to her screen.

"Actually, no," said Alicia. "I wondered if you'd cleared Ginny's desk yet?"

Saffron's eyes snapped back. "Why?"

"Just want to grab a memento. She had a bunch of photo strips we took over the years. You know, those happy snaps you get from photo booths? The last ones were hilarious. We had been out at lunch and—"

"Yes, yes, help yourself." Saffron wasn't remotely

interested in Alicia's prattle. "And if you want to clear out the rest of her junk, ask Frances for a box. She can help you do it."

"Okay then," said Alicia, jumping up. She stepped towards the door, then swung back. "You going to have some kind of memorial?"

"What? No, that's not necessary. I said a few words to the team yesterday. And there'll be a funeral, won't there?"

Alicia cocked her head to one side. "Right. Of course."

Then she turned and walked out, leaving Saffron blinking madly behind her.

What did she mean by that? "Right. Of course"? Of course *what?* What was she trying to say?

Saffron stared glumly at her tasteless coffee, then reached a hand down to her desk's lower drawer…

~

Alicia was not surprised by Saffron's indifference. She had only one interest. No, two. Her magazine and herself. And Alicia knew Ginny had little respect for either of them, had been miserable there, and it was all Arabella's fault. The Human Resources manager wanted to promote more people within the company, so when the Beauty Assistant position became vacant at *Styled,* the decision had been made to offer it to the longtime receptionist and train her in-house. A great idea in principle, but Ginny had been a bad fit and not just because she wasn't nearly snobby enough for that title—with her bawdy humour and dress sense, she would have fit in better at *Lout*—but because Ginny knew Saffron too well and didn't worship at her Pucci pumps like the rest of her browbeaten minions. And that would not have played well with the haughty editor.

Alicia ignored the PA's lingering glare as she made her way across to Ginny's desk where she was surprised to find it had been cleared out of everything but the company phone, computer, keyboard and mouse.

Ginny's in-trays were gone, as were her foreign magazine

piles, her expandable plastic binders jammed with beauty snippets and media releases, the pilfered milkshake glass she used to hold her lurid-coloured pen collection, and the ceramic pink bowl she kept filled with sweets that the office were welcome to help themselves to, encouraged even. The corkboard by Ginny's desk was also bare, not so much as a gold-embossed invite to some glamorous product launch, let alone the photo strips she so cherished.

Alicia glanced across at the beauty editor who had her head down, wading through what looked like mascara samples on her desk.

"Hey, Chloe, how're you doing?"

Chloe glanced up and smiled. It was dazzling. *She* was dazzling, with her razor-sharp snow-white bob, acorn-brown eyes and skin so radiant she could light up a dance floor. Add to that the latest in designer couture and she was a walking advertisement for the *Styled* beauty pages she commandeered.

"Oh, hey Alicia." Her smile faded. "You heard?"

Alicia nodded. Glanced back at Ginny's desk. "Know what happened to her things? Who took it all?"

Chloe was Ginny's immediate boss, so perhaps she'd taken the initiative and boxed it up, but she stared at the empty desk like she'd only just noticed.

"Wow, no. Must've been Frances."

But Saffron's PA said she hadn't done the honours and, when Alicia posed the question, no one would admit to being anywhere near Ginny's desk.

"Could've been Arabella," suggested Frances as they gathered around. "But she must've done it after-hours because I'm always first in and last out, just behind Saffron, and I didn't see her."

"What about Ginny's flatmate Isla-Mae?" added Kora, the Fashion Director—just as stylish as Chloe but smaller, frecklier, not quite as dazzling. "She was here, auditioning for my activewear shoot yesterday. Maybe she used the opportunity to grab Ginny's crap?"

"Doubt it," scoffed Frances. "I mean, it's not really her

job to clean up after Ginny."

She made a good point. Isla-Mae and Ginny had been sharing a home in North Sydney for close to a year, and while Isla did pop into Arial for the odd modelling job, it was hardly her responsibility. Besides, someone would have noticed her do it, surely?

Still, it wouldn't hurt to ask, thought Alicia. Wouldn't hurt to check on Ginny's flatmate while she was at it. She had met Isla a few times, usually at parties or the pub, and always thought of her as a little fragile, a little needy. She was a foreigner, out from England, and Alicia now wondered if she had anyone supporting her through this horrendous ordeal.

Determination in her step, Alicia thanked them for their help and made her way out. But as she left the *Styled* office, en route to the elevator, Alicia didn't notice one set of eyes tracking her movements, watching her closely.

Wondering what it was exactly the little pixie-haired pain in the butt was really looking for.

CHAPTER 4
Mixed Messages

Isla-Mae Cavendish was one of those angular, willowy models who looked like a newborn foal—tall and gangly, long flowing mane, so painfully thin you wondered how she found the strength to swing the front door open, which she was doing now as Alicia stood in the corridor outside Ginny's old apartment, shaking off the rain that had pelted her between the car and the building.

"Oh, hello. Alicia isn't it?" said Isla after a brief blank look, her British accent so rich she could pass for Princess Kate. Her eyes were bloodshot, and she was clutching a crumpled tissue. "From the magazine?"

"From the same publishing house," Alicia said. God forbid anyone thought she worked for *Styled!* "Are you okay?"

The woman nodded fervently, then her face crumpled like that tissue and she fell into Alicia's arms. Or rather, Alicia fell into hers, Isla's long, bony limbs clinging onto her for dear life. She was glad now that she'd checked in on Isla and let her cling for a little longer, then drew her inside and closed the door behind them.

"It's all so dreadful," the woman was saying, grappling for her tissue. "I can't *believe* it. I keep wondering if I missed the signs, if there was something she was trying to tell me and I ignored it."

"It's not your fault, Isla," Alicia told her. "This is not on you."

"I know… it's just… it's so…"

Then she burst into tears again, and again Alicia stepped forward to offer a hug, but this time she shook her off.

"Sorry, I shouldn't be unloading on you. You're probably sadder than I am. I know you two were terribly close."

It's not a competition, Alicia wanted to tell her, but she just shrugged and said, "Shall I pop the kettle on?"

"I'll do it."

As Isla stepped into the kitchen, Alicia glanced about and was not surprised to see her morning cup and cereal bowl were both rinsed and sitting on the drying rack. The tea towels were hanging neatly on the oven rail, and there was not a speck of dust on the floor, the aluminium fridge, the bench tops…

The flatmates had been a perfect match like that. Despite her chaotic love life, Ginny was a neat freak, and that's what she had most loved about Isla. That and her supermodel looks which helped pull blokes when they hit the bars, but that was a whole other story.

And while Isla wasn't looking quite so super now, the apartment was still tidy, and it felt reassuring. At least she hadn't fallen apart completely. Although she was struggling to focus, and Alicia noticed Isla still clutching the kettle to her chest, staring at the pouring rain through the kitchen window.

"We were supposed to be going to a rave tonight," she murmured. "Ginny was so looking forward to it. I can't believe she'd… I can't…"

She crumpled again, and Alicia grabbed the kettle and placed it on to boil. Then helped her to the sofa and asked if there was a friend she could call or someone she could stay with for a while.

"I'll be fine. Honestly. It just keeps hitting me, over and over."

"Me too. It will for a long time. Have you been in touch with your family? Is there someone you can talk to?"

"My folks are currently summering at Saint Barts. I couldn't do it to them." She offered the semblance of a smile. "I'll be okay. Truly."

Alicia wasn't convinced but took the chance to ask about Ginny's things. Had Isla collected them from the office?

"Things? What things?"

"Ginny's desk's been cleared out. You didn't do it?"

The model shook her head, dislodging more tears as the kettle finished boiling. Alicia made them both a cup of black tea, noticing there was no sugar and virtually no milk, just a dribble of outdated soy.

"So you didn't grab her stuff?" she persisted. "When you were in yesterday?"

"When would I have done it? Kora herds you in and out like cattle, gives you two seconds to impress, then it's 'Next!'."

She was referring to *Styled*'s modelling audition, and there was a touch of derision in her tone.

"Did you get the job at least?"

Isla managed a casual head shake like it didn't matter, but Alicia knew it would. She had seen the empty fridge and had a hunch it had less to do with a lean body than a lean bank account. It can't be easy trying to steal jobs from the local girls, and with Ginny now gone, she no longer had a foot in the door.

"When did you last see Ginny?" Alicia asked, changing the subject.

"That's the thing. I saw her that morning. She seemed *fine*. I keep trying to remember if she'd given me some kind of signal or said something—"

"You really mustn't keep blaming yourself. All we can do is think that whatever was troubling her is now over. She's at peace."

Isla nodded, more tears trickling from her bleary eyes, and Alicia realised she wasn't just sad, she was exhausted. A visitor was probably the last thing she needed.

She jumped up and rinsed her cup in the sink, placed it on the rack and popped the tea bags and milk away. "I'll leave you in peace," she told her, heading for the door. "Can you let me know if Ginny's stuff shows up? Maybe her mother collected it."

That got Isla wailing again.

"Poor Gail! This will *destroy* her. They were so close!

What am I even going to say to her?"

"Nothing. Don't say anything. Just give her a hug."

As if to demonstrate, Alicia stepped back and pulled Isla up, wrapping her arms around her again. "You need to look after yourself now," she said as they strode to the door. "Take some time out. Head home if you have to. Or find Ginny's stash of French champagne and guzzle the lot."

She was joking and Isla chuckled, then gasped and said, "Oh my God, I forgot to say congratulations! Ginny told me all about your wedding. It sounded *amazing*. I hope you liked Ginny's gift."

Alicia swung back. "Gift?" She hadn't received a gift from Ginny, nor did she want one. Just having her at the wedding, brightening the place up, was gift enough.

"Yes," said Isla. "She'd been working on it for weeks. All very secretive, wouldn't tell me anything, but she was going to leave it for you at work. Maybe on your desk?"

Alicia hadn't got to her desk when she went into Arial Publishing that morning.

"Was so proud of herself," Isla was saying, a smile breaking through. "Said you'd love it."

"Then I'm sure I will," Alicia said, smiling now too.

She hadn't intended to return to work before her holiday was over, but Isla had given her fresh impetus to pop back in. She couldn't wait to see what Ginny had left for her.

One ray of sunshine in all the gloom.

~

DI Indira Singh took the phone that was being held out to her and read the text message, then reread it, her mood brightening with every read.

"You know I love you, Mum, but I can't do it anymore. I'm sorry." Followed by a love heart emoji.

She glanced up at Gail DeRosso and offered her a sympathetic smile. "Mind if I forward this to my number?"

"Sure. Whatever," said Ginny's mother, a crack in her voice, anguish in her eyes.

And who could blame her? It was hard enough losing a daughter, but to *suicide?* That was a heavy burden to bear, although Singh felt lighter, like she'd lost ten kilos since Gail had produced the suicide note.

And it was clearly a suicide note. No two ways about it. Ginny had texted it to her mother the morning she took her life.

You didn't often get a note with suicides, but boy it helped when you did. It cleared things up; paved the way for grieving. And it also cleared the path for Singh to hand the case over to the coroner, where it belonged, and leave her free to focus on some actual homicides. God knows they were piling up.

But it wasn't really her workload that was worrying Singh, it was her partner, Liam Jackson. Or more specifically, his new wife. Why was it Alicia Finlay was at the centre of every suspicious death she stumbled upon these days? How could that even happen? How was that statistically possible?

Well. Turns out there was nothing suspicious about this one. Ginny's farewell message proved it. She looked across to Jackson, who was now inspecting Gail's phone and had to smother her smile.

He seemed even more relieved than she did. Understandably so. Now he could tell his meddling wife to stay out of it, and she might actually listen this time. There was nothing here to investigate. Alicia's buddy had committed suicide.

Case closed. And hallelujah to that!

~

Ted pulled the phone from his Merino wool jacket as he strode past his executive assistant and straight into his office. Slammed the door shut and pressed his speed dial.

"Hmm?" came a voice at the other end. Soft. Lilting.

"I need to see you."

A slight snigger. "My, my, my… Ebony not performing?"

"It's not funny. I'm serious."

"And I have a very busy schedule, don't you know?" Then a sigh. A soft one. "I'll see if I can fit you in."

Then the sudden, brutal sound of silence, his screen now black. Not so much as a goodbye. Ted chucked the phone on his desk, grumbling aloud. When had the tables turned? When had he lost the upper hand?

Everything was unbalanced, and he didn't like it one bit.

"All good?" came a voice from the doorway, and he looked up to see his executive assistant standing there, holding his morning macchiato.

He didn't bother answering, just offered her a snarl. Didn't have to pretend with Dionne.

She strode in, eyelashes batting behind thick, coke-bottle glasses. "Anything I can do?"

"Nah. I'm sorting it."

"Of course you are," she said breezily, placing the coffee down like that was the real reason she'd popped in, before striding out again.

She would've made a much better wife than Ebony, he thought as he watched Dionne close the door behind her. Cooler, more willing to look the other way.

Pity she's not twenty years younger and a shit-tonne better looking.

CHAPTER 5
Gifts Galore

The gift box was like something from Tiffany and Co but in reverse. It was silky white with a duck egg-blue bow neatly tied around it.

"From Ginny?" Alicia asked as the receptionist held it out to her when she stepped back into Arial Publishing for the second time that morning.

"What? No, no, free sample. Arrived this morning."

Blake handed it over, along with a glowing media release and an obscene recommended retail price, then watched as she opened the lid to reveal a miniature bottle of Eau de Parfum.

"PR girls just presented to *Styled*, giddy with excitement." He snickered. "Wanted you to have one too, in case you do another beauty one-off."

"Fat chance of that."

After producing a Super Summer Hair Special that was "simply mortifying"—Saffron's words, not hers—the *Styled* editor had insisted on taking over all future beauty one-offs, and she'd happily agreed. Less work for Alicia.

Still, it was nice to get a luxury freebie, and she thanked Blake, giving herself a liberal spray before sniffing and wincing and saying, "This is bad, right?"

Blake chuckled. "Sorry. Should've warned you. Chloe's already binned hers." Then, "Why're you back so soon?"

"Sucker for punishment?" she suggested, thanking him, then wafting a hand at her neck as she strode past the communal toilets and tearoom to her office one door down from *Lout*. At least she had Ginny's wedding gift as a consolation prize, she thought, as she strode into the large, open-plan space.

She winced again. The place looked like a cyclone had whirled through. My God, she really had been frantic before heading off on her honeymoon! There were boxes of unsold magazines and free products cluttering every spare space, and her desk looked like it had set up camp as a garbage tip with folders and clippings and god knows what else.

She wished she could blame this on somebody else, but the truth was, Alicia was a slob. Would not have lasted a day as Ginny's flatmate. Luckily, she was the only person who used this office now. It was once a bustling department producing multiple special projects, like puzzle books and fanzines and one-offs devoted to pop stars like Taylor Swift (it was on Alicia's to-do list; she didn't want to think about that just yet). Sadly, Alicia was now the last editor standing, the others all going the way of half the magazines from the pulp era.

It was a dying industry, paperback titles, and Alicia had a begrudging admiration for the likes of Saffron and Hamish who somehow managed to keep their magazines going at a time when news and content had mostly moved online. And not just going, *growing* judging by their booming sales figures and egos.

Crossing to her desk now, she noted it was even more cluttered than she remembered it, and she struggled to find any kind of gift box, let alone a glittering bottle of champagne, which was Ginny's go-to.

Then she noticed the old book. The Agatha Christie book.

The Mysterious Affair at Styles.

Now, normally, a Christie novel would not stand out amongst Alicia's things. She was the founder of the Murder Mystery Book Club after all. But this one did, and not only because she didn't have time to read at work but because it was not her copy. Hers had a different cover and was stashed away back at Woolloomooloo.

Scooping it up, she was surprised to find it was laminated

with a call number printed on the spine. Clearly a library book and one she had not borrowed.

She flipped the cover open, hoping to find a note from her friend, some kind of explanation. But nothing. It was just a book. And a borrowed book at that.

Was *this* the gift Ginny had left for her? Was she trying to be funny? Or had she read it and loved it and wanted to suggest Alicia read it too? If so, it seemed an odd thing for Ginny to do, considering she had never made any secret of her disdain for "Agatha 'Yawn' Christie".

What had Ginny said when she'd been asked if she'd like to join the Murder Mystery Book Club? "I'd rather pull my fingernails out!"

And if this was a wedding gift, Alicia felt like there were wittier Christie options like *A Deadly Wedding Day* or *Death on the Nile*, which featured the honeymoon from hell.

But *The Mysterious Affair at Styles*?

She turned it over and read the back blurb—something about a murder that takes place in a stately mansion called Styles Court—and still felt none the wiser. Did Ginny think it was amusing because she worked at *Styled* magazine? If so, it was very odd.

"Urgh! What's that stench?"

Alicia swung around to find Hamish standing in the open doorway, a mug of coffee in one hand, his thick lips smudged downwards.

"Designer perfume, darlink," she shot back. "It costs a small fortune. You no like?"

"Christ no. Proves what I'm always bangin' on about— money can't buy taste. Almost as bad as the aftershave Saffron tried to offload on us the other day. You'd be better off rubbing yourself in dog—"

"What do you want, Hamish?"

"Just passin'. What're you doing back anyway? Miss me already?"

She held up the Christie book. "Know anything about this? I think Ginny left it as a wedding gift."

His lips smudged again. "Not like her to be a cheap arse."

He pointed to the numbers down the spine.

"I know. It's a serious step down from the Veuve Clicquot she gave me for my thirtieth."

She followed his gaze to the desk where she noticed some other oddities, including a Roget's Thesaurus, a white T-shirt with a smudgy brown image on the front, and a wad of cash. But not real cash. It was Monopoly money.

"These must be part of her gift too," she said, checking them out.

He snatched the shirt from the desk and said, "This is bloody ugly, even for you."

He was right, it was ugly, but at least it was new. Judging by the tag, it was from the discount shop near Town Hall station. The kind that sells beanies in midsummer and is always closing down.

"What're you doing?" she asked as he began riffling through the novel.

"Checking she hasn't stashed a line of coke in here or a gift voucher." Then, "Hold the phone!"

He had the thesaurus in his hands now and was flinging the cover open to reveal a penned inscription: *'Cause there are more words than "sweetie" and "darling". H.*

"I gave this to Ginny. She can't regift it to you!"

As he showed it to her, a yellow Post-it note fluttered out and to the floor, and they both leapt upon it, but it was blank. Hamish looked relieved, like it might've contained a lewd message, and she pushed the thesaurus back at him and told him to keep it. She had one, didn't need another.

"No one needs another," he replied, dumping it on her desk and glancing around. "That's what AI's for. She didn't gift my Oasis hoodie to you, did she? Can't find it anywhere."

"Urgh!" Alicia said, giving him some of his own back. "And you're ridiculing my dress sense?"

"Hey, at least it's worth something. Got it at a Wembley tour, nearly twenty years ago. It's a collector's item. But this crap… I'd bin the lot if I were you."

Alicia shook her head and hugged the Christie book to

her heart. At least *this* Ginny had got right. Sort of. She would reread it and think of her dear friend with the strange sense of humour and the quirky taste in gifts.

"Know anything about the funeral?" Hamish asked, turning towards the door.

She told him not to expect one anytime soon. She'd learned from Jackson that the coroner was performing an autopsy.

"What?" He swung back, eyes wide, lips agape. "But... why?"

"It's okay," she told him. "It's standard procedure for unnaturally violent deaths." And was there anything more unnaturally violent than suicide? "But there might be some kind of memorial. I could ask her mother if you like?"

His jaw tightened. He rubbed a hand against his tattooed neck. "Better you than me. That woman hates me."

"I'm sure that's not true."

"All the mothers hate me. I take it as a badge of honour."

Then he winked and loped out, and Alicia sat stewing in her stinky perfume, staring morosely at Ginny's bizarre gifts, which had proven to be quite the anticlimax.

She couldn't imagine why Ginny would leave her such a motley collection. Was she trying to tell her something? Something about why she took her own life?

Or was there some deeper meaning here?

A cry for help that came too late?

CHAPTER 6
Dinner Dates

"Your brain's working overtime again," Jackson told Alicia when he met her later for dinner at their local Thai restaurant. "Bit like that perfume you're wearing."

Alicia sniffed herself and groaned. "Sorry. Hoped it'd wear off by now. This isn't from Ginny. It's a freebie from work. Bit much?"

"Bit everything," he said, then smiled to lighten the criticism. "But Ginny's gifts are harmless enough. And hardly surprising. She left you a Christie book because you're the biggest Christie fan on earth. It's clearly a reference to where she works, and she probably stumbled upon it in her local library and thought it was hilarious. I wouldn't read much more into it than that."

"Except I can't imagine her even knowing where her local library is, let alone stumbling around in it. And what about all the other stuff? Isn't it just... *weird?*"

"What's weird is how you could find anything on your desk." Another apologetic smile. "Look, you mentioned freebies. Maybe it has nothing to do with Ginny and is some kind of marketing gimmick?"

Now she was scoffing. "A promotor dumped a borrowed library book, Ginny's gifted thesaurus, Monopoly money and a cheap T-shirt on my desk? All without a press release or any explanation? Is that what you're saying?"

"I'm saying none of it really matters. None of it brings her back, does it?"

No, she agreed, it does not. "But what if she was trying to tell me something? Something important? Related to her death?"

Jackson glanced up from the menu he'd started scanning. There was pity in his eyes. "She's gone, honey. I'm sorry, but she chose to go."

"But you don't know that *for sure*."

"We do know. I told you this. Singh checked the CCTV, spoke with the witnesses. It's clear-cut. There's no doubt she stepped out. Of her own free will."

Alicia frowned. Shrugged. Then turned her eyes to the menu.

~

Chloe swept her snowy white bangs from her eyes as she scrolled through Facebook, lithe legs tucked up underneath her on the creamy new boucle lounge, heart in her mouth, dread in the pit of her stomach.

That skanky cow had better have deleted those incriminating photos like she promised she would.

She groaned. God, why had she let it get this far? It's not like it had even been worth it. Not really. And why she'd even agreed to meet up again, she could not say. Was it sympathy? Was she not thinking?

"Come on, Chloe!" she snapped at herself. "Get your act together!"

The *Styled* beauty editor knew she'd be sacked the moment Saffron found out, and she was terrified that moment was coming. That Saffron already knew. Half suspected at least. You could tell by the way she'd been glowering at her in the office all week.

But then again, Saffron always glowered. At everybody.

Mustn't get paranoid, she told herself. Just need to stick to the plan. Make sure the images have been removed and no evidence remains. That's what we agreed. That's what must happen!

She continued scrolling, past all sorts of cringey stuff, and kept thinking about Ginny and what happened to her, how she ended up on the train tracks.

How it had freed her in a way. But it wasn't over yet.

There were more tracks to deal with, ones she needed to cover up.

Stomach roiling, she picked up the pace and continued scrolling…

~

Jackson watched as his new wife stared vaguely at the menu and could see she was not concentrating, nor was she convinced. He knew Alicia well. Knew the subject of Ginny's suicide was not over. Would never be over until she got answers.

She was a truth seeker, Alicia. A mystery solver. And why a seemingly happy young woman kills herself was certainly a mystery.

But it wasn't hers to solve. Singh had made that crystal clear, and he needed to get the message across. For everyone's sake. And he needed to do the ordering, or they'd be here all night. So he suggested their usual, called the waiter over, and with that out of the way, reached into his jacket.

"I'm not supposed to show you this," he said, pulling out his mobile phone. "It's private family business. Do not tell Singho."

He looked up. Smiled. It had become a kind of mantra in their relationship. His smile vanished. "We met with Ginny's mother today. Gail DeRosso?"

"Oh, poor Gail. She and Ginny were so close. How is she handling it?"

Better than you, he wanted to say but just shrugged as he began scrolling through his photos. "She's distraught, of course, but she showed us this." He found the image he had snapped earlier and held it out. "I think it's been helping her."

He hoped it would help Alicia too.

Confused, she squinted at the screen and then took the phone and studied the photo more closely. "What is this?"

"A copy of Ginny's suicide note. She texted it to her

mum the morning she died. It's quite clear."

But Alicia's frown only deepened as she reread the text. "But what does she mean by 'I can't do it anymore'? Do *what*, exactly?"

"Sorry?"

"I'm asking you, what was so hard that Ginny had to throw herself in front of a train?"

"She was probably just talking about life, Alicia, trying to get ahead at work and find love, all the usual stuff that upsets young people. And she was pushing thirty."

Alicia scoffed. "She couldn't care less about work and love and ageing."

"*That you know of.* Honestly, Alicia, we don't always know people. We may never—"

"And why is she just telling you this now?"

"What?"

"The mother! Gail! Why bring it up now? Why not mention this when it happened?"

He dropped his head to one side. "It happened two days ago, Alicia. She's a mother in mourning. Just lost her only child. Cut her some slack."

She nodded. "Of course. Sorry. Yes."

She handed the phone back as the waiter appeared with their wine.

While the waiter filled their glasses, Alicia's heart filled with grief for Gail. Yes, she would be distraught. The mother and daughter were more than close; they were like best friends. Had dinner every week, she told Jackson now. Caught up regularly for drinking sessions at their local pub.

That's what made it so confusing.

Why would Gail wait two days to pass on Ginny's message? A message that was clearly a cry for help. Was she feeling guilty she hadn't acted on the warning? A warning she had received many hours before Ginny stepped in front of that train.

There had been time to save her...

"Listen, there's going to be a memorial," Jackson told her.

"Mrs DeRosso's organising one for this Friday I believe. I'll get you the details."

"That's quick."

"Body won't be released for a while. Doesn't want to wait. I mean, is there ever a good time to memorialise your dead daughter?"

Good point, thought Alicia. And a good idea really. Everyone who loved Ginny must be floundering, as she was, as Isla-Mae was. Coming together might help them try to understand what happened and why. Jackson was seeing it as more of a chance to move on, and he told her as much.

"Maybe after that you can try to let it go. Stop overthinking it, like you always do."

She would have been offended if it wasn't the truth. Alicia was a chronic over-thinker, with a turbo-charged imagination. She couldn't simply watch a woman walk alone at night without taking note of the men nearby, the cars, their number plates, in case she vanishes. If there was a strange sound in the dark, it was never a tree branch or a possum that sprang to mind. It was a shadowy figure, lurking… And if a friend of hers stepped in front of a train, she couldn't possibly have done that deliberately.

There must have been hands at her back.

None of this left Alicia feeling fearful or depressed. It's just the way her mind worked—like a stream of trailers for scary movies you never ended up watching. Or, as she liked to think, preparing for the worst and being pleasantly surprised.

But there was nothing pleasant about suicide, and she just couldn't reconcile it. Not with her friend.

As if reading her mind, he said, "At the risk of sounding selfish, can we change the subject? I'd like to focus on us for a bit. This is supposed to be our happy time, yeah? We've still got a week and a half left of our honeymoon. So I'm going to make a proposal."

"Ooh, another one," she said, trying to sound light.

He smiled, appreciating the effort. Held up his glass. "Let's make a pact. I won't go back into work if you don't fixate on Ginny. I know you care, but fixating won't get you anywhere other than depressed. Please. Just try to let it go."

Alicia nodded and raised her glass, gave his a clink. He took that as a yes and offered her another smile, this one filled with relief. But as they both sipped their wine, she couldn't ignore the scary trailer that was starting up in her head.

Something was off. Something about Ginny and the gifts she had left behind.

Alicia wasn't sure what that so-called suicide message was about, but there was definitely a message behind those gifts. She just had to work out what it was.

And if that meant she was fixating, then so be it.

"One more request," Jackson said. "Bin that disgusting perfume. I don't care how expensive it is. Give it to the kitchen. They could use it to kill rodents."

She laughed and nodded and thought at least this was one promise she was happy to keep.

~

What a dump, thought Austin Smythe as he strode into the Frog & Bucket Hotel and glanced about, taking in the crummy lamps and couches that were supposed to be "bohemian" but were better suited to the tip. Why Ginny loved it so much he hadn't a clue, but he needed to be here tonight. It was the only way to move on.

He strode past the undersized pool table and into the back room where he spotted a familiar face and couldn't help smiling. Brushing quick fingers through his thick locks, he made a beeline for the bar and placed his order.

The barman looked surprised and with good reason. He was Arial Publishing's biggest catch, the head of Sales and Circulation, don't you know. And it wasn't just his lofty title and good looks that lured the chicks. Austin was cool. Everybody said so. And ordering two Aperol Spritzes was the opposite of cool. But needs must, and so he just shrugged and paid for them and took a grimacing gulp of one before making his way across the room.

When he got close to the booth, he dropped his head to one side and said, "Oh, hey, Isla-Mae isn't it?"

Ginny's flatmate glanced up, mid-conversation with another model—a prettier redhead with a flowering frown—and said, "Austin! Hey, what are you doing here?"

He sighed and glanced about. "Waiting for a mate. Been waiting ages though. Think I've been stood up."

"Oh no!" Isla said as the other woman's frown softened.

"Yeah." He glanced at the untouched drink in his hand. "You don't want this, do you? No use to me now."

"Oh wow, thanks. That's my favourite."

She nodded at the lurid orange drink in front of her, and he looked surprised.

"Must be fate," he said, handing it over.

Then he sighed again, glancing about. As he did this, the two women locked eyes and the redhead gave Isla a subtle nod.

"Join us," said Isla. "I mean, if you want to…"

He shook his head firmly. "Nah, wouldn't want to intrude. I'm not one of those losers who interrupts a couple of girlfriends on a night out."

"No, no!" both women chorused back now.

"Please, sit. We'd love it," said Isla. Then she added, "We were just talking about poor Ginny. It's been such a shock." She turned to the redhead and explained, "This is the guy Ginny was seeing before… well… *before*."

The redhead was no longer frowning. "Oh my God, you poor thing! How are you coping?"

He shifted his features into miserable mode as he took the seat across from them.

"Gotta be honest," he told her. "It's like my heart's been sliced in two."

There was a chorus of "awws" now, and he glanced sheepishly at Isla.

"I know we had our issues; weren't perfect. But the truth is I was falling for Ginny. Hard. Was hoping…"

He coughed. Cleared his throat. "Too late now, I guess. I

just have to try to move on."

They both mirrored his misery, and the redhead said, "You'll be okay," as she swept a hand to his forearm and gave it a gentle rub. A suggestive smile.

He smiled back. "You're so sweet. Anyway, enough about me." He raised his glass. "Here's to Ginny. Gone too soon."

They both nodded and raised their glasses too.

Then, as the sweaty hordes swirled around them, he settled back in his seat and turned his smile to the less pretty of the two.

He wasn't here for pleasure, after all. He would get that elsewhere. Later.

Tonight it was strictly business.

~

Ebony Johnson admired her reflection as she pulled the glass door open and then glanced about the bar. He'd be in the back room, of course he would. Always lurking in the shadows.

She fluttered a wave at the leering waiter then made her way across the floor, swinging her tight butt for his benefit, then headed down the corridor and into the overflow room, where she found what she was looking for, seated at a corner table alone.

"Gin and tonic," the man murmured, nodding at the drink in front of the vacant chair.

"You ordered for me?" She was surprised. He could teach her useless husband a thing or two. It had taken two prods to get Ted to order her Mimosa at brunch that morning.

The man slowly blinked. "I think I know you well enough by now, Ebony, and you probably need it."

She grinned wickedly. "You didn't catch the news then? Not anymore I don't." Then she cackled as she slipped into the seat and added, "Ding dong the witch is dead. Everything's back on track."

He didn't cackle along.

Her smile dissolved. "What now?"

He produced an A4-sized envelope from his lap and placed it beside her glass. "She's not the only witch in Oz, I'm afraid."

Ebony glowered. She had seen that kind of envelope before. Knew exactly what it contained. Didn't have the strength yet. She reached for her gin, slugged it back in one, and then pushed her empty glass towards him.

"If you *really* knew me," she snapped, "you would've bought me the whole damn bottle."

Then she held her breath and reached for the envelope.

CHAPTER 7
The Memorial Part 1

Three days later, the Frog & Bucket looked like it had had one of *Styled*'s infamous makeovers. The space was lighter, brighter and much better dressed, largely thanks to the fashionable magazine crowd who were swanning about in the back room where Ginny's memorial was now in full swing.

If anyone thought this pub was a strange choice of location, they clearly didn't know Ginny or her mother, Gail, the one who'd organised it. Not only were the two women regulars—it was just a drunken stumble from both their abodes—but Ginny was tight with the staff and beloved by the publican, Brian, who considered her family she was here that often. Today he and Gail had tarted the place up with buckets of fresh flowers and free Prosecco, as well as platters of mixed sandwiches, mini sausage rolls, cheese and crackers, and right in the centre of the room, a clumsily made photo board featuring happy snaps of Ginny, some as a naked baby, others as an adult, not wearing much more.

Alicia was staring across at the board now, wondering if the missing photo-booth snaps were in the mix and made a note to check as she glanced about.

Despite thirty minutes of agonisingly sad speeches, the mood was finally lightening up, helped along by the free plonk and the crazy stories the crowd were now sharing about Ginny. And she would have loved it, Alicia decided. She would have jumped atop the bar and regaled them with scandalous fish tales of her own.

There was only one group who looked like they had nothing to say—the small crew from *Styled* who stood in a tight cluster on one side, watching everyone like a panicky herd, their alpha female, Saffron, right in the centre, chatting intensely with Arabella.

Alicia had said hello to them all but didn't linger. It was decent of them to show, but it felt more like a compulsory staff outing, and she wasn't sure any of them genuinely cared.

And she needed to be with people who cared today.

"You okay?" Jackson asked, handing Alicia a glass of the Prosecco.

She nodded. "Thanks for being here."

"Of course. I really liked Ginny, you know that. But I'm mostly here for you."

And it was true. Jackson was not there under any official capacity, and he quickly pointed that out to those who knew his vocation and raised an eyebrow or two.

Or ten if you counted the other five members of the Murder Mystery Book Club, who were also there for Alicia, several now ogling the detective suspiciously.

"Looking to see if the killer's lurking?" whispered Perry Gordon, the cheeky palaeontologist in the group. "Isn't that what you detectives do? Infiltrate the wake? Have a little sniff about?"

"Pointless exercise with suicide," Jackson replied drolly, and Perry tutted at him, like he was a killjoy.

"How are you holding up, dear?" Ronnie Westera asked, her heavily wrinkled eyes firmly on Alicia.

"I'm *fine*," she told the wealthy widower. Then, more truthfully, "I don't know why it's knocked me about so much."

"Because she was your friend and because it's tragic," Claire Hargreaves told her, handing her a delicate embroidered hanky that had probably come from her vintage clothing shop and was far too pretty to use. "It is sad, honey. You're allowed to be sad."

Missy Corner's cherry-red locks bobbed up and down as she watched Alicia dab at her eyes.

"Claire's right, possum. You let it all out if you need to. Just like her friends were doing. Gee some of them were *inconsolable* during the speeches. I could barely hear what her poor dear mum was saying."

Missy turned her cat-eye spectacles towards a group of young women, clearly models judging by their height and weight and immaculate complexions. Alicia spotted Ginny's flatmate Isla-Mae amongst the group and was relieved to see she hadn't been sobbing so much as handing out tissues. She looked better today, brighter, stronger, and was wearing a body-fitting black-and-silver dress, her hair swept up in a high ponytail. Alicia also noticed Austin Smythe in the group, dapper in a dark Hugo Boss suit, and she wondered if Ginny's boyfriend also needed consoling. She hadn't been close enough to see.

"But wasn't the mother stoic?" said Perry, staring at a busty woman in the centre, by the photo board, now talking with an enormous man, also in a designer suit—all height and girth and ego. Gail DeRosso looked like she was holding her own with the Arial CEO, one hand rubbing Ted's shoulder, like she was consoling *him*. "Her speech was magnificent."

"Women of a certain age always are," said Ronnie. "What I found surprising was how close she was to her daughter. BFFs, she said. Makes it all the more tragic."

Alicia agreed. She'd been surprised by their closeness, too, when she first met Gail at Ginny's twenty-first birthday party, many years ago.

Aptly named, Gail had arrived loud and late that evening, like a slow-moving tropical cyclone, wearing a flashy dress and an even flashier smile. "Let's get this party started!" she'd roared as she tottered in, her voice rough like she smoked a pack a day—and probably did, judging by the cigarette packet stuffed down her cleavage. It also bore a large tattoo—angel wings by the look of it—and there were more tattoos down both arms and around one ankle. Her topknot hairdo was misshapen, her thick eyeliner badly smudged, and Alicia was pretty certain she'd forgotten to paint in her right eyebrow. But that didn't matter. The birthday crowd had cheered with delight at the sight of her.

Alicia recalled glancing straight to Ginny, who was flirting with some guy in the kitchen, wondering how she'd take it. Would she be embarrassed? Mortified, like Alicia might? But oh no. Ginny looked as delighted as the crowd and had yelped as she rushed over to hug her.

Alicia smiled remembering that. Trust Ginny to have a wild mother and be proud of it.

Gail didn't look so wild now though. Didn't look too rough either. While she still had the plunging neckline, her tattooed wings lying limp against her crepey skin, her makeup was meticulous today, surprisingly subtle, and Alicia wondered if Arabella had arranged to have it professionally done. It was the kind of thing the company would do, taking the concept of free hair and makeup literally. But it wouldn't make up for anything.

Even perfect eyeliner and a stoic speech could not mask Gail's pain.

That got Alicia thinking of Hamish, and she glanced about, wondering where the *Lout* editor was. She'd texted him twice about the memorial but hadn't seen him arrive. It wasn't like Hamish to turn down free booze, she told them all, then winced. It was unfair. He would have paid for kegs of Krug if he thought it would bring Ginny back.

"Listen," said Missy. "Since you're home early, shall we do book club this Sunday?"

The club was due for their fortnightly get-together but had postponed, thinking Alicia would be on her honeymoon.

Lynette tsked. "Really, Missy?"

"No, no, let's do it," said Alicia. "You know how much book club cheers me up."

"But has everyone read the book?" persisted Lynette. "It's just two days away. I can host, but is that enough time for you, Alicia?"

Alicia nodded, as did the others. The club's next choice was a popular modern cosy—*The Thursday Murder Club* by Richard Osman. She'd already polished it off on the flight to Vanuatu. "Besides, what else am I going to do this weekend? Sit and sob?"

"Better than being angry," said Perry, nodding back towards the mother. "Does she look angry to you?"

Alicia looked across and noticed Gail was now alone, staring at the photo board, her head shaking over and over, and while she couldn't hear her from this distance, she could clearly see her lips mouthing the word, "Stupid, stupid, stupid!"

Saffron spotted the woman in the trashy dress, ranting like a crazy lady at the photo board. It was her dead Beauty Assistant's mother of course—the genes were strong in that family—and she tried to get her expression just right as she watched. A little sad. A little concerned. Ever-so-slightly nonplussed. You didn't want to look too judgy. Arabella might snap at her again.

And it wasn't just Arabella she had to perform for. Alicia Finlay's beefy detective husband was also here, eyes darting about the crowd suspiciously.

What was *he* doing here? Was he on police business?

She noticed Alicia hand her glass to him, then stride across the room towards Gail. She wondered why the detective didn't accompany Alicia and clap handcuffs on the dreadful creature.

Gail was more than dreadful, she was a common criminal, and if it wasn't for what happened to Ginny, Saffron would have called the cops on her days ago. Now she didn't know what to do, but she sure as hell wouldn't hug her like Alicia was now doing. Like she was some innocent victim! Couldn't believe Ted had insisted they all show up for this freak show. Easy for him, all he had on his schedule was brunching with his equally dreadful wife.

"All good?" asked her deputy, wearing a frankly disappointing bubble hem skirt from last season. They had an entire fashion wardrobe to choose from. Why couldn't she make better choices? She glanced around. Where was her blasted PA? Oh, that's right, somebody had to stay at work and hold down the fort.

"Can I get you another champagne?" asked Tiani.

"Oh, for goodness' sake this is not a party," Saffron snapped back. "How's that going to look? And let's not pretend it's champagne. It's *Prosecco*. And not even the good stuff. Just a sparkling water thanks."

She smudged out a smile as her deputy scuttled away. Should've left *her* manning the phones, not Frances. If her PA were here, she'd know exactly what to bring her. Exactly what would help. But right now all Saffron had was pasty egg sandwiches and a pathetic excuse for plonk.

"Try not to look quite so pissed off," came another voice beside her, and she dropped what she thought was a decent-enough smile and turned to glower at her boss.

"Well?" she said to Ted. "Did you sort it?"

Both sets of eyes were on Gail now, and they watched as Alicia released the mother from a clearly awkward hug and then reached across to an ice bucket.

"It's hardly the right time, Saffron," the CEO replied through clenched teeth.

Her eyes snapped back at him "There is no *right time*, Ted. Need I remind you how important this is? It's not just my future on the line here, it's yours. Your *marriage*. How do you think Ebony is going to—"

"Just chill," he said, barely moving his lips. "It will all work out. Just take a frigging chill pill."

Then he faked his own smile and strode away as Tiani returned with her water. Saffron snatched it, then remembered to thank her, took a good gulp and glanced across the room again. But it wasn't Gail she was now watching, or Alicia. It was that stick insect that used to live with Ginny.

Ira-Jane was it? Isla-Mary? Mary-May?

Whatever her blasted name, she could also be trouble. No two ways about it.

She glanced from the wannabe model to Arabella, who was giving Saffron a pointed look, and then to Kora, deep in conversation with Pascal. Saffron caught the fashion editor's eye, nodded her over, then leaned in and told her exactly what had to happen. And fast.

It was all about optics, she told her, repeating Arabella's words, mimicking her smile…

As Alicia poured Gail a fresh glass of bubbly, she had a feeling the woman didn't remember her, and it wasn't just the awkward hug. She had an equally awkward smile on her lips and a vague look in her eyes.

"I worked with Ginny," Alicia explained. "She was a very dear friend."

Gail snapped out of it. Her eyes turned sharp. "You're not Saffron, are ya?"

"No." *God no.* "I don't work at *Styled.* I'm in Special Projects. I edit one-off magazines. I've met you before at a few of Ginny's parties. My name's Alicia—"

"Alicia Finlay? Oh, I didn't recognise you, sorry, love. Come here!" The woman dumped the drink and grabbed Alicia by both shoulders, wrapping her in a proper hug this time. "My Ginny talked about you all the time. She loved you, she really did."

Alicia felt herself choke up. She cleared her throat. "I loved her too."

The woman pushed her back and nodded. "How are ya, darl'? You holding up?"

Like this was more Alicia's loss than hers.

"I'm fine," she told her. "It's you I'm worried about." And not just because she was ranting angrily at her daughter's photos. "I know you two were so close."

The woman waved a hand flippantly. Alicia noticed her fingernails were long and meticulously manicured in a fashionable milky beige. "I'll survive, don't you worry about me, love. Been through a tonne of shit in my time and I'll get through this too. But I'll never forgive Ginny, I'll tell you that for nothing."

There was no bitterness in her tone now though, just deep sadness, and Alicia understood the sentiment. She said, "Ginny seemed so happy last time I saw her. At my wedding? In fact, I have some beautiful shots I can get to you. Ginny looked stunning."

"Oh, she knew how to take a good photo, that girl! Right from the start, even as a bub, she'd pop her head to one side, drop her chin just so, and give a flirty smile." She imitated her daughter's pose to perfection, and they both burst out laughing.

God, it felt good to laugh today.

Alicia glanced across to the photo board and said, "Did you find some selfies she and I did at the photo booth in Town Hall? I'd love to pinch one, as a memento, if that's okay?"

"Course, Alicia, although I'm not sure I've seen 'em."

"They weren't with Ginny's work things?"

"What work things?"

Alicia explained about the stuff on her desk, how it had all been cleared away.

"Not by me it hasn't," said Gail, flute halfway to her lips. "Where d'ya reckon it's ended up? Shit! Hasn't been trashed, has it?"

"Hope not," said Alicia. "I really loved those pix. There were dozens of them. They're like a montage of our friendship. I'd love to keep them."

"And you should! I'd give 'em to you now if I knew where they'd ended up. That's pissed me right off that has."

"Oh, I'm sure it will all turn up…" Alicia began, but Gail was having none of it.

"I'm gonna ask that stuck-up cow who runs the mag."

"Saffron? She has no idea."

"You're telling me. Can't believe my Ginny spent her last months working for that tyrant."

Gail's eyes were fixed to the coiffed brunette at the other side of the room—Saffron clinging onto a glass of water, a constipated look on her face.

"You don't think that's why—" began Alicia, and Gail's eyes snapped back.

"Why what?"

Alicia blushed. "Sorry. I'm just so confused why Ginny… *did* … what she did. It makes no sense to me. Do you have any idea?"

Now Gail was glaring at Alicia. "Me? Why would I know? It's not my fault what happened to Ginny!"

"No, *of course not*. I'm not saying that." Alicia was horrified by the suggestion, and she reached across to rub Gail's shoulder. "I'm so sorry. I wasn't implying anything."

The older woman shook her off. "Yeah, of course. Right." Then, "Shit. I told my sister not to come. What's she doing here?"

Alicia stepped back. "I'll leave you to it."

"Gawd, don't do that." Gail wrenched the Prosecco bottle from the ice bucket and bolted towards the toilets.

Alicia chewed her lower lip, watching her go, then turned back to join her friends when an eerily familiar voice stopped her in her tracks.

"Well, if it isn't Alicia Finlay!"

She swung around to find an older woman with a smile as stiff as her black bob and bright resin beads, staring across at her, smirking. Suddenly Alicia was whirling through time.

And not in a good way.

CHAPTER 8
The Memorial Part 2

The Murder Mystery Book Club came about because of one woman. Well, two if you count Ginny, but more on her later.

That woman's name was Kirsten. She was the founder of the Monday Night Book Club, the very club that Alicia had loathed so much she created her own. The last time she'd seen Kirsten was just after Alicia had leapt to her feet in the middle of "question time", downed half a glass of red wine and informed her she was bailing.

And here she was now, all these years later, smiling at Alicia like she was posing for a police-issue mugshot. She was in her sixties and dressed entirely in charcoal-grey linen with thick red beads slung around her neck. If Alicia hadn't recognised her from the outfit, she certainly remembered the smile.

"Kirsten!" she gasped. "My God it's been forever."

Kirsten's lips softened as she approached, so she guessed there was no bad blood between them, and she was right. The older lady waved off the suggestion, telling her, "Oh, you were utterly misplaced in my club. Virginia never should have recommended you. Hell, my niece should never have signed up herself."

Alicia blinked. Hang on… "Ginny's your *niece*?" Was Kirsten the sister Gail had just fled from? How did Alicia not know that?

Kirsten's smile turned mugshot-cold again. "She never mentioned it, hey? I'll try not to take that personally. How else do you think Virginia ended up in my book club? I was trying to bring her up in the world. My sister doesn't have a book in her house that isn't a Harlequin Romance."

She sighed. "Since Lance walked out, she's been a sad ole sop." Sighed again. "Anyhoo, Virginia was even more misplaced in my club than you."

Then she winked and Alicia smiled. She was being facetious, and Alicia liked this side of Kirsten; wondered why she hadn't shown it more during book club. And could not believe this posh lady was related to Ginny, let alone Gail.

Pursing her lips, Kirsten said, "I still have your Peter Carey book, you know."

"Sorry?"

"The day you stormed out. You left your copy of *Oscar and Lucinda*. It's at my place if you ever want to retrieve it."

"I didn't *storm* out, did I?" Alicia winced, remembering back. Well, she might've been a bit snippy…

"Virginia told me you started a new one. Romance is it?" The old Kirsten was back, the disdain dripping from her voice.

"Murder mysteries actually," said Alicia. "But cosies. Nothing sinister. It's the puzzle I love."

"In that case you should puzzle over why the police seem to think Virginia threw herself willingly onto the tracks."

Alicia blinked. "You don't think she did?"

Kirsten's lips puckered again. "Of course not. It's absurd. She didn't have a suicidal bone in her body. Must've been a terrible accident. That I can believe. She was a scatterbrain. Just like her mother and as shallow as a birdbath."

"Even shallow scatterbrains can get depressed," said Alicia.

She tsked at that. "I saw her two weekends before, at Nana's ninetieth birthday barbecue. She seemed perfectly happy then, and I'm sorry but you don't go from Pollyanna to Anna Karenina overnight. I'm gathering you understand my literary references there?"

Alicia rolled her eyes as Kirsten added, "Now if her boyfriend had done it, that I would believe. He was more your tormented Heathcliff."

"Austin?" Alicia blinked. Blinked again. "Are you talking

about Austin Smythe?"

But Kirsten's attention was now taken by something across the room. She glanced back. "Sorry, gotta scoot. I can see my sister attempting to hide behind a pot plant. Must go pay my respects. Lovely to see you again, Alicia."

With that she was gone, her beads clinking in her wake.

Ted Johnson picked up the trilby he'd left on the bar, dropped it to his head and glanced around the pub, ready to take his leave. He'd paid his respects as Arabella had requested, been well and truly *seen*. Enough was enough. He was a busy man. It was time to get back to the real world. Pity though, he thought, as his eyes slithered across the crowd—from the silly little models in one corner to the lovely leggy blonde who seemed to be related to his Special Projects editor Alicia. In another lifetime he might've had a crack. But he had to be careful these days and not just because of Ebony.

His eyes settled on the *Styled* girls still huddled together like they might catch something, Saffron in the centre like the queen bee that she was, her worker bees buzzing around her. Except for one of them, standing to the side, chatting furtively with Ginny's flatmate. He sighed. Talk about lovely…

He crooked his neck. Readjusted his hat. This was not the time to get distracted. He needed to man up and put an end to it. There was no other option. His only chance at survival. But boy he wasn't looking forward to it. He knew exactly how it'd play out.

Could already feel the sting…

"Jug of water please," Alicia told the hovering barman, intending to make her way back to her friends, but then she noticed Tiani slumped on a nearby stool, staring into a highball glass of God knows what. Something strong, she hoped, because *Styled*'s deputy editor did not look good.

"You okay over there?" Alicia called across to her.

Tiani glanced up from her drink, her eyes red and

smudged, then sniffed and nodded and wasn't very convincing. Alicia stepped across to join her, trying to hide her surprise.

So there was someone at Styled *who cared about Ginny.*

As if reading her mind, Tiani said, "I know she had a tough time with us. Always felt guilty, you know? That I didn't stand up for her more."

"Ginny could stand up for herself though, couldn't she?"

Tiani looked away and sniffed again. "Saffron was so mean to her, but I liked Ginny. She was real. Just like our readers. Saffron thinks they're all as glamorous and rich and perfect as her, but they're so not. They're ordinary, everyday girls like Ginny. Frances too. Desperate to look rich and perfect but struggling to pay the bills, lose weight, meet Mr Right. I found Ginny's advice invaluable. Now..." She gulped. "Poor Ginny. I mean, sure she was *a lot*, but she didn't deserve what happened in the end. That wasn't right."

Alicia stared hard at her. Was she referring to Ginny's grisly death? She went to ask, but Tiani brushed her off.

"Sorry," she said, wiping the mascara from below her eyes. Shaking her auburn hair back. "I'm not making any sense. I think I need another drink before I head back to the trenches."

Then she raised a finger to catch the barman's attention while Alicia grabbed the water jug and turned, thinking, she's right. None of it makes sense. There are no words to explain any of this. Just heartache and grief for a young woman whose life was over far too soon and a mother who would somehow continue living but never roar quite as happily again and a group of family and friends and, yes, even the odd guilt-riddled colleague who had lost someone who lit up a room, whether she annoyed you or adored you or anything in between.

And then suddenly Isla-Mae appeared like a vision splendid and offered fresh words.

Words of hope.

"Hey, Alicia," she sang out. "I think I might know what happened to Ginny."

Alicia dropped the jug back on the bar. "What? Really?"

The willowy model nodded, glanced around, then leaned in. "Have you got a second?"

"Of course!" she said, offering her a hug first. "You look so much better today."

"Thank you. That's because I took your advice. Found Ginny's stash. Opened a bottle of her Moet. Not the really expensive one *obviously*. I'd never—"

"You deserve it," Alicia broke through. "Nothing like a drop of bubbly to cheer you up."

"But it wasn't the bubbles. Look, I found something." Isla leaned even closer. "Something that might explain everything. Something... *strange*."

"Strange? How do you mean?"

Isla glanced around and then back. "That's the thing. I don't know. But you might. I think it's best I show you. Can you come to the apartment? Sunday morning? About tennish? I'm on a shoot all day tomorrow. Turns out I did get the *Styled* gig. Kora just told me."

"Good on you," said Alicia. "Is everything cool?"

She glanced around again, then leaned in and whispered, "I can't talk here. I'm getting the evil eye. Come at ten, yes? We can open some more bubbles. But we'll make it her vintage Dom this time."

Alicia was going to tell her she wasn't much of a drinker, certainly not mid-morning, but then Isla gave her a strange, inscrutable look and scuttled out. And Alicia watched her go, feeling utterly confused, then turned to see who was giving Isla the evil eye, but all she could see was Ginny's mother on one side, glaring angrily at Ginny's photos again, and the *Styled* team on the other looking like they couldn't care less.

And she wasn't sure which was the lesser of two evils.

CHAPTER 9
A Turn of Events

Winter in Sydney is relatively mild, certainly blue-skyed and sunny. But not this winter. Not today. The sky was granny grey, the air icy, and rain was drizzling down when the woman stepped out of the building. She hovered for a moment, almost turning back.

How dreadfully miserable! It reminded her a lot of home, and she tried to think of that as she trawled her phone for her tunes, popped in her earbuds, slipped the phone into her jacket and made her way down to the sidewalk.

Besides, it was all her fault she had to be out here this early. Her penance for a weekend of shame. Shouldn't have downed quite so much Prosecco at Ginny's wake, not to mention all those tasty sausage rolls. Then there'd been the catering yesterday. That hadn't helped, although she had stuck to the salads. At least she had *some* restraint.

Still, she wished she'd had more as she pulled on her beanie and tucked her hands into her jacket, shivering a little. Then glanced up at the surly sky. Just a few quick laps of the block, she told herself, then I can nestle back under the covers and watch *Emily in Paris*.

And that's why she stepped out so quickly and didn't notice the car bearing down upon her—she was in a hurry to get back to her streaming. That and her earbuds and the fact that the rain was getting heavier and you could barely see beyond your nose, let alone hear the vehicle that wasn't there just a moment ago.

And as she lay prone on the street soon after, no longer feeling the icy chill and drizzle, she was heartened to see a familiar face hovering above like an angel.

Thank God, she thought. Thank God! Please help me!

And she thought for a moment help was coming as the face lurched closer and hands reached down towards her. But then they vanished below her jacket, and she couldn't feel what they were doing, but she could see their expression, and it was oddly disconcerting.

What did they have to be so grumpy about? she wondered as everything faded to black.

~

Alicia noticed the first red flag the moment she stepped around the corner.

It was more of a blue-and-white flag, in fact, a chequered police tape strung up halfway down the street, preventing pedestrians and cars from going any further.

The second red flag was all the white plastic— the personal protective equipment several people were wearing on the other side of the tape.

And the third? Jackson's old Toyota 4WD, parked bang in the middle of the road.

Oh God. Oh no...

Alicia had awoken that morning, feeling positive, hopeful. And it wasn't strictly because she had her book club get-together that afternoon, something she loved more than anything (shh, don't tell Jackson). Oh no, she was meeting with Ginny's flatmate beforehand, and she could not wait.

Isla-Mae's words at the memorial had provided some solace. She said she had answers, said it would finally make sense! And Alicia couldn't wait to hear them, but first she had to work out how to sneak away from Jackson. She could hardly tell him. He'd begged her to leave it alone, and she'd promised that she would.

Just as *he'd* promised not to go back to work, so she was surprised to find him missing when she opened her eyes, a cold cup of tea by her bed and a note that read:

Got called in, sorry xx.

Alicia would have been furious if she wasn't so relieved.

No need to sneak about after all! And so she had dressed without guilt, then caught the train to North Sydney station before making the ten-minute walk to the red-brick apartment complex where Ginny once lived.

But now, as Alicia turned down the leafy one-way street tucked behind the main drag, her hope was fast evaporating.

Heart in throat, she approached an elderly lady, standing on her side of the ribbon, and asked, "What's going on?"

The woman swept around to reveal a tiny fluffy dog tucked under one arm. "Oh, there's been a terrible accident. Young lass went and got herself run over. Just tragic."

Alicia's heart dropped to her feet. "Do… do you know who?" She held her breath.

The elderly lady shook her head. "You okay, dear? You look like you've seen a ghost!"

Alicia mumbled something but wasn't about to stand there, politely watching. She ducked under the blue-and-white tape and rushed towards Ginny's building. A little further up the street she could see three PPE-clad officers now staring down at what looked like a black patch on the bitumen. Someone was snapping photographs. Someone had a measuring tape.

Trying not to panic, she stopped at the building and rushed up the wide stone staircase where an officer in uniform stalled her with one hand up.

"You can't be in here!" he called out. "This building is out of bounds, ma'am. Please turn around and get back behind the barrier."

She stopped and gulped at him. "But I've got an appointment with someone here." She didn't recognise her voice. It was a high-pitched, squeaky.

He shook his head. "Sorry, no can do. Come back in a few hours." Then, almost as an afterthought, he asked who her appointment was with.

She swallowed hard, crossed the fingers in her head and said, "Isla-Mae Cavendish, apartment three."

Now he looked like he'd seen a ghost and his voice sounded squeaky.

"Oh. Right. Um, wait here. I… I'll get someone."

Then he swivelled and rushed into the building.

As he did so, Alicia slid down onto one step, dropping her head into her hands. "Oh no, no, not Isla. Please, not Isla-Mae."

"Alicia?"

She looked up and around and found Jackson standing at the doorway to the building. "What are you doing here? You okay?"

She nodded, then shook her head, then said, "It's Isla, isn't it? Something's happened?"

He sighed heavily as he propped the door open, then dropped down beside her. Took both her hands and squeezed them.

"She's gone, Alicia. I'm so sorry. Was found just up the block, very early this morning. Hit-and-run we suspect. Lot of head trauma. Looks like she might've stepped out and in front of a car. Would've been instant."

Like that made it all okay.

"No witness yet, so we haven't got a clear picture," Jackson continued. "But a dog walker found her already deceased. It's always a dog walker." He shook his head like people really shouldn't walk their dogs these days. Then he squeezed her hand tighter. "You okay?"

She sniffed and wiped her nose with her sleeve.

He pulled a handkerchief from his pocket and passed it to her. "Can I ask why you're here? Did you get word?"

"What? Oh… no. I saw her at the memorial on Friday, remember? She asked me to meet her here at ten." She wiped her nose and then frowned. "What do you mean, she stepped out in front of a car? Why would she do that?"

He lifted one shoulder. "Still piecing it together, but she was wearing trainers, a tracksuit, the sort of gear you might wear jogging. It was pouring; she had earbuds in place. My guess is she didn't hear the car coming. Why people wear those bloody things on the road I just don't know."

Now he was blaming the earbuds. He released an angry puff of air and squeezed Alicia's hand harder, forcing her to look at him. "I'm sorry I have to ask this, but didn't you say she was distressed after Ginny died? That she wasn't really coping?"

"Well, yeah, but…" Alicia blinked. "You can't think she *threw* herself in front of the car?"

"It's unlikely, of course, but I'm keeping an open mind."

He glanced backwards, through the open doorway, and you could see the front door to Isla's ground-floor apartment swing open as a forensic officer stepped out. Before it swung back, Alicia spotted a cushion on the floor and what looked like a leather jacket.

"We're going through her things now. Just in case."

Just in case she conveniently left a suicide note like her friend Ginny? Is that what he was hoping?

"Isla would not have killed herself, Jackson. That's ridiculous."

"How well did you know her?"

She looked away. The truth was, she didn't know Isla-Mae at all, and he knew it.

"You're a journalist, Alicia. You know about copycat suicides. They're not that uncommon."

He was right, she couldn't deny that. It was the reason suicide was rarely mentioned in the press. There was a band of researchers who believed that just talking about suicide triggered further suicides—the "Werther Effect" they called it. Others believed it helped to prevent it—the "Papageno Effect". So long as you showed positive alternatives, listed numbers for crisis services… Alicia was in that camp.

She pulled her hands away. "Still. You don't think this is all a bit strange? Isla dying mysteriously less than a week after her flatmate? That doesn't ring alarm bells for you?"

"Of course it's alarming, Alicia, that's why Singh got called in. That's why she called me and why I went. I'm sorry I broke our pact, but you were sound asleep. Didn't want to wake you."

She waved that off. It didn't matter now.

He said, "You told me the other day that Isla was inconsolable when you visited her here. You were concerned about her. Her mental health."

"Yes, but…" She paused. He needed to understand this. "When I saw her at the memorial, Isla was much better. Stronger. In fact, she was helping her friends get through it. Don't you remember? She was energised, almost upbeat. That's why I was meeting with her. She had something she wanted to show me. Something important. Something related to Ginny's death."

"She said that to you?"

"Yes! She said she'd found something that might explain what happened to Ginny. But couldn't say more because someone was watching. Said something about evil eyes."

"Evil eyes? Who was she referring to?"

"I don't know, do I? Because I stupidly didn't ask her and now it's too late!"

She felt her heart constrict. Why didn't she demand answers at the memorial? Why didn't she mention all this to Jackson afterwards? Why didn't she get here in time to save the poor girl!

Jackson was thinking along similar lines. "Why didn't you tell me?"

"Hey, you're the one who insisted I stop fixating on Ginny. I couldn't be sure it would lead to anything, and I thought you might try to stop me from coming. Now I wish I'd come sooner. This *has* to be connected to Ginny, don't you see? It's too coincidental."

Jackson didn't nod as she hoped he would, but he didn't dismiss her either.

"You know I hate coincidences. It's the reason we got called in. But you also know they don't always add up to murder. Sometimes it's just bad timing. I don't know why the driver didn't stop and assist this morning, but that might have nothing to do with Isla, or Ginny for that matter. It's highly likely they were over the alcohol limit or driving drugged or unlicensed, and that's why they fled. That's the usual story anyway. But we're checking for CCTV and, like I said, going through the apartment now. If we find anything even remotely suspicious, I promise we will bag it.

But you need to prepare yourself too."

He waited for her to look him in the eye again. "For all you know, Isla just wanted to show you some sad poems Ginny had collected or a message from her boyfriend breaking up with her. Those things might have explained her suicide. It might have been trivial."

Alicia scoffed. Ginny would *never* kill herself over a boyfriend let alone collect sad poems! The idea was laughable. Besides, Isla wasn't acting like she'd found something trivial. Nor did any of this explain why *she* was now being carted off to a morgue.

"Let's stick with the facts," he continued. "The timing is odd, I grant you that. But give me a chance to investigate. We'll need a proper statement from you and—"

"She was on a shoot yesterday!" Alicia just remembered. "A *Styled* shoot! You need to talk to Kora too. She's the fashion director."

He nodded, then reached a hand up to gently wipe the tears she hadn't even realised she was crying. "This has been a terrible shock for you. Let me give you a lift home."

"I'm fine." She smiled gratefully, then stood up. "I think I need to walk this out."

Then she glanced back towards the apartment again. The door was now propped open, and she could see more clearly. There were clothes strewn across the floor, bursting out of a carryall, and she could see cabinet drawers left open, a board game falling out, and not one but three handbags dangling across the sofa.

"Did you guys do that?" She pointed towards it. "The place is a mess."

He followed her finger and shook his head. "It was a bit of a tip when we entered. We assumed she was a slob. Why?"

"She's not a slob. She's a neat freak, like Ginny."

"Yeah, but you said she wasn't coping, so—"

"Even so, the place was meticulous last time I was here, when she was at her saddest. That mess is not normal, Jackson." She gasped. "Oh God, do you think someone's been through it? Maybe searching for something? I could have a look, if you like. See if anything obvious is missing."

"No chance," came a stern voice behind them, and they swung back towards the street, where DI Indira Singh was now standing, two takeaway coffee cups in hand.

She strode up the steps towards them. "Hello, Alicia." Her smile was as stiff as Kirsten's. "Sorry about your honeymoon."

Alicia mirrored her smile. The relationship between the two women in Jackson's life—his new wife and his detective partner—had never been an easy one, and she had a feeling it wasn't going to get any easier with this case.

Singh's smile turned glacial as she handed one coffee to Jackson.

"Alicia knew the deceased," he said quickly, answering her unspoken question. "Was supposed to meet up with her here at ten this morning. I'll explain it all later."

Singh looked relieved at that, and now Alicia was darting icy looks at her husband. Was he excusing her presence? *Apologising* for her?

He held the coffee out to Alicia like a consolation prize, and she crossed her arms, scowling at him, before turning her scowl to Singh.

"I wasn't just *meeting up* with Isla," she told her. "She had something important to tell me. Something about Ginny's death. But now she's dead and can't tell me anything. How strange is that?"

Singh's eyes widened. Once again she was looking to Jackson for the answers.

"I'll get an official statement from Alicia later," he told her. "We'll know more then."

"Good," said Singh. "For now I will need your *wife* to vacate the premises."

There was so much loaded into that word, and Alicia felt like she had just been brought down to size. Like all she was good for was cooking Jackson's dinner and washing his whites.

She went to snap back, but Jackson had grabbed her arm and was now pulling her down the steps.

"Come on, Alicia, let's go."

"But—" She yanked herself free and turned to the DI who was sipping from her cup. "You don't understand!" Alicia called out. "Isla's apartment has been ransacked. That's not just mess in there, Indira. That's a crime scene."

Singh lowered the cup from her lips and said, "All the more reason for you not to be here."

Then she turned and strode into the building.

As Jackson escorted Alicia back down the steps and along the street, she cursed under her breath, ranting about Singh and how the upstart detective had never taken her seriously.

By the time they got to the police tape, Jackson was ranting too. "What is it with you two? Why can't you just get along?"

He snatched at the ribbon, held it high, then dropped it again, turning back to Alicia. "You know what Singh's like. She's by the book. Always was, always will be. Screaming at her is not going to get you anywhere."

"I wasn't screaming!" Alicia all but screamed back.

She caught the eye of the elderly dog lady, who looked delighted by this fresh spectacle, and took a deep breath. Lowered her voice. "I'm serious Jackson, there is something in that apartment that relates to Ginny's death. Isla found it, and now you need to too. That is if it hasn't already been swiped by whoever's just ransacked the place."

"Alicia—"

"No. I'm *telling* you, the two deaths are linked whether you like it or not."

He stared hard at her for a moment, then he, too, lowered his voice. "Okay, I've heard you loud and clear. Now you need to hear me. You need to stay out of it and let us do our job." He held the tape high again and waved one hand through it. "Just go home. Please. No interfering like you always do."

Alicia would have slapped him if it wasn't the truth. She and her book club had "interfered" in homicide investigations many times before, and Jackson came scarily close to losing his job because of it. But this wasn't just about self-preservation. Alicia's club had also come under scrutiny and been raked over the coals. None of it much fun.

And so she had to accept that he was protecting her and her friends too. That his determination to keep her out of it had love behind it.

But she wasn't feeling so loving now.

She was irritable. On edge. And it wasn't just her clash with Jackson or his detective partner or even the death of another young woman. There was something fresh niggling at the back of Alicia's mind. Something else Isla said to her…

Something important.

If only she could remember what!

Nor was Alicia heading home as Jackson had asked. She would make her way to Woolloomooloo where, in a few hours, the Murder Mystery Book Club would gather. And if they happened to *interfere*? Well, who was she to stop them?

But first she had some gathering of her own to do…

CHAPTER 10
The Book Club Is in Session

Lynette had been busy baking all morning, but she had a hunch the minute her sister divulged her news to the rest of the club—because she had been ranting about it since she'd arrived—her spicy ginger cake, cherry clafoutis tartlets and lime muffins with smoked trout would fade to grey. As would their chosen book.

And she was right.

No sooner had everyone arrived and helped themselves to tea and treats, then sprawled out across the snug, mismatched sofas, Alicia had stepped forward and broken the shocking news.

Isla-Mae Cavendish was dead. And in suspicious circumstances.

That brought gasps all round and a query from one— "Who's Isla-Mae Cavendish? Sorry."

This was Queenie Dobson, and there was no need to apologise. The newest member of the group hadn't made it to the memorial and not because she didn't want to support Alicia but because her boss, who also happened to be Claire's husband, had an important conference that day and needed all hands on deck.

So Alicia explained how Isla was Ginny's flatmate, a budding model out from England.

And then Missy sighed dramatically and added, "It's unbelievably sad. She was so young and so pretty."

"Oh, I see," snapped Ronnie. "So if she was old and dumpy, it wouldn't be quite so sad?"

She was winding Missy up, and the younger woman looked mortified, but they all knew what Missy really meant.

It was a tragic waste of a young life, one with real potential.

It was also suspicious, Alicia told them, their eyes widening in unison as she described her last conversation with Isla at the Frog & Bucket Hotel.

"Hold on," said Claire, nearly spluttering her Earl Grey, which was so unlike Claire. "Isla was going to tell you something related to Ginny's death, and suddenly *she* shows up dead? That is beyond suspicious."

Alicia clapped her hands. "*Thank you.* That's what I said! But Jackson thinks I'm overreacting, and Singh is dismissing me like a… like a…"

"*Biatch?*" suggested Perry, winking.

Alicia smiled. She adored Perry. She wouldn't use that ugly word, herself, but was glad he always had her back.

"The point is," she continued, "from the moment I heard about Ginny, I felt like something was off. Didn't make any sense. Why would a happy-go-lucky, twenty-something step in front of a moving train, especially someone as happy as Ginny? And now her flatmate does almost the exact same thing? I'm supposed to just believe it's another suicide or accident or whatever? And I can tell you this—if her apartment wasn't ransacked, I'll eat that Richard Osman book!"

She was pointing at a copy of *The Thursday Murder Club* on the coffee table, and Claire leapt upon it. "I'll just pop this safely away then, shall I?" She plunged it back into her retro snakeskin clutch purse. "Looks like we're not going to get to it today anyway."

There were glances of resignation between them, and Alicia apologised.

"I can't believe this is happening again," she said, reaching into her own bag—a fraying calico tote. "But I do have another book we can discuss."

She pulled out *The Mysterious Affair at Styles* and placed it on the table. Then she reached in again and pulled out the Monopoly money, the thesaurus and the T-shirt.

They watched curiously as she carefully laid them out, then Perry said, "I know the contents of a woman's bag are mysterious, but this is next-level bizarre even for you, Alicia."

Missy giggled, and Alicia rolled her eyes, explaining how these four items were left on her desk by Ginny.

"Isla said they were her wedding gifts to me, but I don't think these are gifts at all. I think they're clues to what happened to Ginny."

Lynette's eyes narrowed. "Really? Because that"—she pointed to the cash—"looks exactly like the kind of wedding gift Ginny would leave you, thinking she was being hilarious."

"And this is not a surprising gift for a wordsmith like you," added Ronnie, tapping at the thesaurus. "Or this. Especially this." Now tapping the Christie book.

Claire frowned and picked it up. "Except you've read this, yes? Didn't we all read this one in the early stages of the club?"

"We did," said Perry. "It was the book we were discussing when Barbara Parlour went missing."

"Who?" asked Queenie, the newest member of the club lost again.

"Long story," said Perry, "but Barbara was one of our original members and just vanished one day. Into thin air! Her husband was acting coy. My God, that had us all in a spin. That was the first mystery we ever investigated."

He swapped misty looks with the other original members, but Missy was less concerned by history than theft.

"She can't give you this," their resident librarian said, pointing to the spine. "Belongs to the library."

"Exactly, Missy," said Alicia. "And the thesaurus is Ginny's own copy, given to her by Hamish"—a quick glance at Queenie—"he's her on-again, off-again, the editor of *Lout*. That's why I think they're a message of some sort."

"Okay and what's the message here?" asked Lynette, pointing at the T-shirt. "That you've got drab taste in fashion?"

She was joking, but Alicia glanced down at her oversized white cotton blouse and back, frowning. Hamish had said a similar thing. "I'm not that dowdy, am I?"

"You're fine," said Claire, the resident fashionista. "You have your own unique, carefree style."

Alicia's frown deepened. She wasn't sure that was a compliment either.

"That's not tie-dye is it?" asked Queenie, bringing them back to the T-shirt, her button nose wrinkled.

"No, it's been printed on," Alicia said, watching as Perry spread it out to scrutinise the smudged brown image on the front. "I'm guessing it's some kind of inkblot. Maybe one of those psychological tests."

Ronnie said, "You mean a Rorschach test."

"That's it. The ones that therapists show their clients and ask 'What do you see?'"

"And what *do* you see?" Ronnie asked.

"A red-hot mess," Lynette answered for her, but Perry was shaking his head.

"I can see exactly what we're supposed to see. It's Jesus." He looked at Alicia. "This isn't a Rorschach test, honey. It's the Shroud of Turin. Or a poor replica of it anyway."

Alicia gasped, snatching it up and holding it out to stare again at the print across the front.

"Oh… right…"

Now that he mentioned it, she did see the vague outline of a man's body, lying, hands clasped in front. She thought back to the religion classes she and Lynette had at school. The Shroud of Turin was said to be a piece of linen cloth featuring the faint image of Jesus after his crucifixion. His burial shroud.

"Was Ginny particularly religious?" asked Claire, now taking her turn to inspect the print.

"Not that I know of," Alicia replied. "And she certainly knows I'm not."

"So why would she give you this?"

It was a good question. A very good one.

Alicia waved a hand across the items. "That's what I'm trying to tell you. I don't think these are wedding gifts at all. I think these are keys that unlock a mystery."

"The mystery of why she killed herself?" asked Missy.

Alicia held up one index finger. "Or the mystery of why she ended up dead on Platform Three. And they are not the same thing."

There was silence now as they all stared back at Alicia.

"What exactly are you saying?" asked Ronnie, clutching at her pearls.

Alicia took a deep breath and tried to get her thoughts in order. Tried to make it make sense. She sat forward.

"So, not long before Ginny dies, she drops a bunch of 'gifts' on my desk. Okay. Fine. Nothing to see here. Except they're not your usual gifts, certainly not Ginny's usual style; they're a motley assortment of random stuff. Except... how random are they? Really?"

Several in the group were now frowning, and so Alicia plunged on.

"What if Ginny's gift to me was a mystery? One I should be able to unlock with all this... stuff? See, that *would* be the kind of thing Ginny would do. She mocked my obsession with mysteries, but she knew how much I loved them. She would have thought it was a laugh, me looking at all these clues and trying to solve it. But whatever it was, she clearly didn't take it seriously or she wouldn't now be dead."

She felt her breath catch as she added, "And neither would Isla. Because here's the thing—just five days after Ginny dies, her flatmate informs me she might know why. Like she's also uncovered the mystery. Said as much to me at the memorial but wouldn't tell me more. Seemed worried about someone at the pub." She held up a hand to stifle their next question. "I have no idea who. Maybe someone from *Styled*, a family member perhaps? Any case, after telling me she had answers, she too ends up dead."

"But what are you *saying*?" asked Ronnie for the second time.

"I'm saying there was nothing funny about whatever mystery Ginny had uncovered. Isla too." Alicia took a deep breath. She sat forward and glanced slowly across the now wide-eyed group. She said, "I think whatever the mystery was, it got them both murdered."

And there it was. The *M* word.

It had been lingering, unspoken for days, but now it was out, and unlike Jackson and Singh, the club knew better than to dismiss Alicia so quickly. Yes, she had a vivid imagination, but she was also uncannily right when it came to wrongdoing.

Still, Alicia gave them a moment to digest the notion, sitting back again, expecting some splashback, but they all just stared at her, half worried, half thrilled, because they were as obsessed with mysteries as she was.

Alicia sat forward again and described how Ginny's desk had been cleaned out so quickly after her death, and yet no one would accept responsibility for that, nor did anyone know where Ginny's things had ended up. Not her mother, her flatmate, her boss or any of her colleagues.

"I think the killer was trying to cover their tracks but clearly didn't realise Ginny had passed some things on to me, otherwise my desk would've been cleared out too."

"Pity," said Lynette. "Your desk could do with a spring clean."

She was joking, but Alicia did not crack a smile. She nodded down at the items. "I think all these things and whatever Isla found at their apartment—and I still don't know what that is—will lead us to the killer's door."

There was an exhalation now. Almost an acceptance, and Ronnie muttered under her breath, "Oh dear, not another one."

"Another *two*," Alicia said. "Although I think poor Isla was just collateral damage."

"And you might be too," moaned Lynette now. "Especially if this so-called killer works out you're onto them and have all this."

"But what *is* all this?" asked Claire, eyes dancing across the items again.

"That's what we need to find out," said Missy, barely able to control her enthusiasm.

"*We?*" said Perry, one eyebrow cocked. He loved a mystery as much as the next person, but he wasn't sure he wanted another *two* mysteries to investigate. He had somewhere else he needed to be. A lovely distraction as it happens.

"We can't let Alicia investigate alone, can we?" Missy said. "We work best as a team, don't we, folks? And who better to look into this little nugget?"

She was inspecting the library book again and had opened it to the inside back cover where she tapped on the barcode for the Woollahra library in the city's inner East.

"Ginny lived in Woollahra?" she asked.

"Used to live nearby, in Paddington," Alicia replied. "Back when she was in her aunt's book club, so I guess that's where her membership is. Not part of your group, is it?"

In the state of New South Wales, libraries are run by the local councils, and Alicia's local—the one where Missy worked—was part of the City of Sydney. Missy was shaking her head as Lynette joined in but for a very different reason.

"Come on, people," she said, pointing at the cover. "A five-year-old could tell you why she took this book out. If what you say is true, Alicia, then it's clearly a mystery she uncovered at *Styled* magazine. And most likely a mysterious affair, if that title is anything to go by."

"Or maybe it has something to do with poison," said Missy. "I remember this book well. It's Christie's first mystery, the one where she introduced Poirot to the world. And listen to this..."

She began reading the back blurb aloud:

"When the wealthy Emily Inglethorp is poisoned in her locked room, the local authorities are baffled. Hercule Poirot ... applies his extraordinary intellect and attention to detail to the case, navigating a web of family secrets, false leads, and ingenious red herrings to uncover the truth."

"That's right," said Queenie. "I remember this now. It takes place in a country manor called Styles Court. Did you know Agatha named one of her houses Styles after this book? One she lived in with first husband Archie."

"Oh, he was entirely unsuitable," said Ronnie. "Thank goodness she moved on to Max."

"There's a second husband in that story too, isn't there?" said Perry. "And a couple of insipid stepsons. Maybe it has something to do with a marriage breakdown?"

Alicia stared at them, gobsmacked. The only thing she remembered about the book was that it sparked her love of Christie.

"Maybe it involves an inheritance!" Missy was saying, pointing now at the fake cash.

"And someone with bad dress sense!" added Lynette, pointing at the T-shirt.

But Alicia had a feeling she was being facetious. She rolled her eyes. "And I'm supposed to be the one with the vivid imagination? Look, Lynny's right, we're probably overcomplicating it. Could be as simple as the title. Let me do some research first. I'll reread the book and see if anything obvious leaps out."

"You don't need an excuse to reread the book, yeah?" said Perry, grinning.

But Missy was shaking her cherry-red curls. "You'll have to get your own copy. Sorry, doll. This one's going back where it belongs. And where I can ask a few pointed questions and see if the librarian has any idea what Ginny was after when she borrowed this book."

Alicia beamed at her, happy they were moving forward and knowing they really shouldn't be. Jackson would be grumpy, but how could she possibly ignore all the clues her friend had left for her or the fact that she was now dead, and so too her flatmate, under shockingly similar and suspicious circumstances?

Oh no, she might have been a simple chick, young Ginny, and OCD-tidy, but she had left behind one very complex, tangled mess.

CHAPTER 11
Things That Go Bump in the Night

Later that night, as she sat up in bed, reading her own well-thumbed copy of *The Mysterious Affair at Styles*, Alicia stumbled upon a quote by Hercule Poirot. He was lecturing the insipid Captain Hastings. She'd never liked Hastings; he was such an unworthy wingman for the brilliant Belgian:

"Beware! Peril to the detective who says: 'It is so small—it does not matter. It will not agree. I will forget it.' That way lies confusion! Everything matters."

Everything matters.

It got her thinking about the clues Ginny had left, how small and trivial they might seem, and yet they had to mean something. Surely?

As she reread the quote, Jackson glanced across from the smartphone he was scrolling and said, "Isn't that the book Ginny left you?"

She glanced up and nodded, although technically that wasn't true. This was her copy, the one she had swiped from her old bookshelf at the end of the club meeting.

His eyes narrowed. "What are you up to?"

"Nothing. I'm allowed to read my wedding gift, aren't I?"

"As long as that's all you're doing."

She scoffed and looked away. It was the safest option. She knew that lying outright to your husband while still on your honeymoon was probably not the best start to a marriage, but neither was bickering, and they'd done enough of that for now.

Earlier, after she'd returned from book club and found him baking pizzas, she'd asked how the search of Isla's apartment had gone, but he had nothing to report. Or nothing he was willing to share with her, and she had to sympathise with that. Jackson's job was on the line. His silence protected himself and her club. There was love echoing all around it.

She just hoped he would remember how much he loved her when he discovered she was beginning to investigate. How could she not? She owed Ginny that, and poor, innocent Isla.

As if reading her mind, he placed his phone aside and said, "I love you, Alicia, you know that…"

"But?" She smiled. She knew him too, and those words were his segue to a caution.

"*But* we haven't found any link between the two women's deaths. Other than the fact they were friends and lived together."

"And both ended up squashed under moving vehicles."

He frowned. "We have Ginny's suicide note, Alicia. And the CCTV footage from the train station. Singh says it's clear as day—she moved towards the train as it approached, then stepped out and in front of it."

Alicia dropped the book down. "Could someone have pushed her?"

He went to shake his head, then shrugged, conceding the point. "They *could* have, but it's not obvious from the footage, apparently. And that's not what the witness statements say either. No one saw a push. Not a soul. And Singh says the platform was chockers."

"Ever heard of the saying 'Can't see the wood for the trees'?" she asked. "Maybe it wasn't so clear after all?"

He sighed gently. "I know you loved her. I know it's hard to accept. But there is no evidence that Ginny did anything but step willingly in front of that train, and not wanting her to is not reason enough, I'm sorry."

"So how do you explain what happened to her flatmate?"

Another sigh. A heavier one this time. "Seriously, honey. We're in the early stages of that one. Give us a chance to properly investigate. It's what we do best."

"Absolutely," she said, picking up her book, "and I'll do what I do best and read some cosy crime."

Then she returned to the novel and he returned to his device, but Alicia had a feeling he didn't believe she was just reading. Or at least she hoped he didn't, or he'd just married a woman he hadn't the first clue about.

Because Alicia wasn't just reading, she was scanning the text closely, trying to find something to explain why Ginny had gone out of her way to return to her old suburb of Paddington to borrow this particular book and then leave it like a glittering nugget under the debris on Alicia's desk.

Was there a character in this book that would ring a bell? A motive? A tiny, teeny theory that would unlock the truth? Something so small Alicia might do as Hastings was prone to do and sweep past it like it was nothing.

Oh no, she had to keep her beady eyes open for a clue, any clue, no matter how small.

Everything matters.

~

Austin Smythe narrowed his eyes at his reflection in the mirror above the bathroom sink and tried not to scowl. He didn't usually scowl. Usually liked his reflection—the chiselled jawline, the thick head of hair, the just-slightly feline eyes that gave him an exotic edge. He was a good-looking man and he knew it. The chicks in the building knew it too. Called him "the Hottie" when they thought he wasn't listening, but he didn't feel so crash-hot today. Hadn't felt good in days. Not since...

He shuddered.

Tried not to think about that. Shouldn't be thinking about anything but the board meeting tomorrow. Needed to play his cards right. Didn't want to go the way of his predecessor. Should be working on his laptop now, in fact, madly prepping the latest sales figures, smacking them into shape, but the only figure he could think about was her—falling, falling, blood and brain matter everywhere. He shuddered again. Closed his eyes. Shook the image away.

Then he opened his eyes, strode back to the bedroom and reached for his mobile, making the call he'd been putting off.

"I've looked everywhere," he said, not bothering with the preamble. "Can't find it."

There was a rush of expletives at the other end, and he let it run its course, wasn't bothered by that now. Was used to it. Then, knowing he was adding fuel to the fire, he said, "But I've been thinking, does it even matter anymore?"

Another stream of swear words, these ones even more imaginative, and he held the phone out and let that, too, run its course. Eventually he said, "Okay already, I hear you. I'll keep on it. Just give me more time."

Then he ended the call and glowered at his mobile, but it was Ginny he was angry with. And Isla. Especially Isla. If only she'd been as obliging as her flatmate. As *loose*. This might all be cleared away by now.

The stupid, frigid bimbo…

~

Gail DeRosso hugged the publican good night, lingering a little too long at his neck, breathing in the scent of sweat and beer and chip fat, hoping he'd invite her up as he used to, but he just pulled away and gave her a pitying look, and she felt a flash of red-hot anger.

She didn't need Brian's sympathy, thanks very much! Hell, she didn't need anyone, not even Ginny. Damn her stupid, stupid girl!

Why had she done it? Was it all her *fault?*

She shook the thought away and her head at Brian, then tottered off down the street, trying to remain on the footpath, managing it for most of the way.

By the time she got to her terrace house, she was feeling better. Stronger. Back to good ole Gail. She was a survivor, she told herself. Had survived the trenches before and she'd bloody well survive them again. And she had some armour this time. Don't forget that! She had a secret weapon.

Just needed to get the pictures up again. The gravy train back on track.

She snickered, not catching her woeful pun but relishing the thought of all the cash that would come rolling in again. And she let out a small "Whoop!" as she toppled into a recycling bin.

CHAPTER 12
Meanwhile Back in the Office

The rain clouds lifted briefly on Monday morning, and it was far too pleasant to be wasted in Homicide Headquarters giving a depressing statement, but that's where Alicia was. Here to "knock it on the head", as Jackson had suggested. And now, as he began searching his computer's database for the requisite form, she glanced around the open-plan office for the other thing she'd like to knock on the head.

"She's working another case," Jackson said, reading her mind. Smirking.

Alicia didn't smirk back. She found it concerning. Did that mean Singh had given up on Isla's hit-and-run already?

Not daring to ask, she just watched as he brought the form up and began tapping her details into it, then glanced around the office again.

The Homicide Squad, where Jackson worked, was housed in the state's Crime Command Centre in Western Sydney. It also housed the Drug and Firearms Squad, the Organised Crime Squad, the Financial Crimes Squad... you get the gist. It was big and it was busy, and Alicia had been here several times before but never for long. It wasn't the kind of place you lingered. Visitors were not welcome in this workplace nor was small talk, and so he got to it quickly, asking her to repeat her final conversations with Isla as he tapped her words in.

And so she did, first describing how distraught Isla had been when she met her at the apartment earlier that week but how that had changed, how she'd seemed buoyant at the memorial. Excited even.

"It sounded like she'd found the answer she was looking for. Like she finally understood why Ginny was dead."

Jackson stopped typing. "Let's just stick to her words, no conjecture, hey?" He said that gently, but it still stung. Alicia had a good sense for this kind of thing, and he knew it. She wasn't just a witness, she was a journalist. Knew how to sort fact from fiction.

"Fine," she said. "I remember exactly. She said she'd found something strange, quote unquote"—she added her own smirk then—"and she wanted to show it to me, said it might help explain what happened to Ginny. That's also a direct quote. She said she was on the *Styled* shoot on Saturday but asked me to drop in to her apartment on Sunday at ten. I asked her if everything was okay, but she didn't want to elaborate. She said, and again I quote"—another smirk—"'I'm getting the evil eye'. Unquote."

She paused as he typed that verbatim, then said, "After that, she said something about having a glass of champagne together when I dropped in, and then she ran out of the funeral—"

"Ran?"

A loud exhale. "Walked swiftly then. Like she was keen to—"

"Walked swiftly," he said, adding a full stop. "Anything else? No calls or texts from her later? No reminder that morning?"

She shook her head.

"Anything else you want to add?"

She shook her head again, so he read over the statement, printed out a copy and got her to read it too, before signing at the bottom.

"What happens now?" she asked.

"The traffic expert's coming in later, so I'd like to hang around for that. Sorry, I know we're still on our honeymoon."

"It's okay. I'd rather you were here, doing your thing. No point both of us sitting at home, bored senseless."

"Thank you," he said, but Alicia was lying to him.

She would go straight home, sure, but she would not be bored. Not in the slightest.

She had her Agatha Christie book to get back to.

~

Saffron could really do with a decent holiday, she thought, as she slumped in her office chair and stared out at the view, at the tourists she could just make out, using the break in the weather to climb the Sydney Harbour Bridge, like they had nothing better to do.

Well, she had plenty to do, thanks largely to Arabella's unexpected group email.

The HR manager was alerting them to Isla-Mae Cavendish's "untimely departure"—her words, she'd never make a journo—and after all the usual platitudes, suggested if anyone had any upcoming fashion spreads with the B-grade model that they bin them immediately. Wasn't a "good look", apparently, featuring a happy smiley model who'd just gone and got herself run over.

Well, it wasn't *Saffron's* fault Isla-Mae was so damn clumsy!

Wished now that she hadn't let herself be talked into using her in last Saturday's activewear shoot. Wish she hadn't bought the line that they "owed her", after what had happened to Ginny. Now Kora would have to go and reshoot the whole blasted thing, and who was going to pay for that, hmmm?

The budget was already as tight as those yoga pants.

She sighed loudly, eyes turning back to the buffoons on the bridge. Why you'd want to do something so mindlessly risky while on holidays the editor could not fathom.

Then again, any holiday for Saffron was risky. She knew from experience. The minute she was climbing a bridge or lolling on a banana lounge, her deputy would be doing everything in her power to bedazzle the publishers and steal her job from under her.

It had happened to her once, early in her career.

Back when she was naive. She'd never let that happen again. Oh no, her deputy was not going to steal her job. Not that Tiani would even try. She was weak, that girl, sniffling away at Ginny's memorial. Honestly what did she have to be sad about? If she thought about it logically—removed all emotion from the issue—she'd see that it was the perfect solution.

Now they were all free.

Chloe was a different matter, of course. There was nothing weak about her beauty editor. She was strong, smart, could write herself into any job she wanted. Just had to make sure she didn't realise it, or Saffron really would be in trouble.

The key was to keep them all one click shy of confident. Never give too much positive feedback. That's what worked. That and fear, it's what bred true loyalty.

Just look at Frances out there, head down, fervently typing. She was a plain Jane, Frances. Her hairstyle too bland, her penchant for tight black leggings doing nothing for her doughy stomach and bum. And she had all the confidence of a twenty-six-year-old who still lived with her father, which she did, as embarrassing as it was. But she was dedicated and hardworking, and *those* were traits to admire.

She was also a little scared of Saffron, and it's just as it should be. Saffron wasn't being mean. It was common sense. Some editors befriended their staff, told them they were fabulous, then wondered why they turned up late and left early, handed in rubbish and spent half the time bitching about them.

Oh no, workers needed a strong leader, someone who could drag out the best in them, not take them out for brunch! Your team was there to make *you* look good. Not to make friends. That was a fact. Look at *Lout* magazine. It was a ghastly rag but seemed to sell like hotcakes, and that was all down to Hamish Keener. And he was the biggest bastard in the building!

She wasn't *that* bad, just tough. Exacting. And in return, her team were falling over themselves to impress her.

Eyes darting back to the climbers on the bridge, she suddenly imagined them dropping from the sky, falling…

Just as Ginny had done.

And now, too, Isla-Mae.

See? she thought. Those two had got too big for their boots. And look where they ended up.

From her desk outside, Frances watched Saffron's back tense as she stared out the window, and she wondered if she should pop her head in and see if everything was okay. Offer her her usual poison. Sometimes Saffron rewarded her with a smile, sometimes she bit her head off. Best to let it go this time.

Truth is, Saffron hadn't been herself since Ginny passed, and it worried Frances. She adored this magazine, more than anything in the world. Hell, she adored Saffron, and she knew you weren't supposed to say that. But she admired her so much. This was the country's top women's lifestyle title. You didn't stay that way by being Ms Nice.

And you didn't stay that way without a good team of people behind you. And she was proud to count herself amongst them. But Saffron had been, well, *odd* lately. Stressed. She wondered if she should talk to her about it, see if there was anything she wanted to offload. But then she shook her head.

"Don't be silly," she told herself. Like her mother used to say, before she took off with the lawn-mower repairman. "I'm not your friend, Frannie, I'm your mother." And that's exactly how she thought of Saffron. As a mother figure. But stronger, so much more reliable.

She turned her attention back to her screen and continued tapping.

~

Hamish couldn't stand anything about the latest issue of *Lout*. The articles. The pictures. Hell, even his art director's usually slick design was pissing him off today. It looked like a dog's breakfast! He wanted to storm into the editorial office and bark at them all, but he told himself to take a deep breath. He was just in a foul mood. And Arabella's depressing email wasn't helping.

Poor, silly Isla. What was she thinking?

Hell, what had Ginny been thinking when she…

He dropped his head into his hands, unable to finish that sentence. Hell, he hadn't even had the courage to show up at her memorial. It was shameful. He should have been there. Fully intended to go. But then he kept thinking of Ginny and that final day, the words he said, the way he hurt her, and he couldn't seem to leave his desk. Guilt weighed him down. Regret was a handbrake that couldn't get him past the door.

How could he face her mother now? Her friends? And, oh Jesus, Alicia Finlay with her bright smile and her tight hugs and her sudden, inexplicable friendship. Like Ginny's death had wiped the slate clean. But it hadn't. He was still a mean bastard, and he deserved nothing but her disdain.

He felt a sudden cold trickle run through his veins.

He wasn't the only culpable one in all of this. There was someone else to blame, someone who was probably front and centre at the memorial, acting innocent. Blasé.

And *that's* the real reason he couldn't go. He didn't want to make a scene.

One glance at that smarmy smile and he couldn't be certain what he'd do. But he knew one thing for sure— it'd be violent.

CHAPTER 13
Hunting for Clues

There is something especially heinous about a hit-and-run, and it has less to do with the crunch of hard metal against soft flesh and bones and more to do with the aftermath.

The running away part.

What kind of animal smashes into someone and then keeps driving without so much as a tap on the brakes? Because that's exactly what the head of the Crash Investigation Unit (CIU) was telling Singh and Jackson now.

A tiny man with a no-nonsense way of speaking, Yong-sun Lee explained how there were no clear tyre marks at the crime scene, not so much as a skid mark to indicate that the driver who hit Isla-Mae Cavendish had even attempted to apply the brakes, let alone stop to check on her.

"Deliberate then?" asked Indira.

Yong-sun swished his lips to one side, then back. "I can't speak to the intention of the driver. But let me say this. You'd have to be blind drunk or just plain blind not to notice a woman in your path. And sure, it was still early, weather wasn't great, bit dark, bit rainy, but even then, once they had hit her, you would expect a brake mark or two. But there was nothing on either side of the impact point. It looks to me like they never applied the brakes."

"So at the very least, callous disregard," said Singh, and he nodded.

"Any clues as to the car, make, model?" Jackson asked now, knowing some vehicle fragments including paint chips and part of a broken headlight had been located at the scene.

The man turned to a page in his report. "We're still analysing the chemical composition of the paint and matching the fragments we located, but preliminary enquiries suggest a white, old-model Toyota."

The two detectives swapped a frown. "As common as blowflies in summer then," said Singh, throwing her pen onto the table.

"I'm guessing no CCTV?" the expert said.

Now she was shrugging. "Nothing along that street. Some down in the main hub though, so we'll go through that and see what we can see."

Yong-sun stood up. "Sorry I couldn't be more useful." Then he stopped and said, "Oh, there was one thing." They both looked up, expectantly. "Part of the headlight had some splatter on it. Faeces. That might help."

"What kind of faeces?" asked Singh.

"Animal. That's all I can tell you at this stage. We've sent it to the lab, along with the DNA we recovered. Most likely a bird, probably pigeon. I have a similar issue in my street."

"Of course you do," she said drolly. "Pigeon shit is even more common than blowflies."

He chuckled dryly as he showed himself out.

~

Across town, Missy was also searching for clues but regarding Ginny's death, not Isla's.

She had Ginny's copy of *The Mysterious Affair at Styles* in her hand and was now staring up at the Paddington library, a historic stone building, painted in pale yellow with decorative archways and columns and a clock tower so magnificent it took her breath away.

But she wasn't here to gasp at the scenery. The young librarian had a job to do! Not that she meant to be quite so diligent. It hadn't even been twenty-four hours since Missy had promised the book clubbers she'd look into why Ginny had borrowed this book, but here she was standing outside Ginny's library, book in hand, ready to make enquiries.

It's just that she had a full hour for lunch today, and it's not like she had anyone to while away the time with.

Her boss liked her, she knew that, but Geraldine seemed to need to be as far away from Missy and her "prattle" as possible on their breaks. Missy didn't take it personally. That's how most people reacted to Missy after a while. Not the book club though. Especially not Alicia. She accepted Missy exactly as she was. That's what she loved most about her and why she was standing here, on her lunch break, doing her good friend a favour.

Or rather, striding in now and presenting the book to the librarian on the front desk, a smiley woman in a hijab, who introduced herself as Fatima.

"Yes, this is one of ours," the woman said. "Where'd you find it?"

Missy explained how it had been left on a friend's desk and how there might be a deeper meaning behind it.

"I'm a librarian too," Missy said, introducing herself, "so I know you're not supposed to release information on your members, and I get it, I totally do. But the woman who borrowed this book was a good friend of ours and—"

"Was?"

Missy nodded. "It's so, *so* sad. The poor chicken, she… Well, the police think she killed herself. A week ago."

"Oh no!"

Missy nodded again. "So you can see why we're searching for answers. We're trying to retrace her last steps, see what was in her head. I'm wondering if you remember her coming in?"

The woman glanced back at the book, turned it over. Said, "Hmmm…" then pulled some silver spectacles on and began tapping at the desktop behind the counter.

"Okay, here it is," she said, shifting the screen so Missy could see. "Virginia DeRosso. She checked it out two weeks ago…" She kept tapping. Said, "Hmmm," again and then frowned. "It was the first time she'd been in here in years. I'm surprised her membership card still worked."

"Do you remember her? Maybe something she said?"

Fatima peered over her glasses. "Missy, you know what libraries are like when things get busy." She glanced at the screen. "And it would've been busy when she checked it out—three forty-three on a Saturday, just before we closed shop."

"Yeah, I know," said Missy, "but Ginny's *really* memorable. She was bright and brash and not easy to forget."

"Well, I don't remember her, and it looks like she took it out using the self-checkout machines."

Missy's face crumpled.

"But listen, I wasn't the only one here. There were two other librarians. Maybe they remember her like you said. They're not in today, but I could put them in touch with you if you think it'll help."

Missy thanked her and then had a thought. "Are either of them men?"

Because she had a hunch that if they were, they'd remember Ginny in a heartbeat.

It wasn't until the following afternoon that Missy got the return call from the library, and it wasn't from an ogling male librarian. It was from an older lady called Carol who remembered Ginny not because of her looks but because of their shared history.

Carol had worked that library for almost two decades and had known Ginny back when she lived in Paddington, she explained over the phone, after first apologising for not calling sooner. She now worked part-time so only just got Missy's message. And was mortified to hear of Ginny's "suicide"—Fatima's words, not Missy's.

"She was such a lovely lass," she told her. "Came in every month like clockwork for a while there, always hunting down some book she was supposed to read for her book club. I'm not sure she ever read them though. They weren't really her cup of tea, that much was obvious. Then one day she stopped coming." She sighed wistfully. "I guessed she'd left the club or moved suburbs or something."

"Both," said Missy. "And now..."

"Mmmm. Yes. I'm so, so sorry. But I'm pleased I got to

see her one last time."

"Yes, do you mind telling me about that?"

"Not *at all*. I was delighted to see her back! Such a surprise, and when I asked her what literary tome she was reading this time, she said, 'No, no, I need an Agatha Christie.' *Had* to be Agatha Christie, she said, but she wasn't sure which one. All very cryptic, so I showed her to the Christie section. And left her to it."

"How many Christie books do you have?" Missy asked. "I mean, would it have taken her a while to choose that one?"

"Oh no, I'd barely turned away when she yelped out that she'd found it. The perfect book, she called it. She had *The Mysterious Affair* in her hands and a big ole grin on her face. She really was chuffed with herself and said that book would give some friend just the right message."

Missy tried not to whoop. Alicia was right! Of course Alicia was right. Her instincts were always spot on. "Did Ginny say what?" Missy asked. "What message she wanted to deliver?"

"Just that she wanted to give someone a surprise. A good challenge, I think she said. And I told her Dame Agatha would certainly provide that."

Then she sighed wistfully again and added, "If only she'd been reading Agatha Christie all along, she might've been happier, you know?"

And if only she'd got that book to Alicia earlier, Missy thought, she might still be alive.

CHAPTER 14
Digesting the Clues

The Orient Express Chinese restaurant was an old favourite of the book club, and they knew the menu almost as well as they knew the similarly titled Christie book, so it did not take long to order.

They were here on Missy's behest. She had already called Alicia with her news but could not *wait* to share it with the others and had even postponed dinner with her boyfriend, Seamus, for this. He was Ronnie's nephew, a man she'd met on a past adventure, and so he knew all about the club and how futile it was to get in the way of their sleuthing.

Just as all their partners did. And most of them had partners now, it was quite lovely! Queenie was still seeing that guy at her office, the one with the cute black curls, and Lynette was dating the head chef of the restaurant she now ran, Rhys Gruffudd (aka Gruffo), a burly Welsh fellow they'd all got to know and love at Alicia's wedding.

That left only Ronnie, a contented widower, and Perry, their eternal single, but the way he was grinning to himself these days made Missy wonder. Was there a new man on the scene? She desperately wanted to ask him, but it would have to wait.

She needed to focus! To tell them all her news about Ginny and Carol and the library book! But before she could open her mouth, Ronnie was steering the conversation towards Isla-Mae, asking if there was any more news from Jackson.

Alicia looked oddly despondent. "He's being really secretive." She pouted. "Won't let me in to Isla's apartment even though I could be useful. And he's being coy about what they've found out on the street. I do know there were no skid marks at the scene and they're looking for a white Toyota but only because I overheard him talking to Singh on his mobile."

"Overheard or listened in?" asked Perry, grinning.

She played coy now and kept going. "Sounds dodgy to me. Even a drunk driver would slam on the brakes at some point, wouldn't they? Might even get out and see what damage they'd left behind, before doing a runner. But to not even stop. That is suspicious."

They were all nodding.

Missy nodded along, then went to speak when Claire asked, "So there are no witnesses at all? No CCTV?"

"Not that I overheard," Alicia said, giving Perry a sly wink. "But I do know Isla's apartment block has a camera out the front, just above the mailboxes, so I'm guessing they didn't find anything on that, or they wouldn't be appealing for witnesses and dashboard camera footage."

"Yes, I saw that appeal on the ABC last night," said Ronnie. "I noticed they didn't name Isla. What's that about?"

"I think they're having trouble tracking down her folks. It's better to get permission before naming a victim, especially if there's a chance it could be suicide." And she rolled her eyes to emphasise how ridiculous that idea was. "Isla did tell me they were holidaying on some Caribbean island, and I passed that on to Jackson. I'm guessing he hasn't found them."

"What a dreadful phone call to receive," said Claire.

They all nodded again, and Missy opened her mouth only to be interrupted by Lynette this time.

"So have they found any connection to Ginny yet?" she asked. "Are they reopening her case?"

"I didn't dare ask," said Alicia. "Wasn't in the mood for another round of cautions and warnings."

Ronnie tutted. "You should be able to ask your husband anything."

"He's also a detective, Ronnie. It's not quite that simple."

She tutted again but left it at that.

"Speaking of Ginny," said Missy just as Perry said, "Did you finish the book? *The Mysterious Affair at Styles.*"

His eyes were on Alicia, but hers were now on Missy. "I'm not sure I have to," she replied, *finally* giving her the nod.

Missy beamed and yelped, "Yes! I have news. Very exciting."

Then she told them all about her visit to the Paddington library. About Fatima and then Carol, and how Carol knew Ginny from back when she was in her Aunty Kirsten's literary book club.

"Get on with it," said Perry. "I haven't got all night."

And she would have frowned at him, she really would, but that had got her excited again—Perry *definitely* had a new beau! "Just hold your horses," she told him and then repeated what Carol had told her verbatim. How Ginny had specifically wanted an Agatha Christie mystery and taken one look at that particular book and said it was perfect.

"That's why I just know Alicia's right and Lynny too. That book was chosen specifically for its title."

"Not necessarily," said Claire, ruining her buzz. "Ginny might have read it before, and the plot came flooding back when she saw the cover."

Now Alicia was scoffing. "She never would have got past page three. No, I think we need to do as Lynette suggested and go with the bleeding obvious—she was clearly, unambiguously trying to tell me about a mysterious affair at *Styled* magazine. An illicit one. Potentially scandalous. Has to be, or it wouldn't've led to two murders. And I'm sure they were murders. I don't care what Jackson says."

"I'm not sure he's saying much at all," sniped Ronnie, like a dog with a bone.

"Any case," said Alicia, "this is why Missy and I have dragged you away from your work"—a quick apologetic wince at Lynette who had a restaurant to manage—"and whatever else is keeping you busy"—a curious glance now at Perry. "We need to work out who was sleeping with whom at *Styled* and why it's a mystery worth killing for."

~

Still holed up at the office, Jackson was staring hard at his monitor, trying to unravel the mystery of why Isla-Mae Cavendish had been hit deliberately last Sunday. They were still waiting on most of the forensics, including the official autopsy and the road expert's final report, but he couldn't shake the feeling that there was nothing accidental about that hit-and-run.

Sure, Yong-sun hadn't quite said that, but it seemed pretty obvious to Jackson, or at least it did in his gut. And yes, it had been raining, but it wasn't that dark. There was some street lighting. Enough to see straight.

Oh no, he had a hunch someone saw her on the road, turned their car towards her, and applied the accelerator. And if that was true, the next logical question was why? What possible reason would someone have to deliberately run down a young woman out for a morning jog?

"Could be domestic violence," Singh called out from her desk where she, too, was still working. "It wouldn't be the first time a woman's bolted from her partner, and he's followed her outside, jumped in his vehicle and mowed her down. Might explain the messy apartment. Could've been a fight first."

He nodded. Okay, that made sense.

"Alicia mention any fellas sniffing about?" Singh asked. "We haven't found one, but she was young and gorgeous." He shook his head. She scratched hers and added, "Of course it could also be some drunken fool who barely registered the hit. Yong-sun did say that too. Either way, a criminal act has occurred and so we stay on the case, but not tonight."

She switched off her monitor and reached for her handbag, adding, "Tonight I have a hot date with my fella."

Singh's "fella" was Miles Henryhan, their chief ballistics expert whom she'd been dating for some time.

They nicknamed him "Scaryhan" because of his gruff bedside manner but never to his face and not in front of Singh now either. She was almost as scary as he was!

Jackson glanced at the clock. "Bit late for dinner, isn't it?"

She sniggered. "Who said anything about dinner?"

CHAPTER 15
Chewing Over Suspects

The tasty Thai cuisine was very distracting, and so Alicia let her friends enjoy their meal before she began listing all the staff employed at *Styled* magazine. The potential suspects.

And the list was a long one.

There was Saffron, the editor, she told them. She was married, had been for more than a decade, to an older investment banker who stayed well out of the limelight. They had no children, and Alicia shuddered at the thought of Saffron as a mother. The only other married staffer was the deputy editor, Tiani, who had a young son. At least she had some empathy, was probably a good mum. The rest of the crew were childless and largely single as far as Alicia knew, including Ginny's immediate boss, beauty editor Chloe, the fashion director Kora and Saffron's PA Frances.

"The only man on the mag is Pascal, the art director," she told them. "But he's gay."

"The only gay in the village?" asked Perry, and he wasn't being cheeky.

Alicia's eyes narrowed. "As far as I know. Why? You think it could be two women trying to keep their affair secret?"

"If one of them was married, maybe?"

That nailed it down to Saffron and Tiani, and she just couldn't see it, but Perry was already galloping ahead: "We like to think the world's open-minded, but that kind of thing mightn't go down so well with some of the mag's posher advertisers. And I can imagine that Saffron would do anything to keep her reputation intact."

"You think Saffron could be a closet lesbian?"

asked Missy, eyes boggling behind her cat-eye glasses.

Now he shrugged as Alicia gave it some thought. Even if that were true, would you really murder two women to hide your affair and retain some ad revenue? It felt like such a stretch. Still, you never knew what people would do to keep their secrets.

They'd learned that time and time again.

"It needn't be that complicated," said Queenie. "It could be a power imbalance. Say an affair between Saffron and one of her employees. Don't know about the advertisers, but HR would definitely frown at that."

"And it might not have been between two people at *Styled*," added Lynette, slurping back some rice noodles. "It could be between someone at the magazine and someone else entirely."

That sparked a fresh round of groaning. Suddenly the case was feeling unwieldy. Then Ronnie tapped her glass with her fork and snapped them all to attention.

"Let's not get despondent, people. Young Ginny did leave us some other helpful clues, so I think we should add them to the mix. Tell us again what they are, Alicia."

Alicia smiled. Ronnie's words reminded her of another Poirot line she'd read earlier in *The Mysterious Affair at Styles*.

"We have found in this room six points of interest," Poirot told Hastings. *"Shall I enumerate them, or will you?"*

And so she *enumerated* them again to the group.

Apart from the Christie novel, there was the thesaurus Hamish had given Ginny, the fake Monopoly money, and the cheap T-shirt with the religious print.

"Any religious zealots at *Styled*?" asked Perry seizing on the latter.

"Or super rich?" added Missy, her mind on the money.

They were all staring at Alicia, and she shrugged, feeling clueless.

"Another assumption we're making," added Claire, "is that it wasn't *Ginny* involved in this affair. She's the one who's dead. I know she had a boyfriend, but what if she was cheating on him with someone on or off the magazine?

Someone who didn't want the truth to come out, and she was threatening to tell all and that's why she was murdered."

"The sleazy CEO!" said Lynette, recalling the leering looks she received from Ted Johnson when Alicia introduced them at the memorial last Friday. "He's super rich, could also be a churchgoer for all we know."

Alicia scoffed at that. No way. Not Ted. At least she didn't think so…

She turned her gaze to Ronnie and asked if the wealthy heiress had ever met Ted in her travels. Ronnie gasped like she'd been slapped.

"My goodness, Alicia. Why do you assume I know every person who has more than a few bob?"

"*More than a few bob*? The bloke drives a Bentley!"

"Still, you cannot assume the well-off all know each other. It's such a cliché."

Ronnie was determined to be offended, and Alicia apologised. "Okay, I'm wealth profiling you, I'll cop it. But do you know him or not?"

Ronnie shrugged. "I might know people who know him."

"Well then, can you get your people to talk to their people and see if he *is* a cliché and sleeps with his pretty young employees?"

"Happy to," she said, offering a conciliatory smile as Perry began tapping his wineglass.

"Moving things along," he said, "I'd like to run the Shroud of Turin angle. See if there's some deeper meaning that we're missing. I have an old friend at Sydney Uni who's an expert on religious iconography. He might have some thoughts. Haven't seen him in ages. Might be fun."

"What about the rest of us?" asked Missy. "We have so many suspects now. Who should do who?"

Alicia held up a stalling hand. "Take a breath, Missy. How's it going to look with you lot wandering in asking questions? It's not like you have an Access All Areas pass to *Styled*."

"I do," said Claire. "Saffron's been trying to drag me in all year. Wants me to feature in her *Styled Queen* section."

Claire paused to explain for those unfamiliar with the magazine that this was a one-page feature celebrating the current looks a local celebrity or "A-lister" was into.

"You're an A-lister now?" said Perry, mock gasping.

She flashed her feline eyes. "I think we can credit my husband for that one."

Claire's husband was Simon Barrier, founder of a large luxury hospitality network with annual revenue in the billions. By snagging Australia's most eligible bachelor, Claire had opened doors for herself and sent her own value skyrocketing, certainly with the likes of Saffron.

"I could take her up on that and throw in a few sly questions."

"Great idea," Alicia told Claire. "You might also get a chance to question the fashion and beauty editors if they style it. See if anyone has any goss on an illicit affair." Then she cocked her head and said, "How *do* you know Saffron?"

"We've met at a few social events, with Simon," Claire explained before laughing. "You can stop scowling, Alicia. I wanted to dislike Saffron, honestly I did, but we really clicked over fashion."

"Good," she replied, "because the only clicking we do is with sabres. Just be subtle. And maybe don't mention me."

Claire chuckled again. "Your name will not come up."

Young Queenie waved a hand in the air. "I could call them tomorrow, if you like, Claire? Set up the meeting? Even come along if that works. I know I'm not your PA, but *she* doesn't know that. It will give me a chance to have a chat with her assistant, Frances I think it is. Us PAs always know who's bonking who."

Claire looked rightfully concerned by that comment, but Alicia was surprised. "You know Frances?"

"Met her at a function on Secretaries Day last May. Seemed okay."

Perry nearly snorted his wine back up. "Secretaries Day?"

Queenie smirked back at him. "It's now called Administrative Professionals Day, but who are we kidding?"

They all laughed at that. They liked that Queenie was more comfortable in the group now, more willing to make jokes and jump in and get involved.

Claire gave her the thumbs-up, and then it was Lynette's turn to start tapping her glass.

"I think we're all forgetting someone," she said. "What about that dude Ginny was dating? The hottie she showed up with at the wedding?"

Alicia frowned. "Austin Smythe? But they were both single. Nothing illicit about it."

"Still," Lynette persisted, "if Ginny was cheating on him with Ted or whoever, he might've been angry. Might've lashed out."

"But they were so sweet together," Alicia said. "I mean, he could've had any woman in the building and he chose Ginny. Despite her reputation. I think that speaks volumes, that and the way they were at the wedding—couldn't keep his eyes off her. He was smitten."

"Was he?" countered Lynette. "It felt a little needy to me."

"Oooh, someone sounds jealous," sang out Perry, grinning at Lynette.

"As if!" she said. "Besides, I was with Gruffo."

She shot Alicia a smile, and Alicia smiled back. She adored Gruffo, they all did, and not just because he was happy to step in for his boss when Alicia came calling. He was completely different to anyone her sister had dated before. Big-hearted, bushy-bearded, totally unpretentious. Turns out Lynette didn't need her big sister to vet the "flops" she brought home, as she once believed. She had Mr Right waiting for her at work. She just needed to look below the surface—and Gruffo was a big man, so there was plenty lurking underneath.

But Lynette made a good point. Having a burly boyfriend on her arm rarely stopped others from checking out Lynette's gorgeous long legs and flowing blond mane. They were like a magnet to most men. Yet Austin's eyes never strayed from Ginny.

"I'm just saying," persisted Lynette, "there's a fine line between smitten and obsessed. What if Ginny was cheating on him and he found out? That'd have to hurt, especially if he knew he was a catch and couldn't believe she'd treated him so badly. He might've reacted."

"And the young flatmate?" asked Ronnie. "How does Isla-Mae fit in?"

Lynette gave it some thought. "Maybe Isla uncovered some nasty messages from him, and he needed to shut her up."

Several of the group were nodding along. This sounded like a decent theory.

Alicia was not nodding.

She had a hunch Lynette was about to volunteer herself to chat with "the hottie" and did not like the sound of that. In the past she'd had no qualms using Lynette as a honey trap, but after their last train mystery, she knew better. Besides, what if Lynny fell for the hottie, like she usually did. She couldn't do it to Gruffo!

So she shook her head and suggested they leave Austin Smythe for now. They had enough suspects to focus on as it was. "Besides," she added, "if we interrogate too many people, my new hubby will become suspicious."

~

Jackson was already suspicious but not about Alicia or her book club. He'd spent the past hour trawling through the digital police file. Not the one on Isla-Mae Cavendish's hit-and-run though. The one on her flatmate, Virginia DeRosso.

And her supposed suicide.

Because Jackson had a sneaking suspicion his wife was right about that too, and this was a lot murkier than Singh suspected. That didn't mean the two cases were necessarily connected—it was all very well for amateur sleuths to jump to conclusions—but he was a detective. A professional. He had to get his ducks lined up first, and that meant understanding where those ducks originated.

And it may very well have started with Ginny.

And so he began poring over her file, because until now he had only heard Singh's interpretation of it. He needed to see it for himself.

First he read through the witness statements that had been taken in the immediate hour after Ginny's fall. There were sixteen in all, but not one had anything particularly useful to say. Five people "thought" she'd stepped out deliberately, three said she "could have" fallen. Many more said she "could easily" have been pushed, but "probably accidentally", it was a busy time. They "couldn't really be sure".

And those were the truest words of all.

Witness statements were unreliable at the best of times, but at that busy hour and in such a busy place, it was clear that no one was really paying attention. They were all just weary workers, scrolling through their phones, desperate to get home.

If it had been a quiet hour, a half-empty platform, a push would have been obvious.

He closed the statements down and then located the Transport NSW's CCTV footage, opening the files Singh had secured from the Northern line. As the relevant timestamp kicked in, he watched the crowd surge down the stairs and escalators and onto Platform Three, looking out for Ginny.

He wondered how on earth he was going to spot her, it was such a crowded hour, and it had clearly been cold and wet out because many were wearing raincoats and hats, beanies and hoodies, so it was hard to see heads, let alone faces.

But then he saw her. Ginny. She was hard to miss in a bright magenta jacket, her hair loose and flowing as she bustled down the wrong side of the stairs, weaving in and out of the pedestrians heading upwards. She was clutching onto something, an umbrella by the look of it, and when she got to the bottom, she shoved it into a large tote bag and began striding along the platform until she got midway. The crowd was slightly thinner here but still three-people deep, and she nestled in amongst them before dropping her head down. Probably looking at her smartphone, he realised, like everyone else.

Not much happened for the next seven minutes, apart from more commuters crowding onto the platform and bodies jostling for space. He wondered how they did it, how they bore it every day. Thanked his lucky stars he could drive into work and had a private car space.

Soon the crowd began to stir and a gust of air caused some hair and scarves to flutter about. The train was clearly approaching, and by now the platform was bumper-to-bumper with mostly coat-clad workers but plenty of tradies judging by the high-vis vests, as well as the odd schoolkids in uniform and a few elderly travellers, some in hats, a few women in hijabs.

As the train closed in on one side of the screen, he watched as Ginny looked up and then ducked around several people, clearly pushing her way to the front.

Typical Ginny, he thought. She was no wallflower. Never one to miss out.

She was staring in the direction of the approaching train, now right at the edge of the platform, first in line to get in and get a seat, and he wanted to tell her "Go back! Get away! It's not worth it!"

But he just kept watching as the train roared closer and Ginny suddenly stepped out and in front of it.

He gasped.

There was an ugly, high-pitched squeal, and he wasn't sure if that was Ginny, an onlooker, or the train's brakes. Hell, he felt like screaming himself. It was not a pretty sight, but he forced himself to keep watching as pandemonium broke out—arms rising, people swirling, the crowd surging backwards. But he wasn't really interested in the aftermath. He was looking to see if someone turned and headed in the wrong direction, away from the train and chaos and finger-pointing.

And there was a woman, a tiny sparrow of a thing,

running in the opposite direction, but she soon stopped at the guard station halfway down the platform. Then he kept watching as she led the way back towards Ginny, two uniformed officers hot on her heels, trying to break through the chaos. He did not recognise the woman. He felt sorry for the officers.

Jackson rubbed a hand across his stubble and paused the footage. Then he took another look, but this time he zoomed back to the minutes *before* the train approached. Again he wanted to warn Ginny, to force her to step back, but he shook that useless thought away and turned his eyes from Ginny to the swirling commuters. This time he was looking for someone furtive. But it was a waste of time. There were lots of people close enough to give Ginny a subtle push, and several of them were hidden beneath caps and hoodies, and at least one short-brimmed hat. But no obvious arms or hands reaching out. No clear nudges or shoulder bumps.

After watching three more times, he gave up.

Closing it all down, he groaned to himself. The truth was if it wasn't for that suicide note Ginny had sent her mother, they could not have said whether she fell, was pushed or did it deliberately.

Despite all the CCTV footage and more than a dozen witness statements, nothing was any clearer. Another thing Alicia was right about—it was impossible to see the wood for the trees.

Or the subtle press of a hand on someone's lower back…

CHAPTER 16
The Way to a Man's Heart

As Kirsten leaned down to air kiss Alicia's cheek, her beads slapping against her right ear, Alicia wondered if the older woman's wardrobe contained anything other than flowing linen and chunky resin.

It was now Wednesday morning. Exactly nine days after Ginny's brutal death, three days after Isla's hit-and-run, and the final few days of Alicia and Jackson's honeymoon.

But who were they kidding?

Jackson had already slunk back into work, pretending he didn't want to, apologising profusely, and Alicia had told him it was "fine! Don't worry about it. I'll stay home and keep reading" when really she was ticking a few things off her own to-do list. Starting with Ginny's aunty, whom she'd arranged to meet at a café not far from her house.

Alicia couldn't believe she hadn't thought of her sooner, considering their conversation at Ginny's memorial. There Kirsten had scoffed at the idea that Ginny committed suicide—"Pollyanna" she'd called her—then likened Austin Smythe to the grumpiest man in literature, Heathcliff, from *Wuthering Heights*!

What did she mean by that?

And so here they were, sipping frothy coffee, chatting about the weather. How inclement, how unseasonal. How more rain was due that arvo. Oh how Ginny would be snickering if she could see them.

Very soon, however, the small talk turned to Isla-Mae. Kirsten had heard the sad news and couldn't believe it.

"And I'm guessing you can't either, which is why I've been summoned?" she said. Then smiled as Alicia's eyes widened. "You did say you were mad about mysteries. You're obviously looking into it. You think something untoward has happened to Isla-Mae? And my niece?"

Alicia smiled. Nothing got past Kirsten. "I honestly don't know, but it feels like a worrying coincidence. I can't just let it drop."

"Good for you!" Kirsten replied, waving a waiter over to order a gluten-free muffin. She glanced at Alicia. "You want some cardboard too?"

Alicia shook her head, laughing. She really liked this side of Kirsten. Could see more of Ginny in her now.

Kirsten sipped her coffee. "So how can I help?"

"Tell me about that last time you saw Ginny. At a birthday barbecue, was it? How did she seem?"

"Absurdly cheerful, like I said. She was with that beautifully dressed man. Austin, I think his name was."

"Austin Smythe. Yes, and you said he wasn't happy. Did Ginny tell you why? Was there something going on between them? Some problem at work maybe? Or could she have been cheating on him?"

As a journalist, Alicia knew better than to ask leading questions, but she was growing desperate and had clearly hit a bull's-eye because Kirsten's eyes were widening.

"That might explain the fight," she said, now tapping a fingernail against her cup. "Oh yes, now it all makes sense."

"What fight?"

"Oh? Didn't I mention it? They had a bit of a tiff, Ginny and her beau. All very under the breath, talking through their smiles, but I could tell something wasn't right. I'm not sure what triggered it, but he pulled her away at one point, and I could hear them arguing in one of the bedrooms."

"What were they arguing about?"

"Well, I wasn't listening in if that's what you're implying."

Alicia smiled. "Of course not. But did anything filter through?"

Kirsten offered her own coy smile. "A word or two, perhaps."

Then she sat back as the waiter brought her muffin over.

She took her time then, slathering it in butter like that was going to help, and Alicia wished she'd just get on with it.

Eventually, after a tentative bite, Kirsten said, "From what I could tell, they were breaking up."

Now Alicia's eyes were widening. "Really?"

That didn't make sense. If they had broken up, why would Ginny have brought Austin as her plus-one to her wedding just five days later? It's not like she didn't have other options. She could have called Hamish. Hell, she could've shown up solo. Ginny never needed a man, that was part of her charm and why Hamish was so heartbroken.

"They really broke up?" she asked again. "Ginny and Austin?"

"That's how it appeared," said Kirsten. "He looked pretty grumpy. Said something about a theft, she'd clearly stolen his heart, and he felt betrayed. 'Destroyed' is the word I think he used." She rolled her eyes. "Young people can be so melodramatic, don't you find?"

The way she included Alicia in that sentiment made her feel ancient, but she encouraged her to continue.

After a few more sips, another grimacing nibble, Kirsten said, "That's right, he told her he'd never be the same again. I guess he felt like she'd led him on, and I'm sorry, but I do think she had. I mean, you don't drag some fellow to meet the family, then expect him to think it's casual. He looked bereft when they reappeared. Quite dejected."

"And Ginny?"

"Happy, like I said. Even a little smarmy." Kirsten placed her cup down and leaned forwards. "I hate to say this about my niece, but I got the impression she was proud of herself for getting in first. Breaking it off before he did. At least that's what she looked like—victorious."

She sighed wistfully now. "That's my last impression of young Virginia. Her wicked, victorious grin."

Alicia sighed along, then asked, "What happened next?"

"Nothing," Kirsten said. "They left soon after. Didn't even stay for dessert! That's what makes me even sadder. If only she'd had one final piece of Nan's creamy baked cheesecake. At least *she* could eat it without her stomach blowing up like a balloon."

Then she stared gloomily down at her gluten-free muffin…

~

Ebony held her wicker basket out to show Dionne and offered her a coquettish smile.

"I know Ted's out until midday," she told her husband's executive assistant, "but I want to prepare a little picnic for when he returns. It's romantic."

Dionne looked at her like it was, in fact, absurd, but knew better than to open her ugly gob. You didn't survive your boss's three wives by being lippy.

So she simply wedged those thin lips into a polite smile, as Ebony knew she would, and waved her in, like the door bitch that she was.

"Thanks, sweetie," Ebony cooed as she strode into Ted's enormous suite, then swivelled, closed the door and locked it securely behind her.

Glancing at her watch, she knew she had just twenty minutes. And that's all it should take.

She dumped the basket on a chair, pulled the blinds closed, then turned back to his computer and started hunting…

~

Alicia was still on the hunt for answers. Had Ginny and Austin really broken up? If so, why hadn't Ginny mentioned it to her? Her good friend told her everything. *Didn't she?* And why had the couple shown up at her wedding, less than a week later, still looking very much in love?

Had Kirsten read that wrong? Had they rekindled?

And if they had broken up, what was the reason behind it?

Had Ginny been seeing someone else at *Styled?*

Had she been sleeping with the sleazy CEO as Lynette had suggested?

All good questions, Alicia decided, and ones she had no answers for. But there was one person who might. So, after leaving Kirsten to her tasteless treat, Alicia made her way back to the Arial office.

"I know!" she called out as the receptionist's eyes widened. "Sucker. Punishment. What can I say?"

Then she swept past him and down to *Lout*.

Hamish Keener had been Ginny's best friend and arch-rival for more than a decade. Again, Alicia couldn't believe she hadn't thought to question him earlier. He was the one man in the building who kept a beady eye on her love life. If he didn't know what was going on with Ginny, nobody did.

She found him at his keyboard, typing furiously with two fingers. He ignored her for a few minutes, then looked up and said, "If you're here to guilt me for not going to the memorial, you can turn around and bugger off."

She shook her head. "Memorials are hard, Hamish. Doesn't matter. It's your business."

"Oh. Right. Okay. Thanks."

"You're welcome," she replied, slipping into the seat in front of his desk. "Having said that, I have an awkward question. Were you sleeping with Ginny again? At the end there?"

Because it had only occurred to her on the drive over that if Ginny *had* broken up with Austin, she could well have boomeranged back to Hamish. It was the usual pattern.

Hamish seemed confused by the question, then irritated. "No, I was not. Why're you asking me this?"

"Just curious."

"She had a boyfriend, didn't she?"

"Never stopped either of you before."

He shook his head firmly. "I wasn't seeing her."

And she believed him this time. The crack in his voice was the giveaway. "What about Ted Johnson? Any chance she and—"

"Christ, woman, wash your mouth out! Ginny wasn't desperate. Why would she shag that old bastard?"

"You're not exactly a young whippersnapper yourself."

He made a *pft!* sound. "I'm not even sure what a whippersnapper is, Alicia, but I bet Ted does. Seriously, he's more Saffron's type."

Alicia's eyebrows swept high. "What are you saying?"

He smudged his lips downwards, crossed his tattooed arms over his small beer belly. "Not saying anything. But you do have to wonder why Saffron gets all the perks. The best car spot and budget and stuff."

"Nothing to do with the fact that her magazine outsells yours?"

He produced a cocky grin. "Not for long, baby. We just did a monster issue. No way she beat me this time." Then he released his arms and sat forward. "What's all this about? Why're you suddenly poking about in Ginny's sex life?"

"Just trying to work out her state of mind when she died. What she was thinking." It wasn't exactly a lie.

"She wasn't thinking. That's the problem. If she was, she would've dumped that gobshite long ago, and maybe then she'd still be alive."

Alicia wasn't sure what he meant by that, but it was now clear that one of her questions had been answered.

"So you don't think she and Austin had broken up?"

He was back to looking confused. "Why would I think that?"

"Her aunt Kirsten seems to think they had. Says they broke up the weekend before my wedding." As she spoke, she realised the colour was draining from Hamish's face. "Are you okay?"

He had a hand over his mouth and nose now, like he was trying to smother himself.

She frowned. Perhaps Kirsten had misunderstood. "So Ginny never mentioned it to you?"

He was shaking his head. He mumbled something, then released his hand and said, "No way. Can't be true. She would've told me if she had."

"I think she was keeping a lot to herself in those last few weeks."

"But I saw her... like, *that* day. The day she... you know? I *spoke* to her. She never said a bloody word." His eyes darted round the room, then back to Alicia's. "Are you sure they broke up?"

"Not really," she replied. "I'm not sure of anything anymore. Does it matter? You think Austin had something to do with it?"

A slow shrug, like he was thinking it through. "Maybe. I mean, if they did break up, it would have been his doing."

"But—"

"What a *wanker*. No wonder she threw herself in front of the train!"

"Hamish—"

"He broke her heart like I said he would! He didn't care about Ginny. Just used her, spat her out. How can he even show his face around here anymore?"

"At least he turned up to her memorial."

Hamish gasped. His cheeks refilled with colour, like he'd been slapped. "Thought you said it didn't matter."

"It doesn't. Not to me. But I have a feeling it matters very much to you, Hamish. And I think you would have benefited from the healing."

"Bloody hell. Now you sound like the mob at *Wellness* magazine."

"Nothing wrong with being well," Alicia said, getting to her feet. "You should try it."

As she walked out, he called after her, "Don't fall for his angelic looks, Alicia! You mark my words—Austin Smythe is the devil in disguise! He's the reason Ginny's dead! No one else! He has blood on his hands that tosser!"

CHAPTER 17
Hunger Games

Lynette's mind was also on Austin Smythe as she watched the lunch crowd stream in and out of the busy sandwich bar across the street from Arial Publishing.

She wanted to talk to the so-called "hottie" and figured this was her best chance. But she had to do it soon, before her sister was back at work and dropping in here to order her usual chicken mayo sandwich. Honestly, Alicia had the taste buds of a five-year-old!

Because Alicia wasn't fooling anyone. She clearly didn't want her baby sister anywhere near the handsome executive. Probably thought Lynette fancied him. But nothing could be further from the truth. He might have been a hottie, but he left Lynette cold.

There was something *off* about Austin.

She had watched him at the wedding and seen some warning signs. While Alicia was charmed by his antics, Lynette did not get the same vibe. There was nothing charming about the way he'd been hovering over Ginny. It wasn't healthy. The only time Ginny got to herself was when she was on the dance floor, kicking up her heels. Other than that, Austin clung to her, barely letting her have a conversation without stepping across and holding on to her tight.

The perfect suspect then, thought Lynette.

Because she knew a little about coercive control, and Austin Smythe reeked of it. And she knew that often led to domestic violence. And *that* sometimes led to murder.

Was Isla killed, too, because she had seen the coercion? Was witness to some fights? Some bruising?

Could point the finger his way?

Lynette shuddered a little as she glanced around. She had chosen a small table at one side of the eatery where she had a good view of the doorway and just hoped Austin hadn't brought his lunch to work, like most of Arial who were now pouring in, ordering rolls and wraps, smoothies and coffee. She'd already seen half the *Styled* girls in here, although they mostly stuck to salads and kombucha.

If Austin did appear, Lynette was going to use the opportunity to catch his eye. Get a better sense of who he was. Whether he had the potential to explode.

Except, after an hour of watching, the only thing exploding were the sandwiches being shoved together by the harried staff.

As she continued watching, she began to wonder if she was wasting her time and not just because of his absence. Now that she thought about it, Austin had ignored her at the memorial, not just the wedding. Hadn't given Lynette so much as a second glance. Perhaps she *was* losing her appeal? Perhaps she wasn't his type?

Or perhaps she wasn't putting herself out there enough, she decided, quickly releasing the top button of her blouse and staring coquettishly at the doorway.

But that only brought more eyes her way, and none of them the ones she wanted.

Groaning, she scooped her handbag from the floor. She didn't have time for this. She had a dinner setting to prepare for, and there was only so many times she could ask Gruffo to cover for her.

As she stood up, a voice called out from the door, "Hey, Lynette isn't it? Alicia's sister?"

She looked across to find a familiar man staring at her. But it wasn't Austin.

This one was older, dressed in black skinny jeans, his hair shaped into a sad attempt at a mullet.

It took her a moment to recognise Hamish Keener. She was no fan of the sleazy *Lout* editor, had crossed his path several times before, but *he* was a big fan of Ginny's, she knew that. And he might just prove useful.

So she dropped her bag back, wedged a flirty smile to her lips and waved him over.

~

After waving goodbye to Hamish, Alicia had dropped back into her office to check there were no more "clues" she'd missed from Ginny. Nope. Just mess. Lots of it. And none she could blame on a ransacker, sadly. And so she'd turned and was on her way out when she spotted Saffron's assistant in the tearoom.

Okay, she could be useful too…

Applying her sweetest smile, she stepped in to join her.

"Hey, Alicia," said Frances, looking up from the kettle. "Thought you were still on your honeymoon."

"Tell me about it," she said, not telling her anything more. "Listen, nothing gets past you, right?"

Frances shrugged as she pulled a silk pyramid teabag from one pocket and dropped it into a pristine white cup. "I wouldn't say that."

"Still, you notice stuff, and I have a question for you. Who do you know that drives a white car?"

Frances snorted as she poured hot water over the teabag. "Half the country, I'd say."

"Sorry, I mean at Arial," Alicia said as Frances began dunking the bag in and out, in and out.

"Oh, that's easy then. Half the company." She sniggered as she started swishing the bag from side to side. "Why're you asking?"

"Just wondering." In fact, Alicia recalled what she'd overheard from Jackson, about a white car being involved in Isla's hit-and-run, and Hamish had just confirmed that Saffron had the best car space. That must mean she had a car. Had she used it that fateful morning?

Of course she wasn't about to tell Frances all that. Instead, she watched as the young PA began dunking the teabag up and down again and frowned.

"Is that, like, a ritual or something?" Alicia asked.

"What? Oh, no. It's just that Saffron likes it the way she likes it."

"Right." God it must be hard working for Lady Saffron. Alicia cleared her throat and tried for a casual tone as she said, "Does, um, Saffron drive a white car?"

Frances shook her head. "Manhattan grey Audi, why?"

"And Chloe? Kora? Tiani?"

Frances shrugged. "Not sure but they all have parking spaces in the basement if you want to check for yourself. Unlike me of course. I have to slum it on the bus with the plebs." Then she smiled and added, "Can't blame me for global warming. Seriously, why do you want to know all this?"

"Just curious," said Alicia, watching as Frances finally pulled the bag out and reached for the almond milk in the fridge. Then she leaned down, level with the cup, and began to slowly drip the milk in.

Alicia shook her head. She didn't have time for this crap. Frances was right; she was supposed to be holidaying! So she turned and left her to the tedious task of being Saffron's handmaid.

~

After ordering himself a "burger with the lot", Hamish Keener grabbed a cola, then dropped into the chair beside Lynette and asked why she was in the area.

"Does Alicia know you're here? Because I just saw her back at the office. You should give her a call."

"Nah, just passing," she said, glancing worriedly towards Arial. Better get a move on! "Listen, while I've got you, what do you know about Austin Smythe?"

"Not you too?" he moaned. "Your sister was just harassing me about him. Tell me you're not into him?"

"Me? No! Besides, I already have a boyfriend. But, um, some girls at the wedding were interested, and I said I'd do some reconnaissance."

She winked, hoping to appear casual. He seemed to buy it and relaxed into his chair, cracking his cola open, spreading his legs wide.

"Yeah, well, tell your mates to avoid the cretin. Not worth the effort."

"Ginny seemed to think he was."

"Ginny didn't always have the best radar." His voice had turned growly, and he took a good slug of his drink. "But nah. Austin's a player. Total scumbag. Tries his luck with every lass in the building."

Lynette had heard the exact same thing about Hamish, but she let that one go to the keeper and said, "You don't think he might've been obsessed with Ginny?"

That elicited a chuckle. "*Obsessed?* Nah, quite the opposite. The only thing he's obsessed with is himself. Oh, and his career. Sucking up to the big boys. Probably shouting Ted lunch at Bistro George as we speak. Tosser."

Ahh, Lynette thought now. She should have been hanging out at the one-hat restaurant up the road, not this lowly sandwich bar.

"Anyway, apparently they'd split," said Hamish after another gulp. "Or that's what your sister said."

Really? Lynette hadn't heard that yet. "Who broke up with whom? Do you know?"

"He broke her heart of course. Why else do you think it happened?"

Lynette stared at him, confused, then she realised he was referring to Ginny's apparent suicide. And she could tell he was hurting. The way his chin quivered and his eyes welled up. She reached across and tapped his hand.

"I'm really sorry, Hamish. I know you and Ginny were close."

He pulled his hand back and tried for a casual shrug but couldn't quite pull it off.

"Hamish!" someone called out from the counter, holding up a brown paper bag. He nodded, then glanced back at Lynette, his eyes suddenly fiery.

"That brown-nosing piece of sh-te did not deserve Ginny,

and he knows it. We all do."

Then he jumped up, grabbed his burger and strode out.

And as she watched him zigzag across the street and back into his building, there were a few things playing on Lynette's mind, starting with the fact that Hamish was not at all as she remembered him. Hamish of old would barely have looked her in the eye, his gaze straying south to her loosened blouse. He certainly wouldn't have shaken her hand away. He would have clung onto it and then added a snaky grin, ignoring the fact she had a boyfriend like she'd said.

Oh, no, Hamish Keener was a very different man today. And he wasn't just different. He was angry. Really angry.

What Lynette didn't know was who he was angriest with—Austin or Ginny?

As she finally took her leave, she decided it wasn't just Austin they should be looking at closely. It was Hamish.

CHAPTER 18
Fashion Faux Pas

The first time Claire was in the *Styled* office she was a wide-eyed twenty-three-year-old who had recently opened her inner-city vintage clothing store. The magazine was doing a piece on repurposed clothes or "upcycling", and she was there to loan them her finest selection. Back then they had taken her wares with barely a thank-you—in fact, quite a few dubious sniffs and at least one "I just can't understand it!"—and they certainly hadn't wanted to hear her views on anything, least of all how to pair her vintage Chanel tweed jacket with a plain white tee, casual denim and loafers.

Today things could not be more different.

"Hello! So lovely to see you again!" Saffron cooed, dragging her forwards and air-kissing both cheeks. "And don't you look *fabulous*. As always. Come… come into my den. I'll get us some bevvies. What's your poison?"

Claire asked for an Earl Grey tea and watched as Saffron clicked her fingers and her assistant came running, taking their orders then dashing off again. Not so much as a please or thank-you. She hoped Simon remembered his manners when he sent young Queenie to fetch for him.

"I was delighted to get your assistant's call," Saffron continued. "This is such a coup. Can't believe you changed your mind."

Claire smiled sweetly but knew what had really changed was her marital status and that she would have been lucky to get a glass of tap water if she hadn't married Simon.

And yet Claire was still surprised at how quickly they had pulled it together. After all, magazines were old-school; they worked several months ahead. Probably already had the next few *Styled Queen* pages in the can.

But she hadn't factored in Simon's diligent PA.

"Oh, easy peasy," Queenie told her on the ride over together that morning. "I told Frances your schedule was super tight and it had to happen this week or it wouldn't happen at all."

Claire laughed back. "So tight I don't have a spare moment to investigate random murders. Well done, Queenie. Now we'll have something to report when we meet up with the club later."

Or at least she hoped they would.

But she'd barely taken a sip of her tea, let alone swapped a few pleasantries with Saffron, when the fashion editor appeared to spirit her into the fashion wardrobe. There they had a wide selection of items "fresh from the catwalks" that Claire had never seen before but was now going to pretend she couldn't live without.

From there she was whisked into a chair for hair and makeup and then in front of a flashing camera for the photographs, followed by a video camera that had been set up in one corner of the office so their resident vlogger could record Claire waxing lyrical about the "fabulous assortment".

It all meant there was not a spare moment to ask a single question about Ginny.

What she did learn was that modern fashion was not her cup of tea, working alone had so much going for it, and that she'd been wearing quite the wrong shade of lipstick her entire adult life.

"This one is more your colour," Chloe told her, topping it up between shots. "See how the shade brings out the lovely caramel hues of your skin?"

Claire had to confess she was right. "Tell me the name of that brand. I'll buy my own."

"Oh, it's not for sale yet. Out in September. But you can have this one. I've got more. It's one of the perks of the job." Then Chloe laughed and added, "Gotta get some perks, the pay is *embarrassing*."

Later, as Kora put the finishing touches to Claire's outfit, the fashion editor whispered, "You're a lucky duck today. The beauty girls are usually pretty stingy with the free product. Maybe with Ginny gone we might all get a look in."

"Isn't that their job though?" asked Claire. "To test everything?"

She pouted. "But how many lippies does one girl need? *Elle*'s beauty team share theirs around. So do *Vogue*'s. Most mags have a little in-house giveaway every few months. Not our lot."

"How does Saffron feel about that?"

Kora snorted. "She gets her own product of course! Now, how tight does that skirt feel?"

As Kora twirled Claire in front of a mirror, the two PAs stood on the sidelines watching.

"How's everyone holding up after that tragic incident with your beauty assistant?" Queenie asked Frances, trying to sound nonchalant.

Frances glanced back at her, surprised. "Oh fine, I guess. I mean, Saffron's heartbroken, of course, but she's such a professional. She'd never let anything get in the way of the important work we do."

Important? If Queenie were Perry, she'd be snorting about now. And with good reason. As far as she was concerned, *Styled* was little more than wasted wood. Give her a copy of *Gourmet Traveller* or the *Financial Review* any day. But she was a professional too, so she nodded solemnly and said, "Of course. Still, it must be hard. I heard Ginny was really popular at Arial."

"Popular with the guys maybe," Frances retorted. "Luckily Saffron's not a guy, so Ginny couldn't win her over. In fact, she went out of her way to do quite the opposite I'd say."

"Oh?" said Queenie, not sure what she meant.

The PA's eyes darted from Kora and Chloe who were now both fussing over Claire and back to Queenie. She smiled and said, "Ignore me, their bitchiness is contagious. I'd better get the lunch orders sorted."

As she returned to her desk, Queenie sighed. It was a pity Frances was also the consummate professional. She would get no gossip from her today.

Finally, after a whirlwind two hours of snapping and vlogging and lying about her love of contemporary fashion, the ordeal was over and Claire was deposited back at Saffron's desk, still dripping with heavy makeup but now happily clad back in her own 1960's Mary Quant-style jersey dress.

"I *absolutely* love your sense of style," Saffron said as she waved her into a seat.

Claire smiled. "Thank you." Then, seeing a potential segue, she quickly added, "You have such style too. Was that a Stella McCartney suit you had on at Ginny's memorial?"

"Yes! Well spotted." Saffron was thrilled that someone had noticed.

"It certainly beat some of the rather… risqué dresses in the room," Claire added, wincing to herself.

She was not a natural bitch, unlike Perry who could pull it off with aplomb. But she needed to draw Saffron out, and it worked.

The editor was now roaring with laughter. "Weren't some of the outfits egregious? Did you catch that frilly number the mother was wearing? Or *not* wearing, I should say. You'd think it was a trashy nightclub opening, not your daughter's send-off."

Claire nodded away. Then threw out another hook. "I guess the apple didn't fall far from the tree."

Saffron's lips parted and she gasped. And for a moment, Claire feared she'd gone too far, but then Saffron leaned in and said, "I didn't know you were so naughty! You're right though. I mean, I'd never talk ill of the dead—"

"*Of course* not."

"But she was never suited to *Styled*, that Ginny. They forced her upon me. She would have been much happier at one of our trashy gossip magazines, or better yet, our hideous men's mag, *Lout*. Much more her style. And I'm not just talking fashion if you get what I mean."

"Slept around a bit, did she?" said Claire.

"Let's just say, no man was safe when she clocked into work." She sniggered, adding, "Very common was our Ginny."

Claire felt herself bristle at that. She despised how this conversation was going and how Saffron would now consider her one of her gossips. She didn't want to encourage that in the slightest. But she had a higher purpose. This would benefit Ginny in the end. So she swallowed her self-loathing and asked as casually as she could, "What about your charismatic CEO, Ted Johnson? Did Ginny ever try her luck with him?"

Saffron's smile deflated at that. "In her *dreams*, darling. Ted would never lower himself to sleep with someone like Ginny."

Then she added a quick sniff like she found the notion offensive, and Claire wondered about that.

Why would Saffron be so offended by the idea of Ted and Ginny?

~

Across town, Ronnie was grasping for gossip, too, as she sat down for lunch with some old friends from her tennis club. She hadn't seen them in ages and was so pleased they could get together at such late notice. Felt dreadful that she'd neglected them of late, what with her book club and her twin nephews who took so much of her time, Missy now glued to one of them. It was a good thing she liked Missy!

Still, these ladies didn't hold a grudge. They were too old for that nonsense. And while they were also too old now for tennis tournaments, they did stay busy, mostly caring for grandchildren and doing important charity work. Because *these* were the kinds of women she hung around with—not the vacuous Ebony Johnson types. Indeed, Ronnie had just as many friends at the Balmain Women's Auxiliary where she volunteered, and they barely had two bob to rub together, that lot.

Having said that, she knew at least one of these ladies, Vanya, did hang with Ebony, or at least live next door to her when she was in town. Their waterfront mansions shared a private jetty and a breathtaking view across Sydney Harbour. So, after the requisite catch-up, Ronnie steered the conversation to the Johnsons.

"How are your neighbours coping after all that drama at Arial the other week?" she asked Vanya, before filling the table in on the *Styled* beauty assistant's "suicide", in case they weren't in the loop.

Luckily, Vanya was, and after a brief discussion about the inadequacy of government funding into mental health services, she told them how Ebony was just moaning to her over the garden fence the other day. "She's most unimpressed with Ted's response at work. Says he's not taking it seriously at all. She's pushing for him to bring in counsellors. Make sure it doesn't happen again."

"Make sure his path to Number Ten Downing Street is secure," murmured another friend, Harriet, under her breath.

She was referring to the UK Prime Minister's official residence and office, and Vanya chuckled at that.

"Ted's plotting a move into politics?" asked Ronnie.

"Not sure about Ted," said Vanya, "but Ebony certainly is. She really doesn't enjoy the time they spend here and wants to get him back to London where she's from. She's homesick, ambitious too. Has him on a tight leash."

Ronnie's eyes were widening. Like Claire she wasn't one for gossip, but this was proving fruitful. "So he was a bad boy once?"

Harriet looked at her like she was dim. "Ronnie darling, you don't get to your third marriage by being an angel, surely?"

"But he's good as gold these days," insisted Vanya. "Wouldn't dare cross Ebony."

Then she glanced around, leaned in and whispered, "She's a little scary. We had a branch fall into their yard the other week, and my goodness, she made a fuss. Luckily my gardener was onto it toot sweet."

"Speaking of trees," said another friend, Denise, "did anyone hear how Randwick City Council are plotting to tear down those grand old figs near my place? It's an abomination! I think we should put our heads together and see if we can put a stop to it."

And off they went, plotting to save Sydney's "floral heritage", while Ronnie could do nothing to save Lynette's silly theory about Ginny sleeping with the CEO. Because if he really was on a tight leash, Ted would not be likely to pull off a mysterious affair at *Styled* magazine now, would he?

~

Perry locked eyes with a weeping angel, then across to a bleeding statue and felt a shiver run down his back. He might work with dead things, but there was something especially creepy about this workplace, at least to an atheist like Perry. He was religious once, until a priest tried to convert him. Not to Christianity but to heterosexuality. Told him he was a sinner, would go straight to hell. He didn't feel like a sinner. But it sure did kill his faith.

It was early afternoon at the University of Sydney, and young students were spread out across the lawn, eating and chatting and flirting between tutorials.

Perry watched them through the arched window of his friend's sandstone office, then turned his eyes back to the religious paraphernalia decorating the room, for want of a better term. There were also piles of books and religious texts everywhere and a desk you could barely see for the folders and papers and multiple computers. And atop it all, the T-shirt Perry had brought in.

"You've brought me a contentious one here, Perry," said his friend Alex, an accomplished art historian and scholar who ran the religious iconography department.

He leaned in to study the image printed on the shirt, then leaned back.

"It's a replica of the infamous Holy Shroud, of course,

the supposed burial garment of Jesus Christ, post-crucifixion. The original imprint is old and faint; you can barely see the outline of Jesus. This one is quite exaggerated, a Disneyland version. Where did you find it?"

And so Perry explained about Ginny and her supposed suicide and how she might have left this T-shirt as a clue to what really happened.

Alex seemed most intrigued by that, then launched into a history of the Shroud and its origins. "I know plenty of historians who scoff at the whole thing and plenty more who believe it's the image of the crucified Jesus."

"So where does that leave you?" asked Perry.

"Not so fast," he said, like he had all day, which Perry did not. "Let's look at the evidence, shall we?"

He leaned back in his chair and proceeded to lecture Perry on the Shroud's origins, how, before being moved to Turin, in Italy, it was first exhibited in a tiny French village in the 1300s and was said to date back to the time of Christ.

"Millions of Christians believed without a shadow of a doubt that the faint yellowing image on the linen really was the remnants of Jesus after being pulled bloody from the cross. Unfortunately for them, carbon dating in the 1980s brought that into dispute, placing its origin closer to the medieval period—so we're talking 1260 to 1390 AD, thereabouts. Quite some time after Jesus of Nazareth walked the earth. However!"

He stood up and began searching his shelves for something as Perry tried hard not to hurry him along. Now he remembered why he hadn't seen Alex in ages. The man could really drone on...

"Ah, here it is!" he said, pulling out a book with a crisp dust jacket. "There's been some fresh research since then using some rather whizbang photography that suggests the Shroud might, in fact, have originated much earlier, around 33 AD." Then he paused to see if Perry would catch it, and he did.

"So the time of the crucifixion then?"

The older man clapped his hands like Perry was his

student. "Very good! Yes. So the debate still rages."

"Okay," said Perry cutting to the chase. "This is all very interesting"—even though it wasn't, at least not to Perry—"but what does it tell us about my friend who worked in women's magazines, do we think?"

Alex shrugged and handed over the book he was holding. "Perhaps she missed her calling and should have gone into something a little deeper?"

He was joking, but Perry was not amused. He felt patronised now and like he was wasting his time. He handed the book straight back, snatched the shirt from the cluttered desk, and thanked Alex for his time, even though everything he'd learned he could have learned from Wikipedia.

As he made his way to the door, his friend called out, "Perhaps she was trying to make some point about not being believed?"

Perry stopped. Okay, that made more sense, kind of. Or perhaps Ginny was up in the sky right now, watching and laughing as she sent them all on a wild goose chase. Whether Jesus was beside her was a whole other question…

"She could also be pointing to fraud," Alex added.

Perry turned. That made even more sense…

"I'm not sure anyone made a dime from the original linen," Alex continued, leaning back in his chair again, "but there's been a lot of money brought in since, from tours of the original Shroud at the *Cappella della Sacra Sindone*, in Turin, to ghoulish knock-offs like that T-shirt of yours. Could it have something to do with money or fraud perhaps?"

Yes, thought Perry, *now* you're talking!

CHAPTER 19
Another Book Club Session

When the book club gathered for another debrief after work that evening, everyone was talking at once, they had so much to share, and so Ronnie returned to tapping her glass and demanding they take turns.

"And I'll do some scribbling," said Alicia, pulling out her trusty notebook where she had already jotted in the names of their suspects.

They were in Claire's inner-city dress shop, the Timeless Vintage Clothing Store, and the only one missing was Lynette, who was busy at her restaurant and would join them later. So Claire had left the front door closed but unlocked, then ushered them into the tiny café at the back of the store where she prepared pots of tea and offered around the leftover treats from her stock.

As they sipped and nibbled, they quickly worked through their findings.

First, Ronnie revealed what she'd learned about the Arial CEO, Ted Johnson. He might have been unfaithful once, but that was all in the past and it was unlikely he was now risking the wrath of "scary" Ebony let alone his potential political career by sleeping with someone as obvious as Ginny. Or so her friend Vanya believed.

And Claire was inclined to agree, telling them all about her fashion shoot. Saffron seemed offended by the suggestion that Ted would sleep with anyone as "common" as Ginny—her vile word, she hastened to add. "You're right about Saffron, Alicia. She is not a nice person. Don't know why I ever thought she was."

"Her PA worships her though," said Queenie. "I couldn't

get much gossip out of Frances, I'm afraid, although she did say something odd about Ginny. I didn't really understand it, but I think she was trying to tell me that Ginny went out of her way to be rude to Saffron."

Sounds about right, thought Alicia, madly scribbling. After that, she launched into her own discussions with both Kirsten and Hamish. Lynette appeared halfway through, and so she repeated most of it, adding, "Hamish is still really upset. He blames Austin for Ginny's death."

There was an unexpected snort from her sister, and Alicia glanced across to where Lynette was now firing up the espresso machine behind the counter.

"Everything okay?" she sang out.

Lynette turned and said, "Sorry, just ignore me. Anyone want a coffee?"

They all shook their heads, and Alicia continued, repeating her conversation with Ginny's aunty. "Kirsten says Austin was heartbroken at the birthday barbecue. That was about eight days before Ginny died. She thinks Ginny was dumping him and he was shattered. Said she'd stolen his heart, destroyed him, words to that effect. No surprise really, considering she'd just dragged him to a family gathering. That's usually a green light, not a break-up sign."

Alicia turned her eyes to Lynette, who was now frothing some milk.

"I owe you an apology, sis," she said. "You might've been right about him. Maybe Austin was obsessed with Ginny and didn't like being dumped."

"Or maybe…" said Lynette, returning to the table with a cup of short black, "Ginny and Austin kissed and made up after the barbie, and it was *Hamish* who lashed out."

Alicia's eyebrows knotted together. "I thought you were gunning for Austin."

"That's before I ran into Hamish."

"How did you—"

"Not important now," she said, waving the question away. "We got to talking about Ginny, and the way Hamish spoke about her…" She slugged back the shot of espresso, then shook her head. "I don't know. It wasn't healthy. He's also obsessed. Possessive even. Didn't think Austin was good enough for Ginny. Like he wanted her all to himself."

Alicia was now confused. And not convinced. Yes, Hamish had a soft spot for Ginny, could be overly protective, but that's why she couldn't imagine him hurting her. It just didn't make sense.

"If that were true, wouldn't it be *Austin* he was pushing in front of a train, not Ginny?" Alicia said. "Besides, she's always had loads of lovers. Hamish has never felt the need to kill her over any of them before."

"Except you said it yourself, this one was serious. Or at least Hamish thought it was. If Kirsten's right and they really did break up, well, Hamish might not have known that. He might've heard all about their closeness at your wedding, feared his chances of ever getting her back were over, so he saw her at the station that day and reacted. Is he a hothead?"

Not at all, she thought as Lynette added, "If Hamish couldn't have her, no one could. Least of all... what did he call Austin? A 'brown-nosing piece of shite'."

"Ouch!" said Perry.

"*Mean,*" said Missy.

Alicia just frowned. Hamish had expressed similar sentiments to her. And he hadn't known about Ginny's break-up with Austin. That was true.

Queenie sighed. "The idea that you'd kill someone because you loved them too much is just awful."

"But shockingly common," Alicia had to concede. "Just ask Jackson. A woman is killed every week in this country by someone who professes to love her. It's nonsense of course. Not love at all."

As the group grumbled about the woeful domestic violence statistics, Perry finished off the last chocolate brownie, biding his time. Lynette's theory was a good one, he thought, but he had another one. A better one. And he needed to present it soon, because he also had a better offer this evening and was keen to get going.

"Hate to throw a spanner in the works," he said, breaking through.

"Throw away!" said Alicia. "We'll take a shovel, too, if you've got one."

He smiled. "I'm wondering if it's not love we should be looking at but fraud."

As their expressions crumpled with confusion, he revealed what his boring buddy Alex had told him about the Shroud of Turin.

"According to him, it's either the greatest find in religious history or the greatest fraud, and that got me thinking. What if this has nothing do with sex? Could the 'mysterious affair' at *Styled* have something to do with financial fraud?"

Queenie clearly liked this theory and was nodding, her perfect little bob dancing about her ears. "That would explain the Monopoly money. Someone could've been stealing money from the magazine."

Alicia frowned. "But how do you steal money from a magazine? It's not like a shop where you can plunder the cash register. Everything goes through the Accounts department. Unless you're talking small change, like pinching a few bucks from petty cash."

"Could add up to a lot over time," suggested Perry. "Who's in charge of the petty cash? The PA?"

"Usually," said Alicia. "And Frances is one sharp cookie. I think she'd notice."

Queenie agreed. "But maybe it wasn't small change. What if it was fraud on a larger scale? Plenty of opportunities to defraud a company if it's not run well."

"Like?" asked Missy.

She began rattling them off. "Payroll fraud, asset misappropriation, bribery. Someone could be misusing the company credit card, say, or manipulating time sheets to get paid more overtime—"

Alicia was snorting now. "What overtime? There's no overtime pay in my world. Just a pathetic salary and an expectation we'll work till we bleed."

Queenie offered her a sympathetic smile. "There's also

data theft, tax evasion… Oh, and another common one is inflating invoices to get kickbacks. That's a cinch when no one is keeping the strictest eye on things."

"How does that work?" asked Perry.

"Surprisingly easily. Someone says they've hired a contractor, like, say, a photographer for two thousand dollars a day. When really it's only an agreed value of one thousand, and the staffer and photographer split the extra thousand."

"But why would the photographer agree to that? They're getting less."

"Yes but then they get *all* the jobs. That's the arrangement."

"But why wouldn't the staff member just keep the extra thousand?" he persisted. "Tell the photographer they were only getting a thousand, then invoice for two and pocket the full amount themselves."

"Because contractors get paid directly," said Alicia, answering for her. "Straight into their nominated back account. They'd have to be in it together."

"And it would only work if the editor and the Accounts department aren't checking the invoices too closely," added Queenie.

"Unless it's the editor doing it," suggested Claire.

Queenie nodded. "But you'd still have to be colluding with someone in Accounts or able to justify the extra money in your budget. It's risky."

"What about this?" said Lynette. "What if the *Styled* staff member *says* they're hiring a contractor but then pays themselves?"

"Sure," said Queenie, "but then they'd have to use a fake name and bank account and do all the work themselves."

Alicia snorted again. "Seriously? You heard what I said about bleeding? In the old days you might've got away with that, but staff levels are anorexic now, and our workloads are obese. When someone resigns, they rarely replace them, just shift the load to everyone else. Especially on a mag like *Styled,* where most of the budget goes to keeping the mighty Saffron Toya-Jones. She's the highest paid editor in the building.

Also married to a wealthy banker. Which is why I can't see her being involved in any of this. She wouldn't need to be."

"Need doesn't always come into it," said Ronnie. "Just because you have money doesn't mean you're not a natural born fraudster. In fact, I'd argue quite the opposite."

"Know anyone in Accounts you could have a quiet word with?" asked Queenie, eyes back on Alicia. "Someone you trust who could do some digging?"

Alicia wavered. Not particularly.

"What about Hamish?" said Lynette, eyes on her sister. "He's a slippery geezer. Could he be misusing his Arial credit card, say?"

"Sure, I've seen Hamish pop the company Amex behind the bar when he wants to impress, but that's a few free drinks. Not that big a deal is it?"

"Depends how much he's drinking."

Alicia tsked. "Ginny would be the first to lap up the freebies. She wouldn't think it was some great mystery I needed to uncover. Don't forget that's what we're trying to do here." She tsked again, hating the way Lynette had her claws into Hamish and not sure why it disturbed her so much. "And Hamish wouldn't kill Ginny to keep it a mystery. They were mates, Lynny."

"Okay, let's return to the boyfriend then," said Ronnie. "The one she was supposed to have broken up with. Didn't her Aunty Kirsten say they'd a tiff at the family shindig, Alicia? And he said something about a theft?"

"Yes, the theft of his heart I think she said."

"Maybe she misheard? Doesn't he work in Accounts? Sales, I think you said. Maybe he meant it literally. He could be a contender."

Now Perry was tsking. "But he doesn't work at *Styled*. Remember the clues, people! *The Mysterious Affair at Styled*. Not *Arial Publishing*. It has to be someone who worked with Ginny, otherwise why leave that particular book? Start there, Alicia. What do you always tell us? Keep it simple, stupid."

"Hey, I may be stupid," Alicia shot back, "but there's nothing simple about any of this."

She smiled, watching as he gathered his things, telling them he had to run.

"Why?" demanded Missy. "Where're you off to?"

"It's called life, Missy. You should try it."

"Hey, I have a boyfriend!" she shot back, still proud of herself for the achievement.

"And don't I know it," said Ronnie. "Will I be seeing you and Seamus at mine for brunch tomorrow?"

Missy nodded gleefully as Alicia also grabbed her bag.

"I'd better get home too. Resurrect what's left of my honeymoon. Jackson's booked a romantic hideaway in the Blue Mountains."

"Sounds like a dirty weekend to me," said Perry, leaning in to kiss her goodbye.

"Hope so," she replied. "It's time we focused on each other and not murder mysteries."

That got them all snorting. If there's one thing they knew for sure, it's that when Alicia got whiff of a murder mystery, nothing else got a look in—no matter where she was, who she was with, and whether she was being paid overtime for it or not.

CHAPTER 20
Whistle While You Work

Alicia's first day back at the office could not come fast enough, and she struggled to hide her enthusiasm as she jumped out of bed and prepared to head in. It was not so much an indictment of their marriage—or at least she hoped it wasn't—but the fact that their honeymoon had been a complete washout, and they had two murder mysteries hanging over their heads.

The newlyweds' dirty weekend had been a bit of a washout too.

Alicia and Jackson had both been distracted, neither daring to mention the elephants that had accompanied them into their hotel room (aka Ginny and Isla)—Alicia because she was supposed to be butting out and Jackson because Singh had sworn him to secrecy.

It had cast a pall over the two days, and Alicia wondered if this was what their marriage would look like going forwards. Not speaking of the things that really interested them, lest they say the wrong thing and set each other off?

So many times she went to express a theory about the deaths or repeat something her book club said, then forced herself to gobble it back down.

It was like she was choking on her tongue all weekend.

So, as she kissed Jackson goodbye that Monday and headed into Arial, she felt a sense of release, like a dog set loose from its leash, free at last to do some proper sniffing.

But first she had to get started on her Taylor Swift special. And so she made herself a strong coffee, then charged her computer to life and opened up a fresh folder she labelled TAY TAY.

She did not get any further.

"God has summoned us to the heavens," said Hamish, poking his head around her door.

Alicia groaned. "Seriously? Back five seconds and Ted's already bogging me down with mindless meetings."

"How else is he gonna justify his existence? Come on, let's go as a pack, that way we can't get eaten."

Alicia laughed and followed Hamish out to the elevators. As they walked, she remembered Lynette's words, her accusations, and tried to imagine him pushing Ginny in front of a train and running Isla-Mae over.

She simply couldn't see it.

Sure, he wasn't going to win any Man of the Year awards, a little too old-school for the modern woman, but he wasn't violent. Certainly not a killer. She was sure of it.

As they rode the elevator upwards, she said, "I can't believe Ted's still in the country. When's he going to choof off back to England?"

She knew that Arial's London headquarters made Seventh Heaven look like a ghetto. Had been there just once, flown in for an editors' conference followed by a lavish retreat at a plush convention centre. That was back when the company had money to splash about. These days everything was done via Zoom, and apart from the top-selling *Styled* team, the rest of them were lucky to get a warm glass of bubbly at Christmas.

Hamish was clearly thinking along similar lines and said, "Maybe he's hanging around to slam us all about our sales."

"I thought yours went up."

"Early figures are just in. Not where they should be. The bumper issue cost a packet, so I'm gonna need some serious sales to cut even. Meanwhile, *Styled* is through the roof again apparently. Heard they just clinched the new Apple campaign off the back of that. Saffron's gonna be insufferable."

"*Going* to be?" said Alicia as they reached floor seven.

As it turned out, the meeting had nothing to do with sales

figures or Apple. Ted Johnson wanted to congratulate his editors on navigating what he called "a dark and concerning period". And he wasn't talking about revenue. He was clearly referring to Ginny's death but never actually used her name, and Alicia felt offended on her friend's behalf.

During this, Saffron stood up the front beside him, nodding like a bobble toy, and now Hamish and Alicia were swapping eye rolls.

"We also acknowledge that a young model who worked across several of our titles has lost her life in an unfortunate incident," added Ted. "And so our thoughts and prayers go to her family and any of our colleagues who worked with her."

Again, no name was mentioned, and Alicia wanted to shout out "Her name was Isla-Mae Cavendish, people! She was Virginia DeRosso's flatmate. She was a beautiful young person, and it was more than *unfortunate*. She was murdered!"

But that wouldn't get her anywhere, except a consult with Arabella, and she didn't really know if Isla had been murdered, so she bit her tongue and continued listening as Ted rattled on about "looking out for each other" and "We don't want this happening again, folks."

He then gave his HR guru the nod, and Arabella stepped forward, a printed briefing in hand, to outline the policies and procedures around mental health, the warning signs, how best to report it…

As she did so, Alicia couldn't help wondering if they were genuinely concerned about their staff's wellbeing or if it was the bottom line that concerned them, because Perry was right—reputation mattered to Arial Publishing. It wasn't a good look having your staff and models throw themselves in front of moving vehicles.

Might lose the likes of Apple if it continued. Might also get sued if a loved one decides the publisher has driven them to it.

Alicia glanced quickly at the head of Accounts, Bob Chalmers, who was seated with the executive team at the front, but he seemed unfazed by the thought of lawsuits, even a little bored, discreetly checking his wristwatch like he also had better things to do. Austin was seated beside him, but Alicia could not read his expression. Annoyingly. He had his back to her and was nodding as vigorously as Saffron.

Finally, when the meeting was over and they were dismissed, Alicia told Hamish she'd catch him later and made a beeline but not for Austin. She wasn't sure about policy and procedures, but she wasn't going to miss an opportunity when it was staring her in the face.

Or at his silver Omega watch to be precise.

~

Jackson leaned against the kitchen bench in Ginny's North Sydney apartment and tried to look at the scene anew. The hit-and-run case had stalled—not a witness to be found—and it was doing his head in.

The police tape outside had been removed, and if it wasn't for the fact that Isla's parents were still making their way from the Caribbean, having finally been located, the place might have been cleared out. But as it was, the apartment was exactly as Isla had left it that fatal morning, and here he was, studying it again when he should be back at work getting on with their burgeoning caseload.

Yet how could he start on a fresh case when this one was so baffling?

They now had Isla's autopsy report, which had stated the bleeding obvious and quite literally. She had suffered blunt force trauma with fatal injuries to the head, spine and abdomen, consistent with a collision with a moving vehicle. Death would have been relatively swift, and that at least was something.

Yong-sun Lee's final report was also in and shed no new light on what he'd already told them, except to confirm that, based on the debris found at the scene, the vehicle involved was likely a white Toyota Corolla (2008–2012). As for the faecal matter found on the debris? That had been passed on to a forensic biologist and was still being analysed.

They were still searching for the hit-and-run driver. Oh, and a motive. That'd help.

Was it deliberate?

Accidental?

Connected to Virginia DeRosso?

Completely unrelated?

And that's what was eating him up. The not knowing. He couldn't let it go. And so he walked around the apartment, searching for God knows what. Yes, it did look messy, Alicia was correct. Whether it had actually been ransacked was a separate question. One Singh remained sceptical about.

"I'm neat too, you know that, Jacko, but even my place erupts occasionally. It was the crack of dawn. She'd worked late the day before. Would've been hard enough getting up for a jog, let alone tidying the place first. Give the girl a break."

So why could they find none of her digital devices? And where were her keys to the apartment and the fob that let you into the building? *That's* what was ringing alarm bells for Jackson. Did Isla drop it all after she was hit? If so, why hadn't they found anything out on the street? Why hadn't someone handed them in?

Oh no, that was definitely suspicious. So too was the CCTV footage out the front of the building. And for the same reasons as the CCTV from Platform Three at Town Hall station.

Too many trees, not enough wood.

Lots of people had come and gone that morning, especially once the alarm was raised and they all surged out for a look.

Jackson had now confirmed that the victim left for her jog at 5:55 a.m. that Sunday, well before sunrise. They spotted her sweeping past the front-door camera four minutes after another jogger, a man, also in running gear, checking something on his wrist, most likely a smartwatch. If he was trying to hide himself, he wasn't doing a good job of it, and besides he was on foot and had no apparent motive. Jackson had thoroughly checked him out. An ageing bachelor from an upstairs apartment, he remembered "the two stunners" well, he told Jackson, but hadn't seen or heard anything until he returned from his jog an hour later to find the street "lit up like a Christmas tree". He sounded unashamedly excited, and Jackson couldn't find any other obvious connection to the women, apart from drooling after them that is.

Isla's body had been found by the dog walker around 6:15 that morning, just metres from her front door, so she hadn't gotten far before she was hit. And the ambulance had arrived six minutes after that, the police about five minutes later—hence all the "Christmas lights"—and it was hard to work out who was who after that as voyeurs streamed in and out of the building. Most used their automatic fob keys so did not appear for long in front of the camera, just a flash as they swished past, some with heads down, some with faces covered mostly by long hair or hoods or umbrellas, because the rain continued all morning.

Had they come out for a look and then returned? Or was one of these "voyeurs" really the driver of the vehicle, heading in to search Isla's now-empty apartment?

If so, they were clever. It was an optimal time to slip in unnoticed amidst all the commotion. And it would be another hour before some equally clever constable connected the dots, realising that this victim shared the same residential address as another recent victim and called Singh, who had then called Jackson, dragging him from his honeymoon bed.

"You're back early; you might as well help with this," she'd said.

Besides, she knew he had a connection to the victim via Alicia.

And it was that connection that had him staring so keenly around the apartment now. Because he did believe Alicia. He was certain there had been an intruder. The question now was why? What were they looking for? Was it really related to Ginny's supposed suicide?

And, more worryingly, had they found it?

He groaned aloud.

Two women were dead within a week of each other, and they didn't have a single motive or suspect. The one thing they knew for sure—that she'd been hit by a white Toyota—was proving as good as useless. He'd already made enquiries. There were plenty of people related to Isla, including in the building, who drove white Toyotas, but none had recently been damaged.

He released a puff of air, frustrated as he glanced around again. Apart from the obvious—the devices, the keys—he hadn't a clue whether anything was missing. But he knew there was at least one person who might.

He picked up his phone and scrolled for the number.

~

Back in Seventh Heaven, Alicia took the seat the head of Accounts was offering in the spacious office he occupied, two doors down from Ted, and in return, offered him a grateful smile.

Bob Chalmers was a funny-looking fellow. Like something from central casting. Weedy. Bespectacled. An outdated suit that would have Saffron raising one eyebrow. Lovely though, and despite his furtive time-watching, more than happy to spare ten minutes for Alicia.

"You're the only editor in the building who doesn't give me grief about your budget," he said as he took his own seat. Then he chuckled and added, "But you didn't hear that from me."

She tapped a finger to her chin and said, "Perhaps I'm letting you off lightly. What do they say about the squeaky wheel? Should I be doing a lot more squealing?"

Bob chuckled again and left it at that, placing his hands prayerlike on the desk, waiting for her to continue. He was a figures man. A man of few words. So she cleared her throat and got straight to it.

"I have a strange question, and please don't take this the

wrong way, but I wondered how easy it would be for someone on one of the magazines, say, to steal from the company or defraud it in some way. Or would that be virtually impossible?"

He blinked at her. Clearly not expecting that.

She quickly added, "I have no intention of defrauding anybody, I can assure you! I'm just talking hypothetically."

The blinking intensified. "To what purpose?"

Good question, she thought, wondering why she hadn't prepped better for this. She realised how suspicious she sounded but could hardly come out and say "Is there any chance Ginny caught someone fiddling with the books at *Styled* and got murdered for it?"

Smiling benignly, she gave her vivid imagination a chance to catch up, and very soon it did. She sat forward, her smile turning confident.

"I'm in a murder mystery book club," she explained. "And we were discussing a plot point in one of the books. A low-level employee puts in all this false invoicing and gets away with it, and well, we just think that's implausible. I said I'd ask the expert. When it comes to money matters, you are the GOAT after all."

If the lie didn't work, flattery just might. And it did. His blinking settled, and he sat back with a pleased smile.

"I'm not sure about GOAT, Alicia, but you're right to question that lazy plot device. Oh no, everything is digitised these days and double checked. Now if someone were to try to defraud a large organisation such as this, one with superb checks and balances, I can assure you, they would have to be pretty senior."

"Like an editor?"

Bob looked at her like she was demented. "Not on my watch. They're the invoices we check most closely. Editors can't so much as charge for extra stationery, let alone long boozy lunches without me knowing about it." Then he winked and added, "You have been warned."

She laughed nervously but couldn't remember the last boozy lunch she had on anybody, let alone Arial Publishing.

She did think Hamish should watch his back though.

"But what about if, say, I was to hire a freelance writer for all my specials," she continued. "And I put in the invoices that I was paying them two dollars a word when really I was paying them just one dollar a word and splitting the difference with them? Would you notice that?"

He smiled. "Considering it's double the going rate, I think I would, then I'd ask you in for a 'please explain'. Oh no," he continued, warming to the subject now, "I think we'd notice if something was amiss. The only way you'd get away with that kind of nonsense was if you were working in Accounts or *with* someone in Accounts. In *cahoots* as they say."

He cackled at the lingo, proud of himself.

"So, if someone was colluding with someone like, say, Austin Smythe—?"

"Young Smythie? From Sales and Circ'?" Bob looked disappointed in her now. "No, no, it would have to be someone directly involved with daily digital transactions, able to disguise or manipulate moneys going in and out. Someone in Accounts, like my 2IC, Helen. Or myself." Then his smile widened and he added, "But I can assure you we're not *that* easy."

And he laughed like there was nothing funnier, and she hoped he kept laughing and didn't put two and two together. Either way, it was not the answer she was hoping for.

Then, about to take her leave, he added, "Or they could go straight to the top, of course, and convince the CEO to do it. Ted's the boss after all. He could get away with murder, that fellow."

CHAPTER 21
The Search Continues

As Gail DeRosso stepped into her daughter's apartment, Jackson tried not to reel back. He'd forgotten how full-on she was—from her flashy tattoos to her slinky dress sense to her frankly whiffy perfume. Yikes. *Was there no subtlety left in the perfumery business anymore?*

"Thanks for coming," said the detective.

"It's long overdue," she snapped at him. "I've been trying to get in for weeks, but you lot wouldn't let me. I should be allowed to finish packing up my daughter's things."

"I apologise for that, but there are some grounds for suspicion regarding Ms Cavendish's death, so we've had to be careful."

Her eyes suddenly flashed. "What kind of grounds? What are you talking about?"

"All hit-and-runs are criminal investigations," he told her and left it at that. "Now, as I explained on the phone, all I need you to do is take a look around and tell me if you feel like something is not quite right. By that I mean something is missing or out of place or—"

"It's all out of place! Apartment's a shambles! Did you do this? Ginny would never leave it in such a state."

He tried to smother a smile. Typical Alicia. Right as always. "If you could just take a look about, Mrs DeRosso."

She humphed and then did as he asked but had little to report. As far as she was concerned, there was nothing obviously missing or misplaced, and after ten minutes she shook her head.

Then her eyes narrowed and she said, "What's really going on? What am I really looking for?"

Again he didn't answer that. Just thanked her for her time and escorted her to the door. As he opened it, she stopped and glanced back into the living room, her tone heavy.

"Truth is, I haven't been back here in months, so I'm not the best person to ask. Maybe reach out to her friends. That Alicia Finlay. She'd know."

Jackson wished Singh were here to witness that comment but simply continued escorting her out of the apartment and down the hall to the front of the building. It was only when they reached the door that he realised what she'd said.

He stopped. Turned. "Why haven't you been back here, Mrs DeRosso?"

"Huh?"

"Did you have some kind of falling out with your daughter?"

Because he remembered how close the two were. She'd said so in her eulogy. Alicia had confirmed it.

Gail's cheeks drained of colour. "What? No! Who told you that?"

He stared at her, waiting, and noticed she could no longer look at him straight.

Eventually she took a step back, crossed her arms over her ample chest, and said, "It had nothing to do with Ginny's death. It didn't. And it definitely had nothing to do with Isla, so I don't think it's any of your business, frankly. Just a mother-daughter spat and one I now have to live with." She released a jittery hand and flung it to her mouth, clearly holding back a sob. Then she swallowed hard and pulled her shoulders back. "Now if you don't mind. I am a busy lady."

He watched for a moment longer, then stepped forward and held the front door open.

"Thank you for coming in. You've been very helpful."

But had she? Really?

It was clear Gail was lying about something, but that's all that was clear. That and the fact that her taste in perfume was as bad as Alicia's.

~

Queenie might have been an executive assistant, but she was doing the work of a lowly courier today, and it didn't bother her in the slightest. Frances had called that afternoon to inform her that the clothes Claire had worn for the *Styled* shoot last Friday had been photographed by the still-life department and were ready to be collected. They were now Claire's to keep.

Of course, Claire hadn't wanted any of them—"Shhh, don't tell Saffron!"—and suggested Queenie keep them herself or donate them to charity, but Queenie wasn't thinking that far ahead. She just wanted another chance to question Frances, so she told Saffron's assistant she'd be in to collect them personally.

And so here she was, back at the PA's desk, clutching onto the bagged clothes, hovering.

Queenie was on a mission. If Alicia was right and nothing got past Frances, then surely she'd know if there'd been a theft or fraud at her own magazine.

But first she had to lay some more bait...

"We had an incident at work the other day," Queenie said as she pretended to wait for her rideshare. "Caught one of our temps trying to steal from the kitty. Simon had to dismiss them."

Frances didn't appear to be listening. She'd handed over the clothes and was now tapping feverishly at her keyboard.

Queenie ignored the obvious cue to leave and added, "Of course that sort of thing happens everywhere."

"Not here," snapped Frances, finally glancing up. "I'm in charge of the kitty. I'd never allow it. Besides I'm good at maths, so I'd know in an instant if something was missing. That's just sloppy."

Queenie had a feeling the barb was intended for her but let it slide. You had to leave your ego at the door when you were sleuthing.

"I know," she said, scraping a hand through her bob, "but they were sleeping with one of the managers, so that's how they got away with it."

It was another lie. She hoped Frances didn't pass it on to one of the gossip mags in the building, but she was desperate for *something* to share at the next book club meeting. They were all so clever, the bookish sleuths, and Queenie wanted to earn her place amongst them.

And sure enough, Frances seemed to soften. She leaned back in her seat and half shrugged.

"Well, we can't be held responsible for what the *senior* staff do," she told her. "That's not in our job description. At least it's not in mine. I'm here to look after Saffron. If someone chooses to break the rules, that's on their heads." Then she added, "You're lucky it was just some petty cash. Round here you can steal boxes of high-end cosmetics and no one bats an eye lid." Then she flicked her gaze across the office, adding, "That's not to say our eyes aren't open to it, of course. We're not all idiots."

Queenie ignored that obvious barb too, then glanced around to see who Frances was glowering at.

CHAPTER 22
Sniffing Out the Truth

"**C**hloe was stealing beauty products!" Queenie announced, the minute the sleuths got back together, which was early that evening in the Timeless Vintage Clothing Store again.

Claire's boutique on Victoria Street was the halfway point between most of their workplaces and an easy drive for Ronnie, so the most logical place to meet, which Queenie had insisted they do, now bursting with her news. And not just that, apologies.

"I'm so sorry, I think I over complicated everything," she told them. "I don't think there's any elaborate fraud. The mysterious affair at *Styled* was simply petty theft."

"But is it really theft when they're free samples that got sent to you directly?" asked Lynette. "She's the beauty editor. Aren't they hers to do with as she likes?"

"Not necessarily," said Queenie. "I looked into it, and it is illegal if you sell samples you received for free so you can make a profit." She beamed as she produced a touchscreen tablet. "I've done my due diligence."

She opened Facebook Marketplace, then tapped "beauty products brand-new" into the search engine and clicked on one of the boxes.

"I think this is her," she said as they gathered around to watch. "She's using the pseudonym 'Beauty Babe', but it's all new product, unopened, and 'exclusive', 'hot off the presses', that kind of thing, including that lipstick she gave you the other day, Claire, the one she said wasn't out for a few months. That's how I found it. Here it is."

She zoomed in on one item where you could clearly see a sticker with the words NOT FOR INDIVIDUAL SALE across it.

"That means she's violating the distribution agreement, the embargo, and probably Arial company policy," said Queenie. "I'm not sure how illegal it is, but it's not a good look."

Alicia agreed and then whistled at the price of several items.

Queenie nodded. "I'd never pay a hundred bucks for an anti-wrinkle cream."

"Hope not," said Perry. "You're, like, twelve, aren't you?"

Queenie ignored that and said, "And look at the price of the primer! It's so inflated, but then it's all very lux, very exclusive apparently. 'Be the first in your group to have it!'"

She was quoting from the blurb, her voice scornful.

It was good sleuthing, and Alicia told her as much, but was it motive for murder?

"Even if Ginny did uncover this, it's not like she's stealing Crown jewels. Chloe wouldn't kill to keep this a secret."

"She might if it means losing her job," said Queenie.

"I guess," conceded Alicia, but she'd have to *really* love her job. It seemed excessive.

Claire had another take on it. "Sorry, Alicia, you're not going to like this, but I have an inkling Ginny was in on it with Chloe."

She proceeded to tell them what the fashion director said at Friday's shoot—how they might have access to free beauty products now that Ginny was gone.

"Kora definitely said Ginny, not Chloe. And really, how would Ginny not know this was happening? She worked in that department and was Chloe's assistant. She must have seen the products coming in and then vanishing. They had to be colluding."

Claire was right. Alicia didn't like this angle one bit. "So what are you saying? Ginny wanted out and Chloe killed her to keep the gravy train going?"

Again it felt excessive. Although it did explain a few things, like why Ginny's apartment was ransacked the day Isla died. If Chloe had killed Ginny over this, she would have wanted to clear the apartment of any evidence of collusion, like boxes of free cosmetics for instance.

Once again, Alicia didn't like where this investigation was heading. Ginny was a lot of things, but she was not a thief. Sure, she'd happily accept a free glass of bubbly courtesy of Hamish, but pilfering all this product and then on-selling it?

It sounded cheap. And greedy. And nothing like Ginny.

She had always been a sharer, Ginny, and generous to a fault. And it went beyond guys and gossip and boiled lollies. She would have given you the shirt off her back if you asked for it, let alone free lipstick and primer!

And even if Ginny *was* guilty of doing this, it was hardly something she'd want to bring attention to. That's what Alicia kept circling back to.

Why would *this* be the secret Ginny wanted Alicia to uncover?

~

Across town, in her waterfront mansion, Ebony tried not to groan as she caught a whiff of her husband entering the house and then the living room. How many *times* had she told Ted to bin that vile aftershave he insisted on marinating himself in?

Still, now was not the time for nitpicking. She simply watched as he pulled the trilby she'd given him from his head, revealing his receding hairline—why else had she given it to him? If only he could wear it at home, in bed— and dropped it on a velvet ottoman. Then offered a light smile and her right cheek to plant his usual sloppy kiss on.

He hadn't yet noticed the magazine on her lap.

"Good day at work?" she asked, and he shrugged, turning towards the home bar at one end of the room.

"Same, same," he called out as he made his way across.

"Hope not," she called back, "for both our sakes."

He stopped, turned. "What does that mean?"

She smiled brightly, then nodded at the bar. "If you're getting yourself a whisky, I'll have my usual G and T thanks. Make it a large one."

Ted watched her for a moment longer, frown slowly developing. He knew what large gin and tonics meant and seemed suddenly wary. As well he should be.

She had seen the fresh pictures of the two of them together, whispering into each other's ears. But it was the *way* they were whispering, the body language, the expressions. That's when her blood ran cold. That's when she realised it was serious.

He stared at her for another moment, then returned to his task, slowly fixing the drinks, before placing hers on the glass coffee table and releasing a long, slow breath.

"So, Ebs. How's your day been?"

She smiled. Using her pet name was not going to help him.

"Very informative," she replied Then she tapped on the magazine in her lap and waited until his eyes registered the spread it was open at.

The photo. Her photo.

He frowned again. Then sighed, slumped in a chair, took a good long swig of his whisky.

"It's not what you think."

"Of course not, sweetie," she said, closing the cover and rolling up the magazine. "It's much, much worse."

Then she stood up, strode towards him and smacked him hard across the head with it.

~

Later that evening, after Alicia had returned home and shared a pasta dish with Jackson, she couldn't help herself. She'd had enough with all the silence. So, as they stacked the dishwasher, she broke their unspoken pact and brought up the Cavendish case again. But she did it by casually asking how he was going at work.

"Anything interesting to report?"

Jackson laughed. "I wondered how long you'd keep it up."

"What?"

"Pretending not to investigate or whatever it is you're doing that requires constant catch-ups with your fellow sleuths—I mean book club."

She laughed now too. "I knew I'd be in trouble, marrying an actual sleuth. So can I ask you a question?"

"You can ask. I don't have to answer."

"That is true. Let's see how we go." She shoved a dirty pot in the bottom of the machine, then said, "When you searched Isla's apartment, did you notice large quantities of beauty products lying around?"

He looked at her sideways as he handed her some cutlery. "It was occupied by two young women, what do you reckon?"

She held up one of the knives menacingly. "I'm being serious, Liam. I mean, *boxes* of the stuff. Suspicious amounts."

He shook his head. "That's the problem. I can't see anything suspicious. Apart from mess. Why, what's this about?"

She shut the dishwasher door and leaned up against it. Took a breath. Then explained what Queenie had learned about Chloe and the pilfered products.

Alicia wasn't thrilled about dobbing the woman in for petty theft so was relieved when Jackson said, "Unless it proves pertinent to the Cavendish case, I have no interest in chasing down a few stolen lipsticks, Alicia, so you can relax."

"Okay, but was it just a few? That's what I'm wondering. And was Ginny involved, and was that the reason behind Isla's hit-and-run?"

She then explained how, if Chloe really did kill Ginny over this, she would want to access Ginny's apartment to clean away the evidence. "Might be why she hit her. To get her apartment key? Might also explain why Ginny's desk was cleaned out so soon and nobody noticed. I mean, who better to do it than the woman at the next desk?"

Jackson mulled it over and had to agree the idea was not completely ridiculous even if the thought of murdering someone over cosmetics was.

"What car does Chloe drive, do you know?"

She shrugged and asked why even though she had a pretty good idea.

He explained how the CIU had flagged a white Toyota hatchback (2008–2012). "If I'd known about this angle, I could've asked Mrs DeRosso too," he added. "I had her in there today, seeing if anything was missing."

"So you agree the place was ransacked?"

He laughed again as he flicked on the kettle to make some herbal tea. "Don't get too cocky. Gail didn't notice anything of interest, although…"

He turned and held up a peppermint teabag in one hand and a chamomile in the other. She nodded at the peppermint, and he dropped it into a large cup, then dropped a black teabag into another. "Gail did say she hadn't been in Ginny's apartment for months."

Alicia was just reaching into the fridge for something sweet and stopped, poked her head back out. "Months? Did you say months?"

He nodded. "Says they had some kind of falling out but refused to elaborate."

Alicia retrieved some dark chocolate and closed the fridge. "Wow. That's sad."

She shook her head as he handed her a cup, and they made their way to the bedroom.

"Did she say what happened? Because those two were thick. Seriously thick. That has really saddened me."

They placed their cups on the bedside tables, and she offered him the chocolate, but he refused as he climbed under the covers and sat up against the pillow, reaching for the television remote.

Alicia broke off a square, popped it in her mouth, then joined him in bed. "I wonder what could have been so bad that she hadn't been in there for months?"

Jackson blew on his tea. "Her taste in perfume?" He then chuckled, trying to return the smile to his wife's face. "It was exactly like that putrid one you should've sold to the restaurant as rat kill."

She smirked back. "Chloe had that perfume online for two hundred smackeroos I'll have you know. I could've been rich!"

Then she reached for her tea and took a good, calming gulp.

As they slowly drained their cups and watched a crime drama in bed—a new ritual they were both enjoying—Alicia couldn't focus on the plotline, let alone deduce *whodunit*, which she usually did with annoying alacrity.

Her mind kept wandering back to Ginny and Gail and how tragic it all felt. If there had been a falling out, it must've been over something extremely serious. They adored each other, those two. She'd never known a mother and daughter so close. And it had been happening for *months*? Alicia's heart plummeted.

'Oh Ginny,' she thought, 'you must have been shattered. I could've helped you. Why didn't you tell me about this? We shared everything.'

Didn't we?

That's when Alicia remembered how busy she'd been the past few months, preparing for her wedding. She'd barely had time to say hello to Ginny, let alone share how she was faring. Hell, who was Alicia kidding? She hadn't shared much with Ginny over the past year. *Years*, really. Ever since she'd hooked up with Jackson and before him the book club. She couldn't remember the last time they'd gone out for cocktails, just the two of them, let alone dinner and the chance for deeper, more revealing conversations.

Had she neglected Ginny? Had she been a terrible friend?

And worse—would Ginny still be alive if she'd spent more time listening to her instead of shoving her aside for everyone else?

She glanced across to Jackson, who was now snoring, and smiled sadly.

Was Ginny the price she paid for a happy marriage?

Tears streaming from her eyes now, she carefully plucked the empty cup from Jackson's hand and switched the TV off, then got up, blew her nose, and prepared for bed—washing away the tears, cleaning her teeth, hopping into her pyjamas—before slipping back under the covers and switching out the lamps.

But sleep did not come easily.

Guilt and sorrow were churning Alicia up, tossing her about for hours, until finally, slowly, she began to drift off, only to be startled by something Jackson said earlier that evening.

She sat up with a start. "The dates don't work!" she cried into the darkness.

"Wha'?" This was Jackson, half asleep beside her.

But she didn't answer. She was doing the maths, and it didn't add up. None of it added up.

Until suddenly it did.

"My God," she said. "Jackson, you're a genius!"

Then she leaned over and kissed him hard on the lips, and he mumbled something about loving her as he returned to his snoring.

CHAPTER 23
Confronting Suspects

The doorbell made a strange, strangled sound like a cat being tortured, and Alicia glanced around at the mouldy, broken-down sofa sitting out the front of the run-down terrace and the weeds sprouting up through the pavers below it and the overgrown grass obscuring the rusty letterbox.

The whole place had a touch of death about it.

She waited another beat, then went to press the bell again when the door swung open to reveal a baffled-looking Gail DeRosso.

Her confusion quickly morphed to surprise and then delight.

"Alicia! Lovely to see you, darl." She glanced past her to the street and back. "How'd you know where to find me?"

"I'm a journo, Gail," she said. "I'm good at research."

In fact, Ginny had given her Gail's address years ago when she was between houses, and it had remained safely in her phone contact notes since.

"Can I come inside for a sec?"

"Course, love. Come, come!"

Gail widened the door and waved her in.

The interior was as bleak as the garden. The wall paint was just the grubby side of off-white and the furnishings a mixed bag of unmatched pieces that wouldn't look out of place in a charity shop. The coffee table was cluttered with empty wineglasses, full ashtrays and a cigarette packet, the stench of stale smoke in the air, but there were pretty things too, including bright cushions and a luxurious mohair throw.

"Want a coffee?" Gail called out, making her way to an adjoining kitchen. "Was just about to fire up my fab new cappuccino maker."

Alicia followed her in and noted the gleaming appliance, incongruous on the old chipboard cabinet. It wasn't the only thing gleaming. There was a Mixmaster that looked straight out of the box and an air fryer with barely a smudge on it.

Coffee made, they settled into two motley armchairs in the lounge room, and Gail said, "If you're worried about me, don't be. Every day's hard, but I'm getting through it. Doin' okay."

Alicia nodded. "Better than okay," she said, glancing across at what looked like a fancy new heater. "Selling beauty products must be a lucrative business."

Gail was back to baffled. "Huh?"

Alicia cut to the chase, producing her smartphone and clicking on the Facebook Marketplace site she'd located earlier, to reveal the pilfered product. Then at the moniker Beauty Babe.

"That's you, is it not?"

Gail opened her vertically wrinkled lips, ready to dispute this, but must have remembered what she said about being a journo so smudged them downwards. "Nothing wrong with spruiking a few freebies Ginny's given me over the years."

"Actually, there is," said Alicia. "It's all under embargo and not for resale. It's illegal, Gail."

Gail looked worried for the first time and reached for the cigarettes. Pulled one out, her hand shaking just slightly. "Yeah, well, Ginny didn't know I was reselling it, not her fault. And she's gone now, anyway, so that'll be the last of it."

She scrambled through the clutter on the coffee table, clearly looking for a lighter.

"Really?" said Alicia. "Have you told Chloe this?"

She stopped. "Chloe?"

"I know she's still feeding you free products, Gail."

"Don't know what you're talking about."

Alicia tapped her phone back to life and zeroed in on one of the sale items, a yet-to-be-released designer perfume that smelt like rat poison.

"So you *didn't* get this from Chloe the other day?"

The older woman was just lighting her cigarette and took a good long drag, staring at her defiantly for a few moments, then her facade cracked. She released the smoke and slumped.

"Ginny always said you were too smart for magazines. How'd you work it out?"

"I didn't. A friend of mine did." She didn't need the details. "And we thought it was just Chloe pushing all this product, but then I had a chat with my partner—Detective Inspector Jackson? I believe you've met?"

Gail looked surprised again, then dragged on her ciggie, like he wasn't important. Except he was. If it wasn't for Jackson's off-the-cuff remark about Gail's stinky perfume last night, Alicia might not have twigged. Although she really should have.

When she'd seen Gail at the memorial, her makeup and nail polish had looked more subtle, more expensive. Completely different to the cheap, garish stuff she'd seen her use previously. It had no doubt come from *Styled*.

"Jackson told me you were wearing this perfume." Alicia tapped on the image again. "Problem is, it came in *after* Ginny died. So how could you possibly have it? Chloe wouldn't just give it to you. I'd already heard she was stingy with the product. Then I realised, you're selling it for her, giving her a cut. Even though you've clearly used it."

"That's reflected in the price," she spat back. "I'm not a crook."

"Neither was Ginny. That's what I can't reconcile— why she'd do it. She was never a thief—"

"She's not a thief!" Gail bellowed, smashing the cigarette into the ashtray. "You leave her out of it! It was all Chloe's fault. Nothing to do with my Ginny."

Except that wasn't strictly true, and after she'd taken a few calming sips of her coffee, Gail told Alicia the whole story.

It all started when the beauty editor saw a chance to make some extra cash by selling the free products that landed on her desk multiple times a day, most of it high-end and worth something. The problem was, Chloe needed some separation, a middleman so she wouldn't get busted.

"Too chickenshit to sell it herself," Gail said. "So she approached Ginny to be her scapegoat. Ginny was too smart of course. She also worked in the beauty department; it'd be just as obvious. Ginny just laughed her off. Told her it was a dumb idea and if she needed extra cash, get an extra job."

Gail sighed then as she stared down into her coffee. "Ginny's only mistake was telling me. We laughed about it together—what a sad sack Chloe was—but then later I started thinking… I could do with some extra cash."

She glanced up at Alicia, chin out. "I don't have a fancy job or fancy man to pay my bills. Since Lance deserted me, every day's been struggle street, and why shouldn't I help Chloe out? Who's it hurting? Really?" She looked away. "I'm the one who approached Chloe one day when Ginny was on a shoot. Didn't want to do it behind her back, I didn't, but I needed the cash—and not for stupid shit like designer bags. I'm using it to pay my bills, that's all."

Alicia dropped her head to the side and stared at the mohair throw and then back towards the kitchen to the espresso machine, the Mixmaster, the air fryer.

"So?" said Gail. "I'm not allowed to have a few nice things like everyone else? Why should I live in poverty when there's all this free shit coming in to *Styled* that nobody needs? Why not sell it to girls who really want it? My God, some of the buyers, they get so excited. Makes 'em feel real special. I'm doing a community service."

Alicia had to stop herself from snorting at that. "Ginny found out though, didn't she?"

Gail slumped again. Nodded into her chest. "She was gutted. It's like I'd been cheating on her with Chloe. We didn't talk for six weeks. The worst six weeks of my life."

"That's why she texted you that message the day she died. *'I can't do it anymore. I'm sorry'*. That wasn't a suicide note. She was going to put a stop to it."

Another nod. "I think she was trying to fix it. Fix us."

A glance up. "I wasn't going to show the cops that note, but then I got to thinking, they'd find it anyway. Better to be ahead of it, you know? So I showed it to that Indian copper, Singh. Told her it was a suicide note. And it sure felt like one. After what she did. Can't believe I drove her to it."

"What?" said Alicia. "She didn't kill herself over this."

Gail looked up, hopeful.

Alicia frowned. "Is that what you honestly thought? My God, how well did you know your daughter? As if Ginny would suicide over something so trivial."

"But... but then why?"

"I don't honestly know, but it can't be that. That's ridiculous. Personally, I think someone hurt her. That she might've been pushed."

Now Gail looked shocked, and worse, deeply worried. "Are you saying... *Chloe?*"

Alicia couldn't answer that, and Gail was scrambling for her cigarettes again.

"But she wouldn't. Not over this! Oh no, please, no..."

"How well do you know Chloe?" Alicia asked.

"I know her. Well enough. She's not a bad egg, Chloe. Helped me do my makeup for the memorial. Dropped into the pub early and spruced me up. She's got a heart, she does. She wouldn't... *Would she?*"

"If she felt threatened maybe?" said Alicia. "For all you know, Ginny told her to stop and she didn't want to, or she was worried Ginny would tell Saffron. And we all know Saffron has ridiculously high standards; she'd sack them both on the spot."

"Saffron has no right to sack anyone!" Gail said, cigarette halfway to her lips. "High standards my arse. That woman has the scruples of an alley cat."

"What are you talking about?"

She shrugged and lit it, took a drag. "Just sayin'. She's no saint. Definitely no beating heart in that one."

Alicia's eye narrowed. "What do you know about Saffron?"

"Nothin'." Took another drag. "Nothing concrete

anyway. But she has secrets of her own, I do know that. Ginny told me there were rumours about her at work. Stuff that never got proven."

"What kind of rumours?" Alicia was remembering what Hamish had said.

"I'm telling you, she never said." Now her eyes were widening again. "Oh damn, you don't think *Saffron* did this, do you?"

Alicia blinked back at her. One suspect at a time, please. "Let's back up a bit. Did Chloe know that Ginny had discovered what you were up to? Was demanding you stop?"

Gail shrugged. "Assume so. Chloe asked me to pipe down for a bit and I was gonna, I truly was but… Look, you said it yourself, this is trivial shit. If you really think my girl was—" A sob suddenly erupted from her lips, and she held a shaky hand to them as though trying to smother it.

Then she took some steadying breaths and finished her smoke. When it was done, she sounded calm, defiant even.

"If you really think someone has hurt my baby, you're looking in completely the wrong direction. 'Cause I can promise you this, Alicia. Nobody's pushing anybody over some stinky perfume. But if my daughter had some dirt that was gonna smudge Saffron's perfect snotty image, well, that'd be a good reason to want to see her gone. You should be looking at *her*. Not us. That shark makes us look like small fry."

~

Alicia watched the "small fry" step into the ladies' bathroom back at work and waited a few minutes to join her. As she did so, she thought of what Gail had said and didn't know what to make of it.

Were her accusations against Saffron just a deflection? A ruse to get Alicia off her back? To absolve herself and her accomplice for her daughter's death?

She wasn't sure. Hamish had also mentioned rumours swirling around the *Styled* editor, but he'd indicated it was old news; there was nothing concrete. And Alicia certainly had no evidence it had anything to do with Ginny.

As far as she could see, there were no dots linking the two. But there were plenty of dots heading to Chloe's door, so she waited another minute, then stepped into the communal toilets.

The beauty editor was standing at the sinks, staring at her reflection in the mirror, when Alicia walked in. She had a Prada handbag on the counter and a small Lady Dior vanity case beside it. Glancing at Alicia quickly, she smiled, her acorn-brown eyes glowing, then reached into the case to pull out a pencil and began to outline her lips.

Alicia stepped towards her and held out a small bottle of perfume wrapped in a duck-blue bow. "I got this the other day," she told her. "It's a bit whiffy for me. What did you think of it?"

Chloe glanced at it and away. "Very little. I agree. It's vile. Trash it."

"Really? Because I heard it could fetch as much as two hundred dollars on Facebook."

Chloe's eyes swept back to her, and she held the pencil still but only for a second. Then she said nothing and kept drawing.

Alicia stepped closer. "Have you sold your sample yet, or are you still waiting for some sucker?"

Chloe's jaw tightened at that but still she said nothing. Just dropped the pencil back to the case and pulled out a lipstick.

As she twirled it open, Alicia said, "I know what you're doing, Chloe. I know you've been reselling beauty stuff to make some money."

Chloe continued to ignore her as she applied the lipstick, her hand not even shaking as she did it, so Alicia added, "I know Ginny found out and was not happy."

Finally that brought a response, a long, embarrassed look, but it was Alicia she was embarrassed for. She dropped the lipstick down and shook her glacial white hair sadly, staring at her through the mirror.

"Oh, honey," she said. "You're really struggling, aren't you?"

"What?"

She put the lipstick away and turned to face her, rubbing her lips together as she did so.

"It has been hard," Chloe said. "I get it. We're all struggling with what happened to Ginny, but…" She offered a worrying wince now. "You're not making a lot of sense, darls. Do you think you need to get some counselling?"

Alicia rolled her eyes. "Don't bother, Chloe. I've just been with Gail. I know exactly what you guys are up to."

But still she bothered, shaking her head sadly before returning to her makeup bag and bringing out a gold compact with the letters YSL looped together on the front.

Clicking it open, she applied some blush to her cheeks and forehead and a tiny bit across her décolletage and said, "If you're talking about Ginny's mother, well, I'd say she's even more messed up than you are. Poor thing."

She paused to inspect her reflection, and Alicia knew exactly what she was doing.

She was biding her time. Trying to come up with a cover story, and she must have, because she dropped the blush back, then zipped the case up and plunged it inside her handbag before turning to face Alicia, smiling. It didn't reach her eyes this time. Not so dazzling now.

"Look, I feel for Gail, I really do. And I feel dreadful landing her in it, but if she's doing something illegal with all the stuff Ginny gave her, it's really not my business."

"Really? So how can you afford that designer handbag on the crappy salary I know you get?"

Chloe glanced down at her large leather shoulder bag. "This? I got it comp, through work of course."

"I don't think so," said Alicia. "See, I'm not new to this game. I used to work in women's magazines myself, and I know they don't hand out boxes of Prada handbags the way they hand out boxes of cosmetics. Kora would be lucky to get a freebie, and I'm guessing there's no way she was handing hers to you. In fact, she doesn't sound happy with you, keeping all the beauty products to yourself. And neither was Ginny, right?"

Chloe's sympathetic look was back. She reached out to rub Alicia's arm. "Oh, honey—"

"Seriously, Chloe!" Alicia slapped her hand away. "I haven't got time for your gaslighting. Gail has already lobbed you in it, so let's just skip to the part where you tell me why you did it."

Her eyes turned flinty. "I'm not telling you anything."

"Okay, have it your way." Alicia turned and strode towards the door. "I'll just take my accusations to Arabella. Or better yet, straight to Saffron. See if she believes—"

"Wait!" Chloe called out, then sighed heavily and strode from cubicle to cubicle, checking they were empty.

When she returned to the sink, she leaned against it and said, "How'd you find out?"

Alicia grappled for her phone and produced the Facebook page.

Chloe looked thunderous. "That skanky, inept old witch! She promised she'd pull it down! Said she'd remove all the photos. And she's *selling* the perfume? I just gave that to her as a goodbye gift. She wasn't supposed to—"

She held up her forefinger. Took a deep breath. Clearly trying to control herself. Then she exhaled and stared down at her chocolate suede knee-high boots.

"Guess how much these Jimmy Choos cost?"

Alicia was surprised by the subject change and feeling suddenly weary. "Honestly, Chloe, I couldn't care less."

"Yeah, well, you're lucky then. I need to care. Unlike you."

Then she stared pointedly at Alicia's scuffed Converse sneakers. "I'm the beauty director of the country's top women's title, remember? I am *always* on display. Every second of every day. I have to wear the very best, but no one's handing that to me and you're right. I certainly can't afford it on my pathetic salary."

"I thought you guys got some kind of designer discount?"

"Oh, you're right! Silly me!" Her voice was dripping with

sarcasm. "With my generous ten percent discount card, it takes the price of these boots from three thousand dollars to just twenty-seven hundred! Totally affordable!" She sneered. "And that's just the shoes. I need to wear the latest in designer couture and drive the fanciest car and—"

"What car *do* you drive?" Alicia was thinking of the hit-and-run, remembering what Jackson said about a white Toyota.

"Pardon?"

"It's a simple question. What car do you drive, Chloe? What colour?"

"A 2023 Beamer. Black. Why?"

"Never mind, continue with your moaning."

"I am not *moaning*," she spat back. "But it's not fair. I'm supposed to look as glamorous as Saffron on a fraction of her salary."

"But Saffron's the editor. No one's expecting you—"

"Of course they are! If I ever want a chance at being editor, and I'm in with a chance, if I play my cards right. Lots of editors start in Beauty. Saffron did, but she snagged herself an investment banker so could always look the part even though *she* was earning a pittance back then. I don't have a sugar daddy, so I have to use my smarts. Sell some freebies to get some extra cash. That's all I was doing. It wasn't hurting anyone."

"Really?" said Alicia. "What about Ginny?"

"What about her?"

"Did you hurt her to keep your side hustle a secret?"

"It's not a hustle and… what are you saying? You think I had something to do with her suicide?"

"*If* it was suicide."

"What else could it be?" Chloe seemed confused, and then suddenly she was gasping. "You're not saying she was pushed into that train? Deliberately? You don't think that I…? Oh my God, Alicia. *As if!* Why on earth would I hurt Ginny?"

"Because she knew what you were doing and demanded you stop. That would mean the end of Prada handbags and

Jimmy Choos and fancy BMWs. Maybe you didn't want that to end. Maybe you were worried she'd dob you in to Saffron."

Chloe scoffed. "She'd be dobbing in her own mother if she did that and probably lose her job in the process."

"Except Ginny didn't really care about her job. It wouldn't have crushed her if she got fired. But I bet it would crush you."

And she bet Chloe would crush anything that got in her path. Because this clearly wasn't just a job to Chloe and a chance to wear designer labels. She'd admitted as much. It was her ticket to the editor's chair.

Just what she'd do for that ticket, Alicia had to wonder.

She was about to enquire further when she heard a loud thump from the other side of the wall. They both stared at it, and when Alicia went to speak again she heard a muffled yell and what sounded like cursing.

She turned and raced out of the women's toilets, nearly colliding with Tiani, who was standing outside the men's facilities next door.

"Sorry," Alicia said, grabbing her before she fell to the ground. "What's that yelling?"

Tiani nodded into the men's room, eyes wide. "It's been going on for a while. Someone's fighting. I–I don't know who."

There was a fresh burst of expletives, and Alicia rolled her eyes and said, "I do."

Then she stepped forward and swung the door open.

CHAPTER 24
Two Dogs Pissing

Alicia could pick Hamish's voice from a mile off. And it had less to do with his cockney accent and more to do with his trademark colourful language, which was now bellowing down the corridor in every shade of the rainbow.

"Hamish?" she called out as she pushed the door wider, then gasped.

He had Austin Smythe up against the toilet wall, one hand at his throat.

She rushed in, the door swinging closed behind her.

"Hamish!" she yelled this time. "What are you doing? Let him go!"

Hamish's head swung around. He was surprised to see her and yelled back, "Stay out of it, Alicia! This is between me and Smugface."

Then he turned back to Smugface and said, "What are you even doing down here? Haven't you got gold-plated toilets on your own floor?"

"I'm not *doing* anything," Austin moaned, face to one side like he was avoiding Hamish's spit. "I was just passing. Jesus."

"Just pissing into the wind is what you're doing. I should slam your head into the urinal, teach you a thing or two."

"Cut it out, Hamish," Alicia cried out. "You're acting like a schoolyard bully."

"He's the bully! Treated my Ginny like crap. Tell her what you just said to me, you gobshite. Go on! Say it!"

Austin glanced across to Alicia and looked suddenly sheepish. "I was just saying the truth. I didn't love Ginny. I never pretended to love Ginny; it was just a bit of fun."

"Not to her it wasn't! You killed her!"

"You think *Austin* hurt Ginny?" asked Alicia.

"Good as," Hamish called back. "This knobhead broke her heart. Why else do you think she threw herself in front of a train?"

"Oh for God's sake!" Alicia blew a puff of angry air through her lips. Did none of them know Ginny at all? "She didn't kill herself over this knobhead."

"Hey!" said Austin.

"Shut up!" said Hamish.

"Sorry," said Alicia to Austin. "But I don't think Ginny threw herself in front of that train. I think she was pushed."

That got Hamish's attention. He released his hold and turned to face her. "You serious?"

"I don't know," she replied as his eyes returned to Austin, who was pulling his jacket into place and readjusting his tie.

He shouldn't have bothered. Hamish had him by the shoulders now and was shoving him back against the wall. "What did you do?"

"What? No!" Austin yelled. "I didn't hurt Ginny! I didn't care enough about her to hurt her!"

"And that's supposed to make me *not* want to hit you?" said Hamish as Alicia grabbed his arm and tried to yank him away.

"I'm just saying," Austin continued, "she didn't care about me either. It was mutual. We'd split... before it happened. I promise you. I was seeing someone else."

Now Hamish's eyes were wide and wild. "You *cheated* on her?"

"It wasn't like that! We'd always been casual!"

But that didn't make sense to Alicia. Why would Ginny invite Austin to her wedding if he had been cheating on her? Sure, Ginny was cool, but she wasn't cold. She had feelings.

And why had Austin seemed so smitten with Ginny that night if he was seeing someone else? And why, according to Kirsten at least, was he so miserable at the family BBQ the week before, whining about how she'd destroyed him?

His story did not add up.

"Who then?" Alicia demanded. "Who were you seeing?"

Austin shook his head. "Can't say." Then a hand up to stop Hamish. "Ginny was fine with it, I promise!"

"So tell us who it is then!" demanded Hamish.

"Can't. She asked me not to." He looked sheepish again. "Look, this one's the real deal. Hottest chick in the building. Way above me. Couldn't believe she was interested. Had given me the cold shoulder for yonks. But she's right to keep it on the downlow. After what happened to Ginny, it would look…"

"Grubby? Like you?" spat Hamish.

He shook his head. "Ginny was just a fling. It was just supposed to be a bit of fun."

"Yeah, great fun, you cheating on her and her now being dead and all. I should knock your bloody block off."

"Come on, Hamish," Alicia said. "You're twice his age and half his size. He could take you in two moves."

She was wondering why he hadn't.

Hamish scoffed. "Yeah, but I'm twice the man he'll ever be with his floppy fringe and fancy suit. You're fooling nobody, you big baby."

"And you're fooling nobody, you old *boomer*, with your fake mullet and your try-hard hoodie."

For God's sake! thought Alicia. Was he trying to set Hamish off?

As Hamish began swearing again, mostly about not being a boomer—"Who're you calling a boomer?"—she grabbed his elbow and managed to pull him clear this time.

Then she marched him to the door and told him Austin wasn't worth losing his job over.

"Oh, I think he is," Hamish growled, one fist waving backwards. "I'd happily lose my job for that wanker!"

"Just *stop!*" Alicia said. "Just go for a walk and chill the hell out."

Then she yanked the door open and thrust him through it, managing to collide him with Chloe this time. She was lurking just outside, clearly listening in, and Alicia gasped as the beauty editor went flying in one direction and her precious Prada handbag went flying in the other.

~

"Might not be over yet," called out DI Singh as she flung a report onto Jackson's desk.

He glanced up from his screen and raised his eyebrows.

"Makes for interesting reading," she added before returning to her chair.

Jackson had been trawling the state's vehicle registries all morning, enquiring about Chloe's vehicle, its make and colour. After Alicia's accusations against the beauty editor last night, and something garbled about Gail DeRosso being complicit as she dashed out of the house this morning, he wanted to look them both up. See what, if any, vehicle they happened to be driving.

Was either painted white for instance? And recently damaged?

But after a little searching, he found himself disappointed. Chloe drove a black BMW and Gail didn't have a registered vehicle, nor did she need one. She was currently on suspension for drink driving. That did not surprise him, but he was annoyed. He'd hoped this would be the end of it.

Why could it never be easy?

Still, Singho was offering him another avenue, and so he closed the page down and picked up the report. It was the latest findings from the forensics lab working Isla's case. Some brainbox had analysed the faecal matter located on the debris found at the crime scene.

"Bat shit," he said, looking up at Singh. And he wasn't being offensive.

She nodded, glancing out from behind her monitor. "The grey-headed flying fox to be precise. Now we have a little more to work with. Wherever that white car is parked, there could be a bat colony of some sort above. If we're lucky that is."

"And if we're not?"

"Then it was a passing bat, because they fly all over this

godforsaken city, splattering everything in sight. Either way, it's worth investigating, because I know you've still got your suspicions."

"Don't you?"

"I do. But I'm keeping an open mind. Wouldn't be the first hit-and-run driver to flee the scene. Doesn't mean there's a motive for murder. Just means they're an arsehole, and there's even more of those in this city than bats."

"Should still bring them in though. They left a woman bleeding out on the street."

"I know that, Jacko. Which is why I've let you run with it. Haven't pulled you onto the drive-by shooting we had last week or the double homicide we had the week before, both of which were definitely deliberate and I could use some help with."

His broad shoulders slumped. "Sorry."

"Don't apologise for wanting to be thorough. That's your job." She sighed. "Just remember though—it's *your* job, yeah? Not Alicia's."

His shoulders heaved up again, and she produced a quick, stalling palm. "Just follow the evidence. The actual evidence. Not your wife's book club's hare-brained theories."

"I'm not—"

She held up two palms now. "I'm trying to help you, mate. I know what you're like. You need to leave your wife out of this. She's lovely and all, but she's also a meddling amateur. I don't want to see this explode in your face again."

Then she ducked back behind her screen, like she was hiding from the shrapnel she knew was coming.

CHAPTER 25
Sneaky Tactics

Tucking into steak and wedges at a pub near Alicia's office that evening, Jackson listened while his wife waxed lyrical about her day and all she'd learned about Chloe and Gail, then the fight between Hamish and Austin.

But he was struggling to concentrate.

All he could think was *Oh God, I need to tell her to butt out, but I can't do it.* He didn't like being Alicia's handbrake. Or Singh's STOP! sign for that matter.

He hated playing piggy in the middle. Was terrible at that game. And now he thought, *This is never going to end. This is my life now. One big tussle.*

Catching his frown, Alicia said, "Sorry. I'm overstepping again, aren't I?" Then she reached for his beer and helped herself to a swig. "And all for nothing. All I did today was learn that Chloe's an ambitious thief with heart, Hamish really is a hothead, and Austin's a pacifist. Oh, and a cheating scumbag. But I'm not sure I discovered anything of any interest. Certainly no evidence of murder. I honestly don't know why I bother."

And then she changed the subject, steering into safer territory—Taylor Swift titbits she'd uncovered in her research—and he found this even harder to focus on. He wasn't a Swiftie, neither was she by the sound of her monotone.

As if reading his mind or perhaps the glazed expression in his eyes, she said, "God I miss Ginny. She's the one I should be boring with all this. She adored Taylor Swift. Went to two of her concerts, did I tell you that? Flew down to Melbourne for the second one. Was so excited when she heard I had a special coming up. Hell, she could've written it for me. What she didn't know about Tay Tay wasn't worth putting in a magazine."

She sighed heavily, and he grasped her hand across the table. "You really loved her. Didn't you?"

"Taylor Swift? *Nooooo*." He rolled his eyes and she smiled. "Yeah, I really did. Not sure I ever told Ginny though. Certainly didn't show it in her final months."

Regret was rippling across her brow, and he squeezed her hand harder. "I'm sure Ginny knew. Deep down."

She shrugged. "Did she though? What would I know? She'd broken up with Austin and hadn't even mentioned it to me. Wasn't talking to her mother and yet not so much as a word. Didn't tell me any of the gossip about Saffron, which she'd usually pass on in a heartbeat. Maybe we weren't as close as I thought. Maybe I didn't know her at all."

Jackson shook his head. That wasn't true. Then he watched as she pushed her half-eaten steak towards him and stared into her empty wineglass despondently, and he thought, no, that was not true in any way, shape or form.

"Shall we get another?" She was nodding at her glass, but he shook his head.

"Come on," he said, "it's time."

As Jackson began the drive home, Alicia felt her sorrow replaced by guilt and regret. Jackson had clearly been less interested in Taylor Swift than she was, and yet she couldn't keep rattling on about Isla and Ginny. It wasn't fair. His job was at stake. She had to keep the two things separate; they both knew it.

That's why it was so strange when he took the on-ramp to the Harbour Bridge and began heading northward, in the direction of Ginny's apartment.

"What's going on?" she asked, and he bat his eyelashes back at her.

"Just need to check something."

She chewed over that and then her lips as he made his way to Ginny's street and then parked across the road from her old building. After shutting the car down, he opened his door and stepped out.

Then he leaned back in and said, "Whatever you do, do not follow me in."

Winking, he threw the car keys in her lap, slammed the door and then marched across the street.

Alicia kept chewing as he approached the apartment block, stopped at the front door, leaned over for a bit, then glanced back at her with a smile.

What was he playing at?

She continued watching as he vanished inside. Then she said, "Bugger this!" and jumped out, locked the car and followed him.

The entrance door to the building had been wedged open with a piece of folded junk mail, and Alicia sailed through, then walked down the corridor to apartment three. She was about to knock when she realised that door, too, was open just a fraction, so she gave it a gentle nudge and could see Jackson standing in the living room, his back to her.

When she stepped inside, he swung around and called out, "Bloody hell, Alicia! You're not supposed to be in here!"

"Sorry! I thought—"

He placed a finger to his lips, then strode across and swept the door closed, sealing them both in.

"What're you up to?" she asked, and he hushed her again.

After listening for a moment, he whispered, "It's called plausible deniability. And it's my only defence for having you here. On record, you followed me in. I get blamed for this, I say you acted alone."

"Judas," she said.

He smiled. "Judas with a good job he doesn't want to risk losing again."

She laughed. "Fair enough. So you *do* want me to check the place out?"

"But I want you to touch nothing. The only reason I'm permitting this is because your DNA is already here from past visits, so you can't corrupt the scene. But I think you're right. I think it's been searched. And Gail's right too. You're the best person to ask if something obvious is missing."

He glanced around and back. "You asked earlier—what would you know? I reckon you'd know more than all of us combined. You knew Ginny. You also knew Isla. You were in this very apartment just days before she died. I think it's absurd not to get you in for a look. But it has to be quick. I'm giving you five minutes, and then we're making a run for it."

Alicia smiled, loving her rule-breaking husband so much in that moment. It's the reason she first fell for him on the SS Orient, back when they were investigating another mystery. The reason she'd left the dashing Dr Anders who, like Singh, was a stickler for the rules.

She wanted to grab Jackson and hug him, but time was ticking, so she mouthed "Thank you" and then took the rubber gloves he was offering.

"I already suspect all the digital devices were stolen," he told her, "'cause there's none in here, despite all the chargers, and that beggars belief. I mean, what self-respecting young person doesn't own at least two? So that might be all that was stolen, but just have a look, go with your instincts."

She nodded and started searching, trying to view the place afresh.

First she surveyed the living area, then the kitchen, then she took a deep breath and walked into first Isla's and then Ginny's bedrooms. But the truth was she hadn't been in either of those rooms on her last visit, so it was unlikely she'd notice if anything was amiss.

As she searched, she called out, "So you do agree the two deaths are linked?"

"I agree they could be," he called back. "Singh's not a fan of that theory. She thinks we're overcomplicating things."

"Yeah, well, life's not always simple."

"And neither is death," he added, his tone low and moody.

Eventually Alicia, too, had to hold up the white flag. "Maybe I didn't pay enough attention when I was here."

"Nah. Don't beat yourself up." He held a hand out for her gloves as he escorted her to the door. "It was worth a try.

Let's go home and crack open some wine. You can tell me more about the scintillating Ms Swift."

Alicia froze. "What did you just say?"

He turned back. "I was just joking—"

"No, about the wine. *That's* what's been niggling at me!"

Alicia swivelled and raced back into the living room. "We need to find Ginny's champagne stash."

She began pulling open cupboards.

"Why?" he asked, also opening cupboards but finding little more than old gaming consoles and board games, half of them upended.

She didn't answer, just chewed her lower lip and did a full circle. Then she gasped and said, "There!" pointing into the kitchen.

Above the built-in fridge was a small cupboard, and she was racing for it now, reaching up and pulling the doors open.

Inside they could see a collection of bottles, mostly brightly coloured spirits and champagne. As Alicia began to reach in, Jackson grabbed her wrist.

"I'll do it," he said and then added, "What exactly am I doing?"

"Just look behind the bottles, see if there's anything there."

He peered in and moved a few bottles around. Then he shook his head and said, "Just lots of grog, Alicia. Top-shelf too."

She frowned, then pulled a stool from the kitchen bench and stood on it so she could see better. "There!" She pointed to a black box with a gold, shield-shaped label right at the back of the cupboard. It was a bottle of Dom Pérignon. Vintage 2015.

He whistled as he brought it out. "This must've cost a fortune."

"Probably a gift, knowing Ginny. Open it!"

Looking doubtful, he did as she suggested, peeling back the lid. Then she heard him inhale as he reached in and pulled out a white piece of paper, folded.

Alicia's eyes lit up as he straightened it to reveal the official Arial letterhead printed across the top. Then they both stared at the names and numbers printed below it, and she grinned with delight as he said, "Damn it. Singho is going to slaughter me this time."

CHAPTER 26
If Looks Could Kill

Detective Inspector Indira Singh was indeed looking murderous.

It was early the following morning, and Alicia was back in Homicide Headquarters, but this was no informal chat at Jackson's desk. She was now planted in an interview room, alongside her husband, and Singh was in the chair opposite, stony-faced. Fuming.

Jackson was suitably sheepish, and Alicia was no longer grinning. But it had little to do with the scary DI. Before Jackson had phoned his partner, she'd taken a good look at the names and numbers listed down the page and realised they were not dubious monetary transactions or evidence of fraud as she'd been hoping.

They were just circulation figures, as far as she could tell, and this was a routine report that went out to all of Arial's editors. Why Ginny had it or even felt the need to hide it was anybody's guess.

Singh was more interested in how Alicia had found it and how she had done it illegally.

"I know," Jackson said, tone suitably contrite. "I shouldn't've done it, Singho. But—"

She held up one finger. "Don't even!" She pointed the finger at Alicia. "Let's get the facts straight first. How did you know to look in that particular cupboard?"

"It was something Isla said at Ginny's memorial," Alicia explained. "She asked me to drop in on the Sunday at ten."

"The day she died," said Jackson. "She said she'd found something and wanted to show you."

Alicia nodded. "But here's the thing. She also said something about having a glass of bubbly together. A glass of 'vintage Dom' she said. I thought that was odd, considering the time we were meeting, but she gave me this cryptic look."

"Now you know why," said Jackson.

"Do we though?" said Singh. "I mean, what exactly is this? Why do we think it's suspicious?"

Alicia said, "It's the May sales figures for the monthly titles at Arial Publishing."

"Yes, I'm not a complete idiot, thanks, Alicia. Anything suspicious in the figures?"

Alicia went to speak, but Jackson now held up a finger. "Hang on a minute," he said, eyes on Singh. "You want Alicia's help or you don't want Alicia's help? Which way you want to play it?"

Both Alicia and Singh stared at him surprised. It was a rare day when he spoke up to his senior partner.

"It's okay," began Alicia, but he shook his head, eyes still on Singh.

"I'm sorry," he said, "but you can't have it both ways, Singho. Either Alicia's a 'meddling amateur' with nothing to contribute or she helps us solve this case. I could say the exact same thing about her book club, by the way. They might not be professionals, but they're all smart with great instincts."

Then he nodded down at the report now sitting on the desk between them.

"That was located thanks to Alicia's instincts. Not mine. Not yours. So let's not keep pretending she's an amateur of no use."

Singh dropped back in her chair, folded her arms, and stared hard at Jackson, and he stared equally hard back at her, his own expression daring, defiant.

Alicia's eyes darted between them, worriedly, then she winced and said, "Actually, I'm not sure how useful I can be."

Jackson's slid across to her. "Sorry?"

She nodded at the report. From what she could see,

everything looked in order. She wasn't an expert—she didn't get these reports because she produced irregular one-offs—but she had edited monthly magazines before and these looked, well, *normal.*

She picked up the page and studied it again.

The list was made up of all fourteen of Arial's monthly publications, and all the usual suspects were there, listed in order of circulation, from top to bottom. One column had the publication title, the next had that month's sales figure (in this case May), and the third had the percentage change from the previous month's sales (April).

Styled was right at the top, as it always was, with an impressive circulation considering how badly most print mags were now selling in the current climate. And while the third column showed a drop of 3.5 percent, which was unusual for them, it was minuscule compared to Arial's other women's title, *Girl Girl Girl,* which had plummeted 12.8 percent from a very low base. Next on the list was *Lout,* which sold slightly less than *Styled* but could at least boast a rise in circulation of 4.9 percent, then *Wellness,* virtually steady at 0.5 percent.

Every other title had dropped, some quite dramatically, including their flagship television guide which was down a whopping 18 percent. Alicia already knew its days were numbered, that the staff were touching up their CVs, and she had a feeling the gang from *Girl, Girl, Girl* would fast follow.

It saddened Alicia, but there was nothing surprising in the report, at least from what she could glean, and she told them as much.

As she spoke, Singh's eyes were back on Jackson, looking smarmy, so Alicia quickly added, "What *is* suspicious is why Ginny had this report, because it's clearly an in-house report, which means it's confidential." She pointed to the Arial letterhead. "As far as I know they don't release these monthly figures anymore. Not publicly, anyway. They usually only report every quarter, sometimes only annually. Depending on the sales I guess, but I do know they often get leaked, especially if they're good and they're trying to lure in advertisers. But I'm not an expert on this."

Jackson waved that off. "So who would normally get this monthly breakdown?"

"The executive team and the editors. So just Saffron at *Styled*. Why she'd give it to Ginny I couldn't say."

"Maybe she didn't," said Jackson. "Maybe Ginny pinched it. Explains why she hid it away."

"But why hide it?" Alicia countered. "For what reason? Ginny was just a staffer, she had no control over sales, not directly. And while sales were down, it's not by much. I guess I could see Saffron slapping them at her, blaming her maybe, or Ginny stealing these to send to advertisers. She could use it as blackmail, I guess, but she wouldn't get far. The truth comes out eventually and, like I said, the overall circulation figure is good. *Styled* is still top of the heap. So what's the big secret? It doesn't make any sense to me."

Then she added, "You know, it's also a moot point these days because you can't really trust sales figures anymore. They used to be audited by an independent body, but that all changed a while back and now organisations like Arial use their own auditors to verify sales."

Jackson tsked. "That's like putting the fox in charge of the hen house."

"Or asking school kids to write their own report cards," Alicia said, grinning as she added, "Not to be trusted."

They'd almost forgotten about Singh as they spoke, and now they stopped and looked across to her, Alicia waiting for the fall-out.

But she'd gone deathly quiet and when she did speak, Singh's tone was as cold as her expression. "Let's leave this for now. For all we know Ms DeRosso stumbled upon that report and used it to soak up the spillage in the back of her liquor cabinet."

Alicia would have scoffed if she wasn't so concerned for her husband and his career. He didn't seem worried though. Just stood up and offered to show Alicia out.

Once they'd cleared the main building and were walking out the front, Alicia took Jackson's hand and squeezed it tight, and she felt him squeeze it back. Once they hit the sidewalk, she whispered, "Thank you."

He turned and pulled her towards him. "No, Alicia, thank *you*. It's long overdue."

"You going to be okay?"

He glanced backwards. "Probably not, but I've had a gutful."

"Fair enough."

"You keep saying that, Alicia, but it's not fair at all. On either of us. I'm sick of being warned constantly about you, and you being told off like a child. It's rude, it's patronising, and it's bullshit. You've helped close more cases in this city than half the Homicide Squad, and she knows it. You received a Commissioner's Commendation for God's sake! Singh should treat you with a bit more bloody respect."

"She's right though. I'm not an *actual* detective."

"Yeah, but you're as good as. Your instincts are scarily spot on. Nothing gets past you. Why can't she see that? *Use* that? Not keep trying to block it?" He growled again, releasing some anger. "Sorry. I'm just sick of having to play nicely and leave you in the dark. You're my wife now. I want to be able to discuss this stuff when I come home from work. Throw ideas back and forth. You're smart. It's why I fell in love with you."

"Really? I thought it was because of my looks."

She was trying to lighten the mood, but he had lost his sense of humour, so she just reached up and gave him a kiss, then thanked him for his support, wished him good luck and booked herself a rideshare.

Later, as she returned to her office, she tried not to think of the wrath Singh was now unleashing upon Jackson. Alicia was so proud of him, though, for standing up for her and her book club. Because he was right, they were all smart. Really smart.

Why couldn't Singh see that?

Foxes were smart too, she thought, her mind zigzagging back to what Jackson had said earlier about foxes and the hen house. It got her thinking of another fox.

Austin Smythe.

He was more than just a big baby in a fancy suit. Austin was also the head of Sales and Circulation. The very person who would have produced those circulation figures they'd found stashed in Ginny's liquor cabinet.

Had to be more than a coincidence, surely?

CHAPTER 27
The Million-Dollar Question

Back in the office, Alicia made her way to the fox's lair. Located in Seventh Heaven, Austin's office was not as spacious as Bob Chalmers', but it was certainly more ostentatious, with a black desk so shiny you could see your reflection in it and equally shiny black and chrome chairs that would not be out of place at a nightclub. Behind him were silver-framed photos featuring Austin grinning beside people Alicia didn't recognise. Probably dodgy tech bros, knowing Austin.

He'd done well for himself, she decided as she popped her head around the door. Austin had to be the youngest executive on this floor by at least a decade. He was relatively new in the top job, had been parachuted in after the previous manager quit suddenly, and he hadn't wasted any time settling in, she noticed as she glanced around.

"If you're here to tell me not to press charges," he sang out, "you're wasting your breath."

She'd forgotten about yesterday's scuffle. "You're calling the cops on Hamish?"

He reached a hand to his throat. "Maybe. You're my witness. It was common assault."

"It was a man in mourning lashing out," she said, stepping in and across to his desk. "Who's it going to help, really? Come on, Austin. He's just hurting."

"Tell me about it." He gave his neck a rub, but she couldn't see any lasting effects. "If he loved her so much, why wasn't *he* going out with her?"

She sighed and slipped into the chair in front of him. "That is the million-dollar question. They were a funny pair, but do not doubt their love for each other. Who knows, maybe they would've ended up together."

He leaned forward. Glanced at the open door and back. "You don't really think she was, like. *murdered?*"

"Don't know. I am worried though. Especially after what I just found."

Alicia pulled out her phone and scrolled through her Photos app for the last image she'd taken—a copy of the report stashed in the bottle of Dom Pérignon.

As she did so, she felt a tiny twinge of guilt. While Jackson phoned Singh last night to report the find, she had snapped it surreptitiously. It was her own stab at "plausible deniability", but genuine this time. She had wanted to tell Jackson but knew it was better for him if he remained in the dark.

She felt another twinge of guilt as she held the screen up for Austin to view. She knew she was sailing close to the wind. He could very well be a suspect; this could very well be important evidence. But Jackson's words had emboldened her. They felt like a green light.

"What am I looking at?" he said.

"You tell me. Aren't you in charge of Sales and Circulation?"

He frowned and leaned closer to get a better look. "Okay, well it's the May circ figures. What's the big deal? I sent them out last month."

She nodded. "But did you send them to Ginny?"

"What?" His brow furrowed. "What're you talking about?"

He snatched the phone from her hand and studied the image more closely, alarm flickering across his face. "Where'd you get this?"

"Ginny's apartment," she told him.

He looked incredulous. "Really?"

She nodded, explaining how it was stashed inside a bottle of French champagne.

He frowned at the screen for a little longer, then tried for a nonchalant shrug and handed it back. "Oh well. Nothing wrong with that. But she didn't get it from me."

Now Alicia looked incredulous, her head dropping to one side.

"What? She didn't! I only send it to management and editors. She was just an assistant."

"Okay," she said, irked by his patronising tone. "Could she have pinched it from your desk or downloaded it from your computer when you weren't looking?"

He blew a puff of air through his lips. "Doubt it. And how would she do that? Like I keep saying, we weren't that close. It's not like she had my passwords or anything. Jesus, it was just a bit of fun."

If Austin used those words again, Alicia was going to leap from her chair and wring his neck herself. Could he be any more dismissive of her dear, dead friend?

"Hamish is right about you," she said through clenched teeth. "You did not deserve Ginny. She was a good person."

He raised his palms defensively. "What is it with you guys? I'm not saying she wasn't. Look, if she had that report, she must've got it from someone else. Wasn't me."

"Yes, you keep saying that. Who then? Who else had access?"

"No one." His voice had a strange new edge. "Look, it's chill. They're just boring sales figures. Nobody cares."

"Really?"

Because he sounded like he did care, very much so.

"Yes! I mean… it's not cool she had that report, it's not hers to keep, but if she swiped it from my bag or whatever, well, she did it without me knowing. I'd never just hand it to her. It breaches protocol. I'm not a bloody idiot."

No, she thought, and you weren't in love with Ginny either, all of which added a totally different slant to the words Kirsten had heard at that last family get-together. Kirsten claimed Austin was upset. Had used the words "theft", "betrayed" and "destroyed". She assumed he was referring to his heart, but Ronnie was right. Kirsten had misunderstood.

Oh no, it was now clear it wasn't Austin's *heart* she had

stolen. He didn't care enough about her. But he did care about his job, she could see that.

Alicia sat forward. "Could this destroy your career, Austin? If it gets out that Ginny stole this confidential report from you?"

Another puff of air, this one long and scornful. "Don't talk crazy. Like I said, it's not a big deal. Jesus."

And yet there it was once more. The strain in his voice, the exaggerated puffing, like he was trying to look more relaxed than he felt. He was protesting too much.

She glanced around the plush office again and wondered if Austin was as ambitious as Chloe, as determined to protect his reputation. Maybe he wouldn't lose his job over it, but this, too, wasn't a good look, letting your "bit of fun" go through your private work reports. Was he embarrassed by it? Did he want to hide the fact from Ted?

And did he kill Ginny because of it, then run down Isla, so he could access Ginny's apartment to try to steal back the report?

Okay, that's where it all fell apart. She kept circling back to the fact this was not international espionage they were dealing with here. It was just some routine circulation figures.

Austin was watching Alicia as her mind did loops, brow furrowed. Then he nodded at her phone and said, "What are you going to do with that?"

"Nothing."

"Okay, well can you delete it then? I mean, it's not important but it's still confidential company business. Stats are embargoed for a few more months."

She made a noncommittal murmur as she got up and made her way to his door.

"At least keep it to yourself!" he called after her, and she stopped, turned back.

"Tell you what, Austin. I'll keep this to myself"—she held up her phone—"if you forget all about what happened in the bathroom yesterday."

She didn't wait for a response. Just left him staring after her, rubbing his neck again.

Back at her desk, Alicia put a call through to Jackson. She was desperate to check in and see how he was doing. Had Singh bitten his head off after she left? Was he still alive and breathing?

Jackson laughed at that and said Singh was "fine! Surprisingly blasé", and now she was really worried. Because she knew Singh well, and blasé was not in her skill set. Then he told her he'd be working late and would not be home for dinner. He had lots he needed to catch up on, now he was "officially" back.

She understood the sentiment and tried to focus on her Taylor Swift special and the pull-out box she was researching dubbed, "10 Surprising Facts for Swifties".

Problem was, the facts of Ginny's case kept getting in the way.

Like the fact that Ginny had possession of some circulation figures that were "chill", "not a big a deal". And yet she had carefully hidden them away.

Was Singh right? Was their appearance in the Pérignon bottle a mere coincidence—she'd just shoved them in there for no good reason? The fact Ginny had left her a bunch of cryptic clues on her desk seemed to suggest otherwise.

And here were some more facts to consider:

Isla-Mae told Alicia she'd found something that *might help explain what happened to Ginny*. Had said those exact words at the memorial. And she'd said them in a room full of Arial staffers, including Austin.

Two days later, she was dead. That was the most horrifying fact of all.

Had someone overheard Isla's words and panicked? Had they taken matters into their own hands? Is *that* why Isla's apartment was ransacked? If so, it had to be Austin.

Who else would care about the report? Why did *he*? Because he clearly did.

What was so special about that report? What was she not seeing?

"Arrrggh!" she groaned, shoving her keyboard aside and

reaching for her phone, clicking on the photo again, staring at the report carefully.

Nothing looked untoward to her. But then what would she know? She didn't edit a monthly anymore. That's when she remembered what Perry and Ronnie both said—keep it simple, stupid! Go back to the clues Ginny left you. Go back to the Agatha Christie book. *The Mysterious Affair at Styles*.

This had to be directly related to *Styled* magazine.

She pocketed her phone and returned to her feet.

Saffron was inside the walk-in fashion closet when Alicia found her, knee-deep in samples, Kora beside her, smiling politely.

"Disgusting, yuck, blah, maybe," Saffron was saying as she swished through each item. Then, "Foul, maybe, no, and no, no, *noooo!*"

These were all Saffron's descriptions of the samples she was wading through, and Alicia watched for a moment from the doorway, noting Kora's smile fast turning panicked.

"Not even this one?" said Kora, wading back to what looked like a beautiful floaty organza dress.

"That was the foul one," Saffron said, swishing past it and on down the line.

Figuring they could be here a while (the cupboard was full to bursting with clothes Kora had sourced for next month's issue, and not much use by the sound of it), Alicia called out, "Hey Saffron, have you got a minute?"

The editor glanced up and away. "Does it look like I've got a minute, Alicia?"

"Not to worry," she replied. "I'll be quick." Then she stepped inside. "So, you know how the editors all get emailed the circ' figures directly every month from Austin Smythe?"

Saffron didn't bother looking up this time as she held out a strapless, pea-green top that Alicia wasn't entirely convinced was a top at all. Was it a skirt? An ugly chamois?

"So?" said Saffron. "What of it?"

"Who gets a copy at *Styled*? Just you?"

Saffron scowled at the top/skirt/chamois and then

flashed Alicia a similar scowl. "I am busy, Alicia. Not all of us work in the cushy special projects department, you know?"

"I do know that." *You keep reminding me every time I see you.* "Please, just two quick questions and I'll let you get back to your super important work."

Alicia tried hard not to glance down at the ugly green strip of nothing that would improve nobody's life, except perhaps its overpaid designer. Her sarcasm spoke for itself.

"Just wondering," Alicia continued, "do you ever hand those reports to your team? Let them have a squiz?"

Saffron stopped then and turned directly towards Alicia. Exhaled dramatically then glanced at Kora and said, "You can shut the door on your way out."

Kora looked surprised then relieved and hurried away.

"What is all this really about?" Saffron asked, pulling off her glasses when the door was closed.

Alicia considered whether to lie, then went for a half truth. "I was helping sort through Ginny's things, back at her apartment, and found an old sales report. I'm just wondering if you gave it to her. Perhaps you give copies to all your staff."

"Why on earth would I do that?"

Because they're part of your team? she thought but just said, "So you're the only one who sees them? What about your PA? Your department heads? Tiani?"

"It's no one's business but mine, Alicia. Why are you asking me this? What's this about?"

Alicia reached for her phone and produced her photo of the report again. She held it up to Saffron, who peered at it quickly and away.

"Sales figures. Big whoop. What's your point?"

"This is last May's report," Alicia said. "I'm just curious, does anything look odd about these figures? To you?"

Now Saffron was glancing at her watch and exhaling dramatically. "The only odd thing here is why I'm letting you waste my precious time."

Still, she slipped her glasses back on and took the phone from Alicia, inspecting the screen more closely. After just two seconds she smudged her matt-red lips downwards and handed it back.

"Looks fine to me."

"Really?"

"Really."

Alicia nodded and thanked for her "precious" time. Left her to it.

But she knew Saffron was lying She had seen the quick widening of her eyes as she inspected the screen shot, heard the sudden intake of breath, before she'd dropped those lips and handed the phone back.

There was definitely something odd about that report. Saffron knew it and so did Austin.

Now she had to find someone honest who would tell her why.

~

The second Alicia turned the corner, Saffron stepped out of the fashion closet and strode across the room to her private office.

"Later!" she snapped at Kora who was following in her wake and quickly scuttled away. Then "Hold my calls!" to Frances, before stepping in, closing the door and releasing a long, slow exhale.

A few breaths in, then she stepped behind her desk, swept open the bottom drawer and stared hard at the contents. She needed a hit, badly. Knew she should not be doing this. Glanced back towards the outer office, but no one was watching, not even Frances with her insipid, judgy smile.

She dropped into her chair then leaned down, plunging her hand into the drawer, rustling through the selection. There was a Mars Bar, a Snickers and a Turkish Delight. She grabbed the Mars Bar, ripped the wrapping off and took an enormous bite, chewing quickly before reaching into her handbag for her reuseable bottle.

After a few gulps of her iced chocolate, she polished off

the bar, then scooped up her phone and made the call.

When it answered she spluttered out a mouthful of chocolatey venom: "You stupid, bloody moron! Do you have any idea what you've done to me?"

~

Alicia found Hamish standing near one wall of the *Lout* office, staring at what looked like a miniature version of his magazine, A5-size print outs, all double-page spreads, pasted on the wall in the order in which they would appear once the latest issue was printed.

She did this herself, before she sent her one-offs to bed. It was a great way to see how the magazine flowed. You could check the order of things, ensure you didn't have too many word-heavy articles clustered together or, too many light pieces in a row. You could check for clashing colours and patterns and, most importantly, advertising. Because there was something rather unedifying about having an ad for weight loss pills right next to a story on anorexia, or a charity's famine appeal in the middle of a bikini spread. (Yes, she'd seen both in her time.) Pasting them up was old-school and foolproof, something you simply couldn't appreciate on a screen.

"Feeling calmer today, are we?" she said, approaching.

Hamish swung around, deep in thought, then offered her a sheepish smile before thrusting his stubbled cheek out. "He had it coming. You know he did."

"No visits from Arabella over it?"

"Not yet. But knowing that wanker he'll dob me straight in to Ted."

"Oh, I don't know," she said. "I have a feeling Austin's just going to let it slide." Or she hoped he would because Ted was the least of Hamish's concerns.

Then she smiled and said, "Can we have a quiet word?"

He frowned but led her to his office and closed the door behind them, perching on the edge of his desk. And for the third time that day, Alicia held up her copy of the report she'd found at Ginny's apartment, but this time she kept that to herself. Didn't want to set Hamish off again and back onto Austin's throat. Because he was smart, Hamish, and he'd definitely put two and two together as she had done.

Barely glancing at her phone, he shrugged as they'd all done and said, "Circ figures. What're you trying to say? I'm not selling enough to get away with my bullshit?"

"Well, that, sure, but take a closer look. See anything weird?"

He looked again, shook his head, then frowned and said, "Hang on a sec." He snatched the phone from her and, squinting, used two fingers to magnify one section. "This doesn't look right." He glanced back at her. "Where'd you get these?"

"Just stumbled upon them." It wasn't strictly a lie. "Is there something wrong?"

"You bet your arse there's something wrong. Look." He held the phone out and then pointed to the name of his magazine. "*Lout's* figures look normal, but this"—he now pointed to the *Styled* column—"this has them dropping. Not by much but I don't remember that. They never drop, that's their whole shtick, yeah? Their big claim to fame?"

"'While others fall, we fly'," said Alicia, parroting their slogan.

"Exactly. And I don't remember them ever falling."

He handed the phone back then dropped down behind his desk, tapping his computer to life. It took a bit more tapping but eventually he found what he was looking for and swivelled back as she heard the printer behind him whir to life. He jumped up and scooped some paper from the tray, then held it out to her.

"This is the May report I saw. The one emailed to me. Exact same figures as your version for all the mags, except *Styled*." She studied the two reports as he continued. "The one I was emailed has *Styled* up 3.5 percent. Yours has them *down* by that amount. That's a bit dodgy don't you think?"

"I do think," she said as he asked again where she'd found it.

Again she refused to tell him, this time adding, "You have to trust me on this, Hamish. I'm doing this for Ginny. So which report is correct? The one you were emailed? Or the one I found?"

"I'm guessing if you're Saffron Toya-Jones and you want to keep your advertisers and your big annual bonus, you'd say mine was." He was pointing at the report he'd just printed, with *Styled* up 3.5 percent not down by the same amount. Then he raised his bushy eyebrows and said, "But is it? That is the question."

Yes indeed, thought Alicia, another million-dollar question.

And this time she meant that literally.

CHAPTER 28
Lobster and Lies

Set on the iconic and now upmarket Woolloomooloo Wharf, FishFishChew was a seafood restaurant with prices just as upmarket and food that was fast becoming iconic, thanks to its executive chef and manager, Lynette Finlay.

Tonight Lynette barely had time to breathe as she darted from the kitchen to the floor and then to the back table where the book club had all gathered to digest the case, along with the exquisite cuisine. Courtesy of the chef, of course. At least half of them couldn't afford Lynny's exorbitant prices, sadly!

Alicia was desperate to share what she'd learned that day, and Lyn was desperate not to miss out, so it seemed like a happy compromise. And it was. Especially for their stomachs, and as they revelled in the pan-fried garlic prawns, buttered lobster and apple and Gruyere salads, Alicia got them all up to speed while Lynette stopped every now and then to listen in before dashing off again.

And what a story it was. Alicia started with Chloe and Gail, wanting to get them out of the way, because as bad as they were, they were little more than greedy opportunists, she'd decided. She told them about Gail's foul perfume and how it had led to her door and then to her confession. Yes, she was selling beauty products for Chloe, and Ginny had found out, but no it had nothing to do with her murder. Or Isla's for that matter. At least she didn't think it did.

Which brought her next to Austin.

After gobbling down a mouthful of lobster, she told them about the fight she'd witnessed between Hamish and Austin in the men's toilets, but as they gasped at that, she assured them it was more about Hamish throwing his weight around, lashing out because he's angry and hurt and can't get Ginny back. Again, she didn't believe it was related.

What was related, though, she was sure of it, was the circulation report she'd discovered later that evening.

After a refreshing sip of insanely priced Chablis, also complimentary, she described how Jackson had driven to Ginny's apartment that night and surreptitiously encouraged her to follow him in. How that had led to her finding the sales report hidden in a champagne bottle.

"You think *that's* why the place was ransacked?" asked Missy, breaking through and giving Alicia another chance to get some food in. "Someone was looking for that report?"

Alicia nodded as she gobbled.

"Lucky he let you in then," Missy added.

Ronnie tsked beside her and dabbed a napkin to her lips. "It was long overdue. Jackson should have got you in from the start, Alicia. You were one of Ginny's best friends. Of course you were going to notice something like that."

Alicia felt her heat sink because she wasn't sure she had been much of a friend in those final days. At the same time, she felt her hackles rise, wanting to defend her husband as he'd defended her to Singh.

She thought of him now and the brief conversation they'd had over the phone earlier. How he'd laughed off her concerns about Singh. Alicia had a terrible feeling it was the calm before the storm, but as he hadn't held up his trusty STOP! sign, she wasn't going to waste a moment of the calm, worrying.

And so she pushed it all from her mind as Perry held a hand up.

"Sorry to sound dim, but why was Ginny hiding a sales report with her bubbly? And why do we care?"

Good questions, Alicia told him. "I was wondering the same thing myself. So I asked Austin. He puts that report together, after all."

She then recalled how evasive Austin had been, how *defensive*, as had Saffron, both insisting there was nothing wrong with the report. Oh no, nothing to see here! How it wasn't until she showed it to Hamish that the truth was revealed—the report Ginny was hiding was ever-so-slightly different to the report that had been emailed to the other editors.

But Alicia was a journalist and she knew to check and double check. So, after swearing Hamish to secrecy—no mean feat as he'd wanted to run straight to *Styled* and rub Saffron's nose in it—she'd nipped into *Wellness* magazine and asked their editor, Mirabella, to show her the May circulation report she had also been emailed. It was identical to the one Hamish had received.

And very different to the one Alicia had found hidden away at Ginny's apartment.

"The report dates are the same, every other magazine's figures are the same. The only one that's been modified is *Styled*."

"Someone's falsely inflating their sales figures then," said Queenie, who was good at this stuff and had noticed Missy was now looking confused. "They're faking how well *Styled* is really travelling, probably to secure more ad revenue. Now *that* is what I'd call fraud."

Alicia added, "And that 'someone' has to be Austin. He's the head of Sales and Circulation."

"But why would he do it?" asked Ronnie. "It's his neck on the line."

"Ah," said Alicia now smiling. "This is where we come back to our first motive—sex. He did it for his lover. Saffron Toya-Jones."

She sat back and chuckled as they all blinked, disbelieving.

Then Missy gasped. "The mysterious affair at *Styled*?"

Alicia nodded. It's the only thing that made sense. Austin had already confessed he'd been cheating on Ginny with someone else. Someone "above" him, he'd said. What other motive could he have for falsifying Saffron's sales figures and risking his job?

"She must have talked him into it," explained Alicia. "Probably targeted him because he was in a position to make her look better in exchange for sexual favours."

"Urgh," said Claire.

"And it might not be the first time," Alicia added. Rumours had been swirling around Saffron for years, according to Hamish. Ginny had obviously heard them too. "Maybe Saffron did a similar thing with the previous sales manager? Or at least tried to. He left quite suddenly. Makes you wonder."

"Okay," said Lynette, dropping back down and catching up. "So Saffron was shagging Austin so he'd fiddle with the figures and not just hers." She locked eyes with Perry, and they sniggered. "Wouldn't it be obvious to the Accounts department if you claim to be selling more copies but you're not actually getting the revenue? I could claim to have sold thirty lobster dishes tonight, but if the cash isn't there…"

Her eyes were on Queenie now, and the smart PA shook her head. "The sales figure is exactly the same, it's just the change in circulation that has differed. They've said it's gone up, when in fact it's gone down."

"So what's the big deal then?"

She sounded like Austin, and Alicia was now shaking her head. "It's a really big deal, Lynny, because movement in circulation has a massive psychological impact. Especially for the advertisers whose marketing budgets are finite. Brands like Gucci and Chanel and Revlon have to make smart choices about where to put their ad dollars. And not just them. Apple, Mercedes, Netflix… And they're spoiled for choice these days. *Styled* competes heavily to win those campaigns from all sorts of other mags, not just *Vogue* and *Elle*. *Lout*'s also in the running, as are travel mags, home decorating titles, newspapers. And that's just the *print* media. They also have to battle with online magazines and sites, social media influencers, Instagram and the like, not to mention digital billboards, TV, film, streaming services…"

She took another breath and with it a gulp of wine before continuing. "Advertisers want to stick with the winners, the movers and shakers, the people who are doing better not worse. And here's the thing, *Styled* has consistently grown, year in, year out, unlike almost everyone else. That's been their selling point for at least five years: 'While others fall, we fly!' So if they appear to be falling too, it could seriously damage their brand, let alone their revenue. And who knows how long this has been happening, right? Is this the first time they fiddled with the figures, or are they on a downward spiral?"

Missy gasped at that, but Ronnie was tsking again, so too Perry.

"I know," said Alicia. "Who really cares? It's just a fluffy women's mag. But Saffron cares. Greatly. And not just to win over advertisers or get her annual bonus. I think Saffron has been on top for so long she would do anything to cling to her perch. It's all about ego. If her mag really is dropping by around three percent a month, she could soon be outsold by *Lout*." She mock gasped. "That would be *scandalous!*"

"So she lures in young Austin?" said Claire, button nose turned up.

Alicia nodded. "It certainly explains his secrecy. And Austin's clearly ambitious. Must love the idea of bagging the country's top editor."

"*That's* why he clung like glue to Ginny at your wedding," said Lynette. "He knew she'd pinched the report and wanted to make sure she didn't blab."

"And yet she did," said Alicia sadly. "At least indirectly, because I think *this* has to be the secret she left for me. The clues add up—the mysterious affair, the fake money, the T-shirt which was all about fraud as Perry suggested."

She still hadn't worked out the thesaurus though, but she didn't need it now. This was more than enough. At least it was for her, but Perry still didn't seem convinced.

"I don't really know this Austin fellow," he said. "I remember him from the wedding and the memorial, but I'm struggling with all this." He brushed some food off his goatee and sat forward. "Do we really believe he'd shove his ex-girlfriend into a train, just to shut this down? And then drive over her flatmate so he can sneak into their apartment and steal back the report? It's so extreme. And as far as I recall from the memorial, he seemed pretty friendly with Isla that day. Couldn't he have flirted his way in, then searched while she was on the loo? Why kill her?"

Perry was right. It did feel like an overreaction, and she recalled how passive Austin had been when Hamish bailed him up in the men's toilets. He hadn't even tried to fight back. But Ginny hadn't been shoved; it was gentler, more subtle than that. And he didn't drive over Isla so much as *not stop*. There was a degree of detachment in both murders. Not exactly arm-to-arm combat. And they were women, after all.

Maybe he was the true misogynist at Arial. Not Hamish.

"Ginny had evidence of fraud," she told Perry. "Isla clearly found that evidence. If the truth got out, Austin and Saffron would both lose their jobs. It would be an enormous scandal."

He was still shaking his head. "No offence, Alicia, but like you said, it's just fluff. Does anyone really care? I mean, set aside Austin for a moment—would *Saffron* kill over this?"

Alicia laughed. That's where she knew she was in safe territory. "Oh my sweet delusional friend," she said, reaching for a prawn, "I think Saffron would kill for a lot, lot less."

By the time Jackson got home from work, Alicia was also back, tucked up in bed, pretending to be immersed in her Christie book, when really she was waiting up for him.

Back in worried mode.

It was now midnight, way past her bedtime, but she needed to see the whites of her husband's eyes, to really talk to him this time, and it had less to do with what she'd uncovered—although she was desperate to reveal all— and more to do with Singh.

But when he walked in, he looked like a crumpled wreck.

"Are you okay?" she asked. "Can I get you a tea? Back massage? Blood transfusion?"

He laughed—that was something!—then shook his head. "I'll be okay. Just need some sleep. Gotta be back at work at the crack of dawn."

"Do you want to talk about it? How it's going with Singh?"

His head was shaking again. "Not tonight. I'm beat. But everything's fine. Don't worry. Get some sleep."

Then she watched worriedly as he brushed his teeth and washed his face and then simply dropped his clothes by the bed and sank into it, not even bothering to pull on his pyjamas. She continued watching as he shut his eyes and promptly fell asleep.

Lucky him, she thought, her mind racing again.

She didn't know what was happening at work, how much trouble Jackson was in, and she didn't understand why he wasn't talking to her about it. Why he was pretending everything was hunky-dory.

She had known Singh now for several years, and there was simply no way his proud boss was going to let it all slide. Something was afoot, she could smell it, then she could see it—her mind bubbling over with images of Jackson being fired and having to find low-paid work as a security guard. His mental health declining, his body widening, his joie de vivre extinguished for life. She could see him now, slumped on the couch, beer in hand, miserable. And not just miserable—angry. Mostly with her…

She shuddered.

Stop it! she told herself, then reached for her book and continued reading. She was more than halfway through *The Mysterious Affair at Styles*, and Poirot was about to head off to hunt down fresh clues. Hastings was frustrated as usual, but the clever Belgian was giving nothing away other than to say:

"Well, *mon ami*, a good deal you can guess for yourself. … We have cleared away the manufactured clues. Now for the real ones."

She thought then of the thesaurus Ginny had left her and jumped up, tiptoed to the living room where she'd left it. She opened the cover and reread the inscription scribbled in the front. The one from Hamish.

'Cause there are more words than 'sweetie' and 'darling'. H.

"Why did you leave this for me?" she whispered silently to her friend. "What are you trying to say?"

Is this a manufactured clue? she wondered.

Or a real one?

CHAPTER 29
Tay Tay Comes Through

Ted Johnson watched his shaggy-haired editor sprint across the foyer and throw herself into his elevator car, and he reached out to stop her from tumbling into the corner, almost crushing his new hat in the process.

"Sorry," she spluttered, steadying herself, then turning to the operating panel and tapping at the number four.

He popped the trilby safely on his head and checked his watch. It was not yet eight a.m.

"You're in early," he said.

She turned, stepped back and smiled up at him. "Well, that's why I get paid the big bickies, sir. I like to get a head start."

His eyes narrowed. *Was she being facetious?* Because he knew exactly what salary package Alicia Finlay was on, and it wasn't that big. Nothing like Saffron's for instance.

He glanced away. Tried not to think of the *Styled* editor and all the trouble she was causing. Had Ebony in quite a state the other night. Bloody Ebs and her blasted ambitions. He wasn't even sure he wanted to go into politics, let alone be the next British PM. He knew what *that* bozo earned, and there was nothing "big bickie" about that either.

He wondered if Ebony had factored a massive pay cut into her ambitions.

Alicia was staring hard at the elevator doors now like she was desperate to get out, and that cheered him up. He liked to keep his editors just the right side of terrified.

He and Saffron were alike in that way.

Clearing his throat noisily, he said, "How's the Tay Tay special coming along?"

Her eyes swept across to him, surprised. "Oh, er, it's fine, sir. That's why I'm here actually. Getting a head start on it."

"Good. There's a lot riding on that special. I'm looking forward to reading it."

The elevator let out a loud *ding!*, and she stepped towards the door like she couldn't escape fast enough.

"Enjoy your day," he called out, and she turned back, giving him a strange little salute before she vanished from sight.

Oh my God, thought Alicia as she stood staring at the closed shaft, hand still to her temple. *What on earth am I doing, saluting the CEO? He must think I'm an idiot!*

It's just that she felt guilty. She wasn't in early for Taylor Swift at all. Jackson had left home at the crack of dawn, and failing to return to sleep, she'd decided to get up and get on with her sleuthing.

But she could hardly tell Ted that! The guy was intimidating enough as it was. And it wasn't so much his enormous presence—he'd taken up half the elevator—but the fact he knew exactly what she was working on. With fourteen national publications to keep abreast of, let alone another twenty across the UK and Europe, that was pretty impressive. She admired his enthusiasm too. He'd sounded almost excited by her Taylor Swift special!

She sighed, passing through the empty reception and on towards her office, feet dragging behind her, thinking, *lucky him*.

Five years ago, Alicia skipped down this corridor, genuinely thrilled by the idea of switching from monthly magazines to creating fresh content regularly, but her heart was no longer in it. She was too old for fanzines, and you could tell from her lacklustre content.

Then she shook her head, thinking of Ted again. The CEO was twice her age and had been here for decades. How he maintained his enthusiasm she did not know, especially in an industry as challenging as this one. Perhaps it's because he knew his product. Always had.

That's what made Ted such a success, such a survivor. And *that's* why she shouldn't have been surprised he was across her workload. Of course he was. They might bitch that he spent his time calling mindless meetings, but that's how he stayed across the entire global operation. Nothing got past Ted Johnson. Nothing.

She stopped.

She gasped.

And suddenly she was racing back down the corridor and towards the elevators again, her finger now bashing at the Up button.

~

Jackson placed the takeaway coffee on Singh's desk, and she barely glanced up from her keyboard, murmured what sounded like a "thank you", then kept tapping.

He went to say something, thought better of it, and turned away.

Things had been awkward since his outburst, despite what he'd told Alicia. But he was starting to grow weary of Singh's stewing. He'd now apologised three times, and three times she'd told him it was fine, and three times he didn't believe her. But then she'd dumped a fresh workload on his desk and told him the hit-and-run would have to wait, so too reopening the DeRosso "train incident".

They'd had four homicides since then, and it was time for him to get on with it.

And he wanted to. He really did. But after a sleepy conversation with his wife that morning, he now had grounds to investigate further. If Alicia was correct and Ginny had uncovered fraud at *Styled* magazine, there might very well be a motive for murder.

But he wasn't about to tell Singh that. She wouldn't have been able to hear him anyway over the assault she was performing on her keyboard, slapping at it like she wanted to inflict grievous bodily harm.

He wondered if she envisaged Alicia every single time her

fingers belted the keys.

Or was it *him?*

~

By the time she got to floor seven, Alicia's nerves had caught up with her, and she was half hoping to find Ted's pit bull, Dionne, sitting at the desk out the front of his office, growling that she needed to call back for an appointment.

But no such luck.

The executive assistant's chair was empty. She clearly hadn't got the memo that Ted would be in early. His door was wide open though, and he spotted Alicia from his desk and waved her in.

Damn it.

"You stalking me?" he said as she tentatively stepped inside.

"Just wondering if I can have a quick word?" Her voice was raspy, and she couldn't feel her legs anymore.

Please say no, please say no, she thought, but he just nodded and said, "Sure. Take a seat," then continued working.

He had some stationery on the desk and was scribbling something down with a gold Montblanc fountain pen. She wobbled her way to one of the two armchairs—designer Astons if she wasn't mistaken, genuine Italian leather—and then watched as he held a fat finger up to stall her.

"Just give me two minutes."

And she was glad to. Alicia needed the time to swallow her nerves and collect her thoughts.

What on earth *was* she thinking? Singh's quite right, she decided. I am an interfering fool! I should take my theories to Jackson and let him take over the hot seat. Not try to interrogate a man I've always been far too shy of.

"There," Ted said, signing the letter with a childish flourish, then folding it carefully and looking up at her. "So. What can I help you with?"

Alicia's mind went blank. She almost stood up and fled, but he misread her expression and said, "If it's more money you want for your specials, forget about it."

"Sorry?"

He threw the pen on his desk and leaned back in his enormous leather chair. This one an original Eames. Saffron had the exact same chair. Alicia had the cheaper replica.

"Your department bleeds us dry enough as it is," he told her, "and you're going to have to hope to God that Taylor Swift special sells to keep you in employment. So I'd be careful with any revenue requests."

There was a smirk on his face, but she wasn't smirking along. She was starting to feel annoyed. Who was bleeding whom, exactly? Ted spoke as though he was doing *her* the favour, that she was lucky to have the job, and she felt a sudden flash of anger. She'd worked for this company for more than ten years. Had been a big part of their success, and he was acting like she was a leech, an *inconvenience?*

The head of Accounts had already admitted she was the least greedy of all the editors, but it didn't take a mathematician to know she cost them diddly squat. Her once-thriving department now comprised just her, a casual designer, and some lowly paid freelancers when she could afford them. Hell, she did most of the work herself! And for a pittance of his salary.

How much more blood did Ted require?

She certainly didn't need a lecture from a man wielding a $2,000 pen in an office the size of her apartment. And don't get her started on the designer bloody chairs!

Alicia took another deep breath, but it was her anger she was controlling now and not her nerves. In fact, she was glad he'd said it. The jitters were gone, and she had the perfect segue.

"Does it *really* matter how well the special sells?" she asked, offering a casual smile.

"Course it does," he barked back. "Poor sales aren't just bad for the bottom line, you know that. They also don't give our diligent advertising team anything to work with."

Oh? she thought. Is this the same team that earns twice her salary but would have absolutely nothing to sell if it wasn't for her content?

"Can't we just give them fake figures?" she said instead. "Then it wouldn't matter so much, right?"

He stared at her blankly. "What the hell are you talking about?"

"I'm talking about following the *Styled* template."

That wiped the blank look from his face. His eyes suddenly widened, his jaw dropped, and he looked like a deer caught in headlights.

And that's when she knew she had him.

But he wasn't giving up easily. Soon he was blinking the look away and shaking his head and saying, "You're talking gobbledygook, Alicia, and I've got work to do. You can shut the door on your way out."

She smiled. She stood up and walked to the door, shutting it as he asked, but she wasn't going anywhere.

Not yet.

Returning to her chair, she said, "Sorry for the *gobbledygook*, Ted. Let me make it clearer. What if we pretended my department sold 3.5 percent more than it did, and you got Austin Smythe to help you fudge the sales figures, then no one would know, right? The diligent ad team would love it, the advertisers wouldn't know so they'd sign on happily, and that way revenue would be up and we wouldn't need to worry about selling as many, because that would cover the costs and then some. How does that sound?"

Ted was now statue-still and equally as quiet. She wasn't even sure he was breathing. But then something flickered behind his eyes, and when he spoke, his voice was deep and scary.

"Are you trying to be funny, Alicia?"

She shook her head. "Nope. I'm deadly serious. I saw the report. The real circulation report. Ginny had it hidden in her apartment. I know exactly what you and Austin and Saffron have been doing."

And suddenly, without warning, he erupted.

Lurching to his feet, Ted flung his formidable form

across the desk towards Alicia, forcing her to rear backwards, nerves jangling again. She'd forgotten how monstrous he was, how tall and large and imposing.

"How dare you speak to me like this!" he boomed, his face just inches from her own. "After everything I've done for you! This meeting is over. Get out!" Then he pulled himself back and shook his head at her like she was a recalcitrant child.

Alicia was back to shaking, her heart pulsating wildly. Ted had been her boss for so long, and she'd never seen him like this. He was apoplectic! She withered under his fury and quickly struggled to her feet, made a beeline for the door when he bellowed:

"And get a resignation slip from Dionne on your way out!"

CHAPTER 30
Not So Fast

Dionne Barnes was humming to herself as she made her way to her desk, pulling off her cashmere coat and reaching for the rack when she heard her name called out. She glanced at her boss's door, not surprised to see it closed. She always locked it after Ted left and always on his orders. But she was surprised to hear voices coming from behind it this early.

Was that Ted she could hear? Yelling at someone?

The EA hung up her coat, then stepped behind her desk to check his diary. He hadn't scheduled a morning meeting, as far as she could see, and it was a little early for theatrics. Early for Ted, to be honest. He didn't usually come in until well after nine, his third wife keeping him busy until they'd breakfasted together, like that was going to salvage their marriage.

Dionne wondered briefly if that was Ebony in there he was bellowing at. She strained her ears. It didn't sound like it.

Still, she wouldn't be surprised if they were having another barney. She ignored the yelling and sat down at her desk, tutting to herself as she did so.

Dear silly Teddy. What had he been up to this time?

He had an abysmal track record, her boss, simply couldn't help himself. And while he'd been good of late, she knew that—had not had to lie *once* to his current wife—Dionne recognised the signs and knew something was afoot.

Ebony could hold all the romantic picnics she liked, but that wasn't going to save her. A leopard didn't change his spots. And the sooner she realised that, the better for all of them.

Why Ted had married bimbo number three she could not

guess. Ebony looked like a miniature poodle, and her posh English accent wasn't fooling anybody.

Oh no, Dionne did not like Ebony one bit.

But that didn't mean she didn't want to save her beloved boss from bimbo number four. Because there was always one lurking. He never saw them coming. But she did.

And she was always good and ready…

~

Alicia's back was ramrod straight. One hand on the door handle, the other in a fist by her side. She dropped her right hand, turned and glowered, Ted's threat of termination the final straw.

The moment he suggested the resignation slip was the moment Alicia lost the last of her jitters. Her fury was back, and it was bigger than his bluster.

"How dare *you*!" she cried, storming back towards him. "I've given my blood, sweat and tears to this company! *Years* of loyal service. And now you want to dismiss me! Like *I'm* the one in the wrong?"

He gulped back at her, and she shook her head furiously. "This meeting isn't even close to being over, so you might want to sit back down. Ted."

The CEO was clearly shocked, and not just by her revelations. It was true. She had never so much as said boo to the man in a decade, always the yes-girl, happy to work harder and longer for less and less. She wasn't being so amenable now, and the fire in his eyes flickered out. When he dropped to his seat, he took a quick glance at the door, and she wondered if he was relieved it was shut or if he was hoping to make a run for it himself.

Alicia took some more deep breaths, tapping back into her anger. Letting it fuel her. She yanked the obscenely priced chair out and stepped in front of it, looming over him this time.

"You asked before if I was being funny? No, Ted, I'm furious! The rest of us have to work our butts off to get sales, to drag in advertisers and prove our worth. And you just fiddle with Saffron's figures and ta-da, she's a bestseller!"

"So bloody what?" he snapped like a petulant child. "We're not the only ones. Everybody amends the stats. Who even cares?"

"I care! Hamish cares too. Incredibly. You play us all off each other like it's a competition. Saffron hogs all the revenue, gets the highest salary, the best bonuses, all the glory, like she's some kind of goddess when she's just a fraud. That ridiculous soiree you held for her at the Opera Bar last month, making us all show up and toast her success when I know, *for a fact*, her sales had gone down that month, not up! At least *Lout*'s are still rising. *Hamish* is the one you should have been toasting. But he doesn't get a shindig at a fancy bar. He's lucky to shout himself a few beers without threats from Bob Chalmers."

"Oh those Opera Bar drinks were just a stunt for advertisers. Just smoke and mirrors. Grow the hell up, Alicia."

"You grow up!" she spat back. "Children cheat, Ted. Grownups face the music!" She took a deep, calming breath. "Was any of it real? Has Saffron been lying about the stats for months?"

He looked away again. Couldn't meet her eyes.

She gasped. *"Years?"*

"It's not her fault!" he roared again. "*Styled* is a bloody good publication, and I don't want it to die!"

"So Ginny and Isla had to die instead?" she roared back.

That shut him up. His jaw dropped. He was back to looking confused. "What? What are you talking about?"

"I'm talking about Virginia DeRosso, *Styled*'s faithful beauty assistant and my friend." She let that sink in for a bit. "Ginny discovered what you were up to. I don't know if she was blackmailing you—that's not her style—but I'm sure she was taunting you. She would have been amused by it. Thought it was good gossip. A great mystery for me to uncover. But you needed it to stay a mystery, didn't you? All three of you? For your careers, for your ambitions.

It's a good motive to want her dead."

"But Ginny killed herself. Didn't she?"

"Or did one of you push her off the platform?"

Ted was gulping so much he looked like a giant puffer fish. He seemed confused. Genuinely so. And she watched him for a moment, catching her breath.

The truth was she couldn't imagine him hiding under his silly hat, furtively pushing Ginny anywhere. He was too large for furtive. Too lofty too. Ted was the top dog. A delegator. He would have ordered someone else to do it.

"I had nothing to do with what happened to Ginny," he said, watching her closely. "Nothing. Okay? And this little circulation… matter. It's irrelevant too." He leaned forward. "What do you really want, Alicia. Is it money? We can sort something out."

She stared at him shocked. Disgusted. *Disappointed.* He might know his magazines, but he didn't know the first thing about his editors. He never took the time to find out.

"Of course I don't want money. I want the truth."

"The truth is Austin's a bloody fool and Ginny's a little snoop! I knew she was trouble when Austin started shagging her. I told him to keep a wide berth. Hell, even I knew not to be tempted by that little slut."

Alicia winced at the words, but he was on his way to some kind of confession, so she had to hold her tongue, as hard as it was.

"Ginny thought she was clever," he was saying. "Whispering in my ear at the Opera Bar. Teasing me with what she knew. I told her to keep it to herself. I'd give her a nice fat bonus. But she didn't want that."

Of course she didn't! Another employee he hadn't bothered to get to know. Ginny was never motivated by money either. She just wanted to play games, and it got her killed.

"She was a foolish young girl," he said, reading her mind, "but I didn't push her. I can't believe you'd suspect me of something so heinous."

"Yeah, well, I guess it's not quite as heinous defrauding

sales figures, lying to your advertisers and sleeping around on your wife."

"What?"

"You're having an affair with Saffron, aren't you?"

Because it was just occurring to her that she'd been wrong about Austin. He wasn't sleeping with Saffron; he didn't need to. Could get sex anytime he wanted it, and what had he called his secret lover? The "hottest chick in the building. Way above me". You'd hardly refer to Saffron that way. She was an ageing editor whose success—he well knew—was all smoke and mirrors. Oh no, Austin wasn't fudging the figures for Saffron, she realised now, he was doing it for *himself*, to advance his career. To keep his corner office and fancy lunches. She wondered again if that was why his predecessor had left so abruptly. Because he wouldn't play ball as Austin had.

But Ted didn't need to advance his career. He was in the top seat. So why risk it all by helping make Saffron look good? There had to be more to it. More to them.

"I am not sleeping with that woman," Ted said matter-of-factly. Too matter-of-factly.

She smiled. "But you did in the past, didn't you? I've heard the rumours about both of you. You were players. Makes sense that you played together once. Is that all this was? One more game with your ex-lover? Or was it darker than that? Was she holding it over you? Threatening to tell your wife if you didn't 'amend' her circulation figures."

He scoffed suddenly, amusement in his eyes. "My wife doesn't care about *affairs*. How do you think we hooked up? Oh no, what Ebony cares about is power. Measuring up the curtains for Downing Street."

He sighed and glanced away. "She uncovered the reports, just like you did. Hired some fancy PI that really did earn the exorbitant sum I paid him. He snapped photos of us, apparently—Saffron and me, having a little chat last week. I don't know how Ebs put two and two together, she can barely add up, but she knew we were up to something, and it wasn't an affair. Sadly. So she lied her way into my office the other day, had a little forage…"

He rolled his eyes. "You think you're angry? Ha! You should've seen Ebs the other night. Slapping me over the head with it. Said I've destroyed all her grand ambitions, like she was the one who was going to run for Parliament."

He scoffed again, then swivelled completely to stare out at the panoramic view. It was the same view Saffron had but even more stunning from this height. He seemed distracted now. Spent.

Too bad, she thought. This wasn't over yet. "Who else knew Ginny had stolen the real report? Apart from your wife and Austin? Did Saffron?"

Because she could definitely see Saffron hide under a hoodie and shove Ginny into the path of a moving train.

"Of course she knew," he murmured, not looking back. "Wanted to sack her on the spot, but where would that get us? Ginny wouldn't go quietly. I told Saffron to bide her time. Austin too. Told him get that evidence back from the little tramp and make sure she didn't tell a soul."

Ted swivelled back, deep furrow between his eyes. "But I didn't tell him to *hurt* her. That's not what I meant." He gulped. "My God, do you think *that's* what's happened?"

Alicia watched Ted for a moment, unsure how to read him. Was he genuinely worried Austin had taken him too literally? Or was this all part of an act? A way to shift the blame to his sidekick?

She wasn't sure, but it certainly put Austin back at the top of the suspect list. Because his boss had told him to make the problem disappear.

And there had been two young women standing in the way of that.

CHAPTER 31
The Impossible Truth

"It can't have been Austin Smythe," Jackson told Alicia over the phone later that afternoon. "He has an alibi. For both homicides."

Alicia dropped her head to her knees and groaned, not even mollified by the fact that her detective husband was finally calling them homicides.

She was now back at her old house, perched on the sofa, Lynette frowning beside her, Max curled up at their feet, completely unfazed. Just as Ted's assistant had been when she strolled into his office that morning and found her boss, flush-faced and gulping while one of his subordinates loomed over him.

That must have been an unusual sight, but Dionne didn't bat an eyelid. Simply purred, "Apologies for interrupting, Ted. Can I get anyone a coffee?"

Yes! thought Alicia, triple strength! But she wasn't going to linger.

She'd just dropped a bomb at her boss's feet and needed to get to shelter. Hell, she needed extra protection, and so she'd fled the building and headed straight for her sister and the safety of Woolloomooloo.

As Lynette fired up the espresso machine, Alicia put in the call to Jackson, telling him everything that had transpired that morning, including Ted's confession to fraud and the instructions he'd given Austin. How he'd ordered him to shut Ginny up, along with all hint of the scandal.

Had Austin taken him literally?

That's when Jackson got excited too. He told her to sit tight while he looked into it, then he asked to speak to

216

Lynette. Alicia couldn't hear him, but he must have told her not to let Alicia anywhere near Arial Publishing.

"Oh, I'm tying her to the couch," Lynette had informed him.

And she did, in her own way, keeping Alicia content with cups of coffee, then pots of fresh tea and her favourite food, including pillowy scones and chicken mayo sandwiches. And they sat there for the rest of the morning and half the afternoon, slurping and eating and going over the case in minute detail.

Lynette agreed with Alicia. It was the only solution. Whatever Saffron and Ted's involvement, Austin had to be the culprit. The one who did the killing.

And yet now Jackson was telling Alicia otherwise, Lynette listening in via speakerphone beside her.

"We brought Mr Smythe in after you called," Jackson said, "and we questioned him regarding Isla's hit-and-run."

"And?"

"And I'm telling you, he has an alibi. He was in bed with Chloe Anderson that morning."

"*Chloe?*" Alicia nearly fell off the couch. "So *that's* who he was cheating on Ginny with? That's who he said was above him? Chloe?"

"Appears so. According to Austin, they've been seeing each other for about a month. Claims he was at Chloe's place the morning Isla was killed. They woke around ten, had brunch at a nearby café. She resides in Watsons Bay. Nowhere near North Sydney. I'm corroborating his story now, but I don't like your chances. He sounded cocky."

"Yeah, well, he always sounds like that."

"Oh, and you're not going to like this either. He drives a Porsche. A red one."

"How surprising."

He chuckled and she just sighed. Wow. She never would have put Austin and Chloe together, and yet it made so much sense. Chloe could easily be called "the hottest chick in the building",—and it wasn't just her glacial beauty. She was hot property, Chloe. Definitely on the rise. As ambitious as

Austin, with morals as shady. And it would explain what he was doing on their floor the day Hamish bailed him up in the men's toilets. Chloe was in the adjoining bathroom, clearly primping herself for their rendezvous.

But why all the secrecy? "Could they be in it together?" she asked now.

"Maybe, but she drives a black Beamer, yeah?"

She scrunched her eyes shut again. "What about Ginny's death? Has she alibied him for that too?"

"Claims he worked late that Monday. Told me to check with Arial security. They'll confirm he never left the building until well after eight that evening."

"And Chloe?"

"Not sure yet."

"Has to be Chloe," she said. "Maybe she was cleaning up his mess for him."

"That's easy enough to check. But, Alicia, I'm not so sure. Like I said, he's cocky. Worse than that, complacent. If he did do this, if his lover helped, they've been very smart about it. I'm not sure we're going to find evidence."

She groaned and dropped her head again as Lynette patted her gently on the back.

"What about Saffron?" Lynette called out. "Did you check her alibis for both murders?"

"In the process," he called back, then, "Hang on."

They heard some muffled voices in the background, then he returned.

"Everything okay?" Alicia asked, head up.

He assured her it was, even though he didn't sound it, then said he was heading to Arial now to question Saffron about the fraudulent circulation figures.

"She'll deny it," said Alicia. "Certainly won't roll over and purr. Be sure to triple check her alibis for both murders, and don't believe a word she says. What about Ted Johnson?"

There was a weary release of air. "Can't find him. He left the office soon after you did."

"That's incriminating."

"Business as usual, according to his assistant. She said he

had an important appointment but can't quite remember where." Alicia scoffed at that, and he murmured his agreement. "I did ask her about his whereabouts during both deaths, and she claims he was home with his wife. Haven't had a chance to verify, but the EA insists Ebony Johnson will back him up."

"And Dionne's right. Ebony will back him all the way to the PM's office. But again, you can't necessarily believe her or any of them for that matter."

"Well, the Johnsons have CCTV at their home apparently, so I'll request a copy. But I don't like our chances. They'll certainly lawyer up. And the truth is, I've seen Ted for myself. He's a monster of a man. Would stand out like Shrek on any of the CCTV, and I did not see him—not at the train station or on the footage at the front door of Isla's building."

"He could've hired someone, or his wife could've done it. She sounds more monstrous than him, but she's tiny. Honestly, Jackson, it has to be one of them. All the clues fit."

"Look, I've really got to go."

"Okay, but how's it going with Singh. Are you in trouble?"

"I'm gonna be fine, Alicia. Just take care of yourself, okay? And do not go back to the office. I no longer trust anyone in that building."

"You can trust Hamish," she insisted. "He'd look out for me. He would." She shot her sister a pointed look then. "And you can trust most of the gang at Arial. They're not all evil."

"Still," said Jackson, then "Lynette?"

"I'll keep her here!" she sang out.

Then they both wished him good luck, and Alicia added, "There must be something we're all missing. How can two people be killed in public and no one notices a thing and there's not a shred of evidence? It's impossible!"

After he hung up, Alicia was left with the bitter taste of disappointment. She was so sure she'd just solved two murders. The deaths of Ginny and Isla *had* to be related to the report Ginny hid in her apartment and Isla had clearly uncovered.

What other reason?

There couldn't be *two* dark secrets at *Styled*, could there? Then she remembered Chloe's theft and thought, oh yeah there really could be.

And wasn't it interesting how Chloe was at the centre of both?

CHAPTER 32
A Storm Brewing

Frances kept her expression pleasant, her hands on her keyboard—tap, tap, tapping away—as she watched her boss storm in and out all morning. First, Saffron had a meeting on floor seven, or at least that's what she'd said, but she'd reappeared not five minutes later and looked fit to bursting. She barked at Frances to bring her "my usual!", then slammed the door between them and holed up in there all morning, glugging the iced chocolate from the discreet drink bottle Frances quickly provided. Like she was sculling fresh water.

The PA wondered if she should remind her how many calories it contained but had only done that once and barely lived to tell the tale.

Around lunchtime, just as Frances was getting up to fetch Saffron's salmon and quinoa salad from the Bistro down the road (more for show, let's face it, Frances usually gobbled the rest of the salad down when no one was looking), two cops showed up, detectives they'd said, and that got the PA struggling to hold her expression.

But Saffron waved them in with a bright smile, like they were there to chat about fashion, and closed the door behind them. So Frances arranged to have the salad delivered, too scared to leave her post. She knew something was up and not just because she knew her boss's smile, and that was the fakest one she'd seen yet. The sugar hit clearly wasn't helping.

Oh no, something strange was going on, something worrying. And everyone had noticed.

"Did they say they were *detectives*?" whispered Chloe,

lingering by her desk.

"Couldn't say," Frances replied, tap, tap, tapping again.

"Wonder what they want?" asked Kora, also lingering, eyes now on Chloe.

"Why are you looking at me?" Chloe gasped. "How would I know?"

Then she'd scurried across to her desk, scooped up her ridiculously large handbag, muttered something about some product that needed collecting and fled.

Okay, that was definitely suspicious.

Ten minutes later, Saffron's door swept open and the editor stepped back out, her smile more genuine this time, the two detectives behind her. As every eye in the office watched, she asked Frances to show them her diary for the day of Ginny's accident.

That brought a few gasps from the room, but Frances was a professional, so she simply nodded like it was the most ordinary request in the world and flipped back to that Monday. She ran her finger down the page and then tapped at the words CHANEL LAUNCH: 4:00 P.M.

Saffron snatched up the book and waved it in front of their faces.

One detective, the beefy bloke, looked disappointed, but the other, the Indian woman, seemed unsurprised, even a little smug. Then she thanked Saffron for her time and all but dragged the guy away.

Saffron stood rigid then, staring after them, then she threw the book back at Frances and barked, "Find Ted! I don't care where he is or what he's playing at, I want to speak to him, and I want to speak to him *now*!" Then she held up a finger and added, "And don't you let Dionne fob you off! That woman knows more than she's telling!"

Then she slammed her office door and Frances began making some calls. She wasn't upset by her boss's tone. She was happy.

If there's one thing Frances liked, it was being useful. She was good at useful.

And so, after the salad arrived and she'd quietly slipped it in front of Saffron, she then closed the door gently behind her and made a beeline for Seventh Heaven.

Dionne could ignore her calls all she liked, but she wasn't fooling anybody. There was no way in hell she didn't know exactly where her boss was that very minute.

She was even more devoted than Frances.

~

When Jackson returned to his desk that afternoon, he wanted to update Alicia. He knew she'd be chewing her lower lip to shreds, worrying, but he couldn't very well call her from his desk. And he didn't want to get busted like last time, chatting to her in the stairwell.

Singh had flashed him a look then that spoke volumes, but he said nothing and didn't volunteer any information. They had an agreement now, freshly penned, but neither was going to risk it.

So he got on with some work, still trying to track down the vehicle registrations, and was finally making progress when Singh called out, "We found him!" as she slammed her desk phone back down. He raised his eyebrows. "Ted Johnson's hiding at his beach house apparently."

Jackson scoffed. "Hiding his head in the sand more like."

She nodded. Might have smiled at that once, but things were different now. "Just got a call from his solicitor, who assures me he'll be in here first thing tomorrow to provide a statement."

"You believe him?"

"*Her* actually. And what choice do I have? We haven't got enough for a warrant, you know that."

He winced, feeling wounded, like he wasn't living up to both her and Alicia. Because they were right—where was the bloody evidence? For both homicides!

And he wasn't humouring Alicia earlier. He believed they were homicides now. Was positive. But apart from the amended circulation figures, he could find nothing else to link anyone to the slaughter of two women in public.

That's the thing that kept sticking. Alicia was right. How could the victims be effectively assassinated in daylight hours, one of them under the trusty gaze of three different cameras and at least sixteen witnesses?

How was that even possible?

The evidence had to be there, staring them in the face. If only they could see it.

He sat up straight. Perhaps it was… He brought his computer to life. Perhaps we've been looking at this from completely the wrong angle…

Then he pulled up the CCTV footage from Town Hall station and began trawling through it again. But this time he wasn't looking at the Monday evening of Ginny's "incident" but the morning instead. Jackson wondered if the killer travelled into work the same way they left the city that afternoon. Via Town Hall station.

If that was true—and it was a very big if (they might have bused in that morning or driven)—then they'd hardly bother hiding their face because they hadn't yet killed a woman.

And so he began studying every frame, every angle, trying to note the faces of the people arriving for work that Monday. And he had his job cut out for him because even if his assumption was correct, it was a crapshoot. He didn't know what time they headed in or from which direction they were arriving.

Still, he did have some things to work with. He knew from Alicia that Arial's general office hours were nine to five, and the building was a six-minute walk from the train station. So he concentrated on the twenty minutes either side of nine o'clock that morning and focused on the CCTV footage at the nearest exit to Arial.

He was studying every face streaming out of the station, trying to find a similarity to one he'd noticed near Ginny on the afternoon she was pushed. Not finding any or none that stood out at least, he went back another twenty minutes and kept watching.

And then he got his first break.

At 8:13 that fateful morning, a familiar face glanced up

and towards the camera, expression relaxed. But it wasn't the expression that caught Jackson's attention. It was the hoodie they were wearing—or not wearing at that hour—the hood down because of course they hadn't yet performed a criminal act.

That black hoodie was eerily familiar. Especially the tiny white box with the band name printed on the top left-hand corner.

Heart racing, he made a few notes, took a few screen shots, then clicked out and brought up the later footage, the images of Ginny's last moments. And it was just as he remembered, someone in the exact same hoodie was standing close to Ginny just before she was pushed.

He couldn't see the face this time, but the hoodie was more than enough. It might've been black, but it had the same band name, this time printed across the back.

Still, he couldn't get excited. Not yet. He had one more thing to check.

Clicking out of the Town Hall footage and then out of the DeRosso folder entirely, he returned to his database and brought up the case file for Isla-Mae Cavendish. There he located the footage they had copied from the camera outside her apartment block on the morning she was run over.

It didn't take long to find what he was looking for.

It was early. Just 6:22 a.m. At least ten minutes after Isla had been struck. A small figure hidden behind a black hoodie was using a fob key to let themselves into the building. It was the exact same figure, he was sure of it. Exact same hoodie.

And the person wearing it was an Arial employee. Jackson knew that now and sighed heavily. Resignedly.

Alicia would not be happy.

CHAPTER 33
An Arresting Decision

It was Friday morning, the rain had finally cleared, the sun cheering Sydney up, but Alicia was feeling grumpy. Jackson had collected her from Lynette's house late the night before and refused to tell her anything other than to say the case was "progressing nicely". They were "close to making an arrest", and all the other clichés they used to fob off pesky reporters. But she wasn't a reporter, not really. She was Jackson's wife and an integral part of this investigation.

He'd said as much himself.

Still, that wasn't why she was grumpy. In fact, the news had her excited, picturing Ted and Saffron, Austin and even Chloe, all in handcuffs, being dragged away.

She hoped someone got it all on camera.

Oh no, the grumpiness set in when she told Jackson she was heading back to work that morning. She might as well have said she was joining a satanic cult.

"That's a seriously bad idea," he said. "Can you work from home for a bit?"

Yes, she could, but why should she? *She* hadn't done anything wrong. Why was she the one in hiding? Besides, Arial was a busy, bustling place. The key suspects already knew they were on the police radar; they weren't going to do anything silly like knife her at her desk. Because, yes, she'd already imagined the whole scenario. Could see any one of them sneaking up behind her, yanking her head back, slitting her across the throat… Had already decided to reposition her desk so her chair was facing the door, her letter opener at the ready. Just in case.

And sure, she had unfinished business with her boss,

but she knew Ted was being questioned at the station that morning, so she didn't fear him, at least not physically.

Whether she still had a job was a whole other question, but she did have bills to pay and a Taylor Swift special to finish. She wanted to get on with it, and sitting at home hiding wasn't going to help. Besides, her imagination needed a distraction!

"Trust me," she told Jackson. "I'll be safe. There's an office full of people. What could possibly happen?"

He'd rolled his eyes at her cliché this time, then finally relented but only after insisting on dropping her at the front door of Arial. It was fast-moving vehicles he was most concerned about. As he did so, he finally held up his STOP! sign, and it didn't improve her mood any. Alicia was not to utter one more word about the case, he told her. Not in person, not over the phone. Not to her colleagues, her book club and Lynette.

That had her especially miffed because she told her sister everything, and the book club had a right to know too—they'd helped get the case to this point.

"This is not me asking," he'd said. "This is the law speaking. If you overstep now, it could jeopardise a conviction."

She nodded. Okay, she got it. But she didn't have to be happy about it.

"So it's definitely someone at Arial?"

"Can't tell you, babe, and you need to respect that. Just focus on your own work, I'll do my final checks, and you'll know everything soon. I promise."

She agreed, of course she did, but as she sat at her desk now and opened up the Swift special, she knew she'd have trouble focusing. She was more than just grumpy, she was discombobulated.

It was a *good* thing Jackson was close, that an arrest was pending.

So why wasn't he more excited? And why couldn't he look her in the eye that morning?

~

Chloe was back at her desk, pretending to be immersed in an article about the importance of quality anti-ageing lotions, but not even her snappy sentences or the beautiful images she'd sourced could keep her entranced.

She really didn't want to be there, but she couldn't skive work as she'd done yesterday. Saffron would get suspicious. But gee it had been hard, walking back in this morning, waiting for the axe to fall, because it was going to fall, she knew that now.

And she was beyond furious with Austin!

How *dare* he blab about their relationship. And not just to Alicia, although that was bad enough. But to the detectives! My God, what was he thinking?

He'd promised to keep their fling a secret. She liked it better that way. Liked Austin, too, if she were being honest. They were *ridiculously* compatible. My God, their conversations ran into the wee hours, they had so much in common, identical plans and ambitions. But she also had a reputation to uphold. She was the rising star at Arial, a potential future editor. He was the company eye candy, and she was damned if she was going to be seen as just another notch on his bedpost.

He might declare his undying love for her, insist he'd lusted after her since he'd first arrived, but it hadn't stopped him from sleeping with Ginny had it? She shuddered just thinking of the two of them together.

Another example of his appalling choices.

And why were the detectives even *talking* to him? It was "nothing" he'd told her. "Unrelated". But she didn't believe him for one moment. Everything was related, didn't he see that? It was all coming full circle. Everything was closing in. All her great plans and ambitions were at risk of imploding. She should never have trusted Austin. Or Gail for that matter. If only she'd kept her distance.

And if only Ginny hadn't found out.

She glanced across the office again and locked eyes with

her nemesis. Tried not to scowl. But oh how hard she'd worked to be in just the right position at the right time. Was so close to taking over the big seat…

Now it felt like the ridiculous lotions she was writing about. A giant waste of time and money and energy.

~

Saffron watched Chloe give her the evil eye and felt like storming over and telling her to pack her things this instant. But she hadn't got where she was by being melodramatic. So she slapped her with a hard look and glanced away.

Besides, it wasn't Chloe she was really angry with. It wasn't even Austin or Ted, the loose-lipped, weak-bellied… She let out a long exhale.

It was bloody Alicia Finlay. The frumpy, meddling annoyance! Thwarting all their plans!

And who the hell did she think she was, bailing Ted up like that yesterday? Marching into his office and screaming at him "like a banshee"—*his* unimaginative simile, not hers. Frances had finally tracked him down to the rock he'd slithered under, and they'd had quite the heated exchange, Saffron and Ted. He'd ranted about binning the circulation reports and keeping her head down and how he wouldn't be back in the office until the dust settled.

"Do not say a word!" he'd yelled over the phone even though he'd clearly just blabbed his heart out.

She thought he was smarter than that. What happened to "Bugger off, Alicia, I'm busy!"?

She'd done it. Austin too.

But oh no, he had to get a bad case of the Truths. And to *Alicia* of all people. She was the biggest tattletale in the building. Jesus, she was married to a police detective— what was he *thinking?*

That had Saffron particularly worried. Not the detective or Alicia but Ted's behaviour. He was usually so unflappable. Ebony even more so. In fact, it had been Ted's wife who did most of the yelling. And with a startling amount of venom.

Like Saffron was the one who'd opened her big mouth and spewed it all out to the lowly Special Projects editor!

The hide of them all!

She took more gulping breaths, then a giant chunk of the Turkish Delight she was no longer hiding. Pointless now, she thought, as she stared out at the view before her. The rain clouds had vanished, sunshine twinkling across the Harbour, but she couldn't see any of it. Not today. Instead, she was envisaging her future—dark and bleak if she didn't play her cards right.

She stuffed the last of the chocolate into her mouth.

Nope.

No way.

She wasn't going to lose all this. Not over something so trivial. It's all she had. She certainly didn't have a life, or a marriage. Didn't even have kids. Her husband never wanted any. What had he said the other day, just before he'd flown off to Singapore or Geneva or wherever the hell he was off to this time?

"You got your fancy house, Saffron, your fancy job. What more do you want from me?"

A little attention would be nice, she thought. Some company. The occasional cuddle.

But she'd married a man utterly devoid of emotion, totally devoted to his work, and she'd learned to be those things too. *Styled* was all she had now. Without it she was…

She shook her head. Nope. No. Don't even think it!

Then she wrenched the drawer out again and reached in for the remaining Snickers.

~

As it happens, Alicia was able to focus on her work and was soon lost down a Taylor Swift rabbit hole.

Who knew the woman was so generous, so brave? Standing up to those record company bullies, not to mention helping the needy, the marginalised… In fact, Alicia was so far down the rabbit hole she almost didn't notice a voice booming from the corridor outside.

She looked up. Frowned. That voice sounded worryingly familiar.

It boomed again, and she leapt from her chair, dashing across the room to poke her head around the door. Jackson and Singh were there, striding towards her, and there was a man in handcuffs between them.

She gasped. "Hamish?"

The *Lout* editor was wild-eyed and pale. "Alicia!" he cried.

"What's going on?" she demanded of Jackson as she rushed up.

"Stay out of it, Alicia," said Singh, sweeping past.

"They're saying I killed Ginny!" Hamish cried out. "And Isla! But I didn't! I wouldn't! Jesus, Alicia, tell your man to back off!"

They had reached the elevator, and the reception area was now crowded with ogling onlookers, some gasping, some shaking their heads, one or two smirking like they weren't at all surprised. Chloe was watching too, but she had a strange look of relief across her face.

"Seriously, Jackson?" Alicia said, watching as they forced him into the lift. "You think Hamish did this?"

"But I didn't!" he called back. "Please, Alicia, you have to help me!"

Those were his final words as the elevator whisked him away, and Alicia was left standing there, staring at the closed doors, thinking, *But how can I help you if I have no idea why you've been arrested?*

CHAPTER 34
Walking It Out

Alicia's first thought was to follow the detectives to Homicide Headquarters and demand some answers. But she soon worked out that would be pointless. Jackson would be holed up all day, questioning his so-called suspect—because she really was struggling to believe it. And it wouldn't exactly improve relations with Singh.

So she called an emergency meeting of the book club instead.

Ronnie suggested they meet at her place this time, largely because she was the only retiree and the first to respond to Alicia's group text.

"Jump straight in a cab, and I'll have the tea brewing," she told her. "You sound most distressed, so it's my calming passionflower and lemon balm mix for you."

Alicia thanked her and booked a rideshare, then fielded apologies from the rest of the group. And understandably so. It was now mid-afternoon and they had jobs they needed and wanted to do.

"Keep us in the loop!" they'd all texted back except for Lynette, who phoned from the Sydney Fish Market and wanted to drop the barramundi in her hands and come running.

"Stay where you are," Alicia told her as the taxi drove west, towards Ronnie's suburb of Balmain. "I won't know more anyway, not until Jackson calls."

And she knew he would call eventually, because he knew her. And he knew this arrest would be eating her alive.

No wonder he couldn't look her in the eyes that morning!

"There's *no way* Hamish did this," Alicia ranted as she strode back and forth in Ronnie's living room soon after, leaving scuff marks in her plush pile carpet. "It couldn't be him. It just *couldn't*."

It might've been the ninth or tenth time she'd said that because Ronnie was looking weary. She released a gentle "tsk".

"Do you believe that because you believe in Hamish, Alicia?" she asked. "Or because you didn't guess it so it can't be right?"

That stopped Alicia in her tracks. "I'm not that narcissistic, am I?"

Ronnie smiled. "Not at all, dear. But you are clever and you're usually the first to work out whodunit. And if I'm not mistaken, it was Lynette this time. She really had a bee in her bonnet for Hamish, and yet you kept insisting he was tickety-boo. My real question is, why? From my vantage point he has all the tropes of your classic killer. He's a man. Obsessed with the victims, or at least with Ginny. Tendency to violence judging by his antics in the office loos the other day. I don't understand why you're so shocked."

Alicia slumped into one of the plush lounge chairs. She didn't understand it either.

Was it really sour grapes because Lynette had solved the crime first? She shook her head. No, she was proud of Lynny. It had nothing to do with that. She gave it some thought as Ronnie brewed fresh tea. Perhaps it had more to do with the loss of pride in herself.

Alicia felt like she was floundering. She was relatively young, newly married. It should be the happiest time of her life. And yet, increasingly, she felt like a failure. And getting this mystery wrong did not help.

Sure, Alicia wasn't into her writing so much anymore, but she *was* into mysteries. Solving them was what she was good at. Her expertise. Judging by the recent arrest, however, she was failing at that too. Because she would have bet her house Hamish was not involved.

Perhaps she wasn't as much of an expert as she thought.

After several more hours of tea drinking and carpet thrashing, Jackson finally called, his tone hushed.

"I'm on a break," he said. "Haven't got long but wanted to fill you in. This is off the record, Alicia. We did not speak."

"Of course," she said, feeling even sadder.

He released a long exhale, then explained the reasons why Hamish was arrested.

"His Oasis hoodie gave him away," he told her. "He said it was stolen from his chair the day Ginny died—"

"Yes! It was! He told me too."

"Well, we don't believe that's true. We have him arriving in the hoodie that morning, then wearing it again at the pivotal time that afternoon. His face is covered, but it's clearly him—same size and height and shape. He enters the platform a few minutes after Ginny, then slowly makes his way to her. So slowly you almost can't pick it. Very subtle. It's like a slow shuffle until he's the one standing just inches from her when she falls. It's him, Alicia."

"But if his face was covered, how can you be sure? And there must be thousands of people with Oasis hoodies. They toured last year."

"His is from their 2007 tour, back in England. Pretty distinctive. Pretty rare. That's his hoodie, Alicia, and that was him in the hoodie that day at the station."

But that wasn't all. Hamish had no alibi for the time of the murder.

"He claims Ginny left a message for him that Monday afternoon, asking to meet him at a laneway not far from Town Hall station at 4:45 p.m., and we do have him exiting Arial at that time."

"Was he wearing the hoodie then?"

"No, but he had a gym bag over his shoulder. It must've been in there. Says he walked to the laneway and waited for forty, forty-five minutes, then gave up and returned to Town Hall to catch the train home. We're checking CCTV now, but that laneway has none, and even if we spot him at

Town Hall at the time he says he arrived—about five thirty—that doesn't mean he wasn't there earlier, pushing Ginny onto the tracks. He could easily have then slipped out and back again. The place was pandemonium. It's all being double checked, of course, but we've got our man, Alicia, I'm sure of it."

"And you've checked Ginny's phone? To see if the message really came from her, about the laneway?"

"Her phone was crushed under the train, but here's the thing. He says the message was handwritten and left on his desk and he's since thrown it away. There is no paper trail, and isn't that convenient? I mean, who leaves handwritten messages these days? I can't imagine Ginny doing anything but texting. Honestly, he's got to come up with a better alibi."

"But his hoodie was stolen, he told me that. Anyone could have been wearing it that afternoon."

"Here's the thing, Alicia. You are the only one he mentioned that to. You also happen to be married to a detective. You don't think he was playing you? Slipping that in?"

She sat back, stomach clenching. Perhaps Jackson was right. Had Hamish set her up from the beginning? Was she *that* gullible?

"We did find some interesting texts on his phone," Jackson continued. "Messages he sent Ginny in the weeks before she died. They were becoming increasingly aggressive, mostly about Austin Smythe, what a loser he was, how they needed to break up, etcetera, etcetera. He was obsessed with her."

"But he's always been obsessed—"

"They had a fight, Alicia. We have witnesses. They were heard arguing in his office three hours before she died. Again, more stuff about Austin and him not being good enough."

"But she'd broken up with Austin!"

"Well, he didn't get the memo Claims she never said a word to him. Which doesn't help his motive any."

Now Alicia sighed. Of course Ginny didn't mention splitting with Austin. She would have enjoyed rubbing Hamish's nose in it, stringing him out. It's a game they played. Perhaps she was trying to force his hand. To make him finally step up and proclaim his undying love.

No wonder he'd paled when Alicia revealed the news about the break-up. If he really had killed Ginny over this, he'd done it for no good reason.

She squeezed her eyes shut. Oh dear... now it was starting to make more sense.

"What about Isla-Mae's hit-and-run?" She squeezed her eyes tighter, not sure she wanted to know.

"Still looking into that. He alleges he recently sold his vehicle, which is why he was using the train, but we do know he owned a cream Honda Civic, which is not dissimilar to the Toyota Corolla, so maybe the experts were wrong. Any case, he alleges he sold it nine months ago, but I'm still confirming that. Look, I have to run. But please, keep this to yourself. Just for a little longer."

She sighed but promised to.

And after they hung up and she turned to Ronnie's wide, curious eyes, she shook her head and said what she'd never said to a book club member before.

"I can't say anymore. I'm sorry. I promised Jackson, and I have to honour that. For once."

She thought Ronnie would tsk. She'd been tsking about Jackson all week. But she just nodded and said, "Of course you do."

Then she'd hugged her tight, like she hadn't just been slapped in the face.

Later that evening, back in her apartment, Alicia was striding restlessly again, this time through every room, looking over the new life she was making with Jackson. Feeling sad and confused, when she should now be happy, when the case should now make sense.

Yes, Hamish was rough, feisty, obsessed with Ginny. Had made a point of telling Alicia about his stolen hoodie—

it's almost the first thing he said to her when he spotted her at her desk the day she found Ginny's clues.

The signs were there, but what about the motive?

There had to be more to it than fury over her fling with Austin. Ginny had had multiple flings in her time. He'd always laughed them off. Why would this particular fling trigger him suddenly? That's the bit that didn't make sense. That and the fact that none of it helped explain Ginny's clues—the ones about fraud and money. They pointed to what Ted and Saffron were up to. So how did that fit in with Hamish? Were they just red herrings?

Did they have nothing to do with her murder?

"Urrgh!" Alicia growled aloud, making another circuit of the bedroom.

And that's when she noticed one of those clues, now resting on her bedside table. It was the thesaurus Ginny had given her.

She stopped. She gasped.

No, she thought. It was the thesaurus *Hamish* had given Ginny. Perhaps Ginny was pointing to Hamish all along. But why? What was Ginny trying to tell Alicia?

Grabbing it now, she flung herself on the bed and opened the cover to reread the inscription he'd written inside.

'Cause there are more words than 'sweetie' and 'darling'. H.

She read it and reread it, but it didn't make anything clearer. In fact, it left her more convinced that Hamish was not the culprit. This gift was smarmy, sure, but he was trying to help Ginny be a better writer. Deep down, the gift was kind. And so was Hamish, beneath the bluster.

Could he really have pushed his great love into a train? Then driven a car into her innocent flatmate? That wasn't the Hamish she knew. The Hamish Ginny loved.

Alicia felt even sadder thinking of all the years she and Ginny had worked together, all the years they laughed in the tearoom and Hamish poked his head in and told them to pipe down, fake frown on his face, twinkle in his eye.

If Hamish really was guilty, if he couldn't prove his innocence, he'd be gone too.

Then where would that leave her? Bantering at the microwave with Blake and Kora and Tiani? It just wasn't the same.

And she realised then why she was clinging on so strongly to her belief in Hamish. It's because he was the closest thing she had left to Ginny. The only other person who loved and accepted Ginny exactly as she was.

If Alicia lost Hamish, it would feel like she was losing Ginny all over again.

She lay back, heart hollowed out, and began idly wading through the thesaurus, sighing at all the words now lost to Ginny. Wondered if she'd ever even opened the book.

She was about halfway through when she noticed a word had been circled heavily in purple pen with silver stars drawn around it. *Stooge.*

Laughter burst from Alicia's lips. So she *had* opened the book! She had looked a word up. And she'd used her ridiculous coloured pen to deface it. Typical Ginny!

Why a beauty writer would need to look up synonyms for *stooge* she could not guess, but it felt like a ghostly whisper, a connection to her friend, so she kept flicking, backwards and forwards, hoping to see more, hear more, connect more, but it was the only word that had been circled.

Frowning, Alicia returned to *stooge* and read the words beside it: underling, minion, subordinate, assistant, henchman.

She sat up suddenly, frowning.

Was this meant to be a clue too? A "small" clue, like Poirot spoke of, but one that actually matters? Not manufactured but genuine? She thought now of the yellow Post-it note that had fallen out when she first showed this to Hamish in her office. Had that stickie been marking this word? And if so, what was Ginny trying to tell her?

Scrambling back to the living room, she grabbed her notebook, then jotted in the synonyms for stooge:

Underling.

Minion.

Subordinate.

Assistant.

Henchman.

As she scribbled the last word, her heart suddenly skipped a beat, her mind spiralling in a totally different direction.

She could think of one person who fitted all these descriptions perfectly. One person who was a minion and a subordinate. Definitely an underling. And would happily be a henchman.

And it certainly wasn't Hamish.

He was nobody's stooge.

That evening, Alicia broke her promise to Jackson, calling another meeting with her beloved book club, and this time they all showed up.

It was just after nine p.m., and they had chosen Perry's Surry Hills home for their rendezvous. Or rather, he had suggested it, deciding it was finally time to reveal his "big surprise", like they hadn't already guessed he was seeing someone. They weren't sleuths for nothing.

But when they got to Perry's whitewashed terrace house, they realised they weren't quite as clever as they thought. Perry's "someone" wasn't just anyone. It was a tall, silvery-haired fellow with a dapper dress sense and a Poirot-style moustache.

"Tag!" cried Lynette, forgoing the hand he was holding out to hug him and then stepping back so the others could too. "It's so great to see you again."

Alan J. Taggart was an amateur palaeontologist, a fellow traveller they had all met while on Alicia's hen's party aboard the Indian Pacific. Well, all of them except Queenie, who was promptly introduced, then asked if he was staying awhile.

He chuckled. "I suppose I could zip back to my place in Freo tonight, but as it's almost four thousand klicks across the country, I think I might bunk in here for a bit."

"More than a bit," said Perry, grabbing the fossil hunter by the hand. "Tag's rented out his pad in Western Australia and applied for a teaching job in Sydney, so I might just be able to keep him."

They cheered, happy for Perry and not just because they had all grown to like the talkative quipster on their last adventure. Love had eluded Perry for too long. It was his time.

"But I mustn't distract you," Tag said. "I hear you're close to solving yet another mystery, you clever clogs, and as I still haven't been awarded an honorary membership, I shall take my leave. But you will find a pot of my famous hot chocolate on the cooktop. Oh, and a bottle of the finest Glenfiddich for those who need something stronger."

Then he swept up the stairs, and they all turned to Perry, winking and smiling, and he rolled his eyes like he couldn't care less, but you could tell he was chuffed. Really chuffed. It was important to all of them that their partners got along with their book club friends because God knows they'd be seeing enough of them and at all hours.

Speaking of which…

Perry tapped his watch and said, "Alicia, my darling. You have the floor."

She nodded, relieved to be talking the case over, hashing it all out. Her confidence was now so whittled away she wasn't sure if she was imagining everything or on the right track.

Hamish was not the killer, she told them. It was someone else entirely.

At least, she thought it was.

And so, as they sipped hot chocolate, then followed it down with tumblers of single malt Scotch whisky, they went through every detail of the case from the top. Every *where* and *when* and *why* and, most crucially, *who*.

And now just one question remained—*how* were they going to prove it? Because they might be smart, but the culprit was smart too, and Alicia didn't have a shred of evidence, she told them. Wasn't sure she ever would.

"We need them to slip up and confess," she said. "But how do you make a killer confess when they're way too smart for that?"

Eventually Perry found the answer, back in the classic

Agatha Christie book.

"We return to where it all started," he told them. "Where the killer feels most comfortable. Where they think they are in control."

CHAPTER 35
A Stooge Revealed

Styled magazine was swathed in darkness when Alicia stepped into the office, and so it should be. It was seven o'clock on Saturday morning, and the staff were most likely at home, tucking into a leisurely breakfast or still tucked up in bed.

All except one.

Or at least that's what Alicia hoped as she set to work switching on the lights and streaming some music, making it feel as ordinary and normal and safe as possible.

She pottered around some more, then fetched herself a tea and sat behind the reception desk and waited.

And waited.

And after two full hours, she began to doubt herself. Had she misread the clues again? Was she on the wrong track entirely?

By the time the clock ticked ten o'clock, Alicia was in a full-blown panic. Oh God, she thought, dropping her head to the desk, Singh will never let her live this down. Or Jackson! He'll be the laughingstock. Her book club will be—

Ding!

Alicia looked up, her body flooding with relief, then nerves, and she took some deep settling breaths as she pushed her cold tea away and stepped out from the reception desk towards the elevator.

Then she felt a second rush of relief as the doors swept open to reveal Saffron's personal assistant. Frances.

The young woman was wearing chinos and a sloppy sweater today. Had her hair in a loose ponytail, a bag of dry-cleaning draped over one arm, and not a stitch of makeup across her freckled face. She looked fresh and pretty and startled to see Alicia, but not worried. Not in the slightest.

"Not like you to work weekends," she said as she stepped out.

"That's true," Alicia replied. "I avoid this place at all costs. Unlike you. Always going above and beyond for your boss." Then she tapped her watch and added, "Although this is a tad tardy. I hope Saffron doesn't find out."

Frances smirked at her and then down to the dry-cleaning. "I've been running errands for her all morning. I think you'll find she'll be very pleased with my performance."

Then she swept past and on to the *Styled* office. And it was only after hanging the bag on a coat stand by her desk that she realised Alicia had followed her in.

She stared at her, palms out, as if to say "What?"

Alicia smiled and said, "That's important to you, isn't it, Frances? Pleasing Saffron?"

Frances now gave her a "duh!" look and sat behind her desk.

"In fact," Alicia continued, stepping closer, "I'd say you'd do anything for your boss. Possibly even kill for her. Have I got that right?"

Frances was just switching her computer on, and her hand stopped, as if frozen in time, then she pulled it back, placed it on the desk and looked at Alicia like she'd lost the plot.

"I wouldn't go *that* far." She rolled her eyes dramatically. "But I am loyal. I make no apologies for that. Saffron works hard and expects us to as well."

"Fair enough," said Alicia, glancing around. "So where is she? This hardworking boss of yours? Because from what I can see, you're the only one in here. The only one who ever comes in on weekends, I'm told."

Frances tapped in her password and sighed. "Can I help you with something, Alicia? Because like I said, I'm not here for my health."

"Sorry, I'm just trying to work out why you are so dedicated to the magazine when you're just the lowly PA."

Something flickered behind her eyes then. Frances did not like being called lowly.

As she reached for the mouse and began navigating her way to a file, she said, "I don't need to apologise for caring about my job, Alicia. And I think you're being incredibly rude. There's nothing lowly about what I do, or *Styled* for that matter." She flashed her a pointed look. "I know you think we're a joke."

"I don't—"

"It's so *obvious*. Every time you walk in, you have this superiority about you. Looking down your nose at all of us. God knows why. I mean, what are you working on right now? *Taylor Swift?*"

Good point, Alicia thought, but let her rattle on, because she was rattling now, listing the many awards *Styled* had won and the ceilings they had shattered and how it was the best-selling women's lifestyle magazine per capita in the world.

"The *world*, Alicia. That doesn't *just happen*. That's all Saffron's doing. And mine."

Alicia's eyebrows swept upwards. "Yours?"

"Of course! If it wasn't for me, Saffron wouldn't be able to do her job. Who do you think keeps this place running so smoothly? It's certainly not Tiani! I'm the one who comes in first and leaves last, who gets everything ready for the week ahead. I go through Saffron's diary, her to-do list, make sure she has all the supports she needs in place."

She glanced at her screen now. "You have any idea how may emails Saffron gets each week, let alone phone calls and messages? It runs in the thousands. And I have to be across all of it. Every single one. They don't answer themselves. That's why she hired me."

"So you're like the wind beneath her wings?"

She glared at Alicia. "You can mock me all you like. You're the one stuck in *special* projects, doing one-offs because nobody wants to buy a second one, but I'm in here doing something valuable, something revered. I'm helping Saffron help everyday girls live their very best life. That's what we do. It's important work, and I'm happy to do it. Honoured, in fact."

Wow, thought Alicia, it was like she was assisting the Secretary-General of the United Nations. She wasn't just honoured, she was willing. And it's that willingness that helped Alicia solve this case.

Because when she saw the word Ginny had circled—*stooge*—she knew it didn't apply to any of her suspects, except perhaps for Austin. But he didn't work at *Styled*. And it was the Mysterious Affair at *Styles*. Not Arial Publications.

It's a strange word, *stooge*, incredibly old-fashioned, rarely used today. And that's why she'd looked it up in her Oxford Dictionary and found it meant more than just an assistant or subordinate, it also meant "unquestioningly loyal". And while she couldn't be sure this was a real clue or a coincidence, she did know it perfectly summed up the woman who was now feverishly tapping at her keyboard like the loyal minion she was.

Alicia wondered if she stepped around the desk, to stare at Frances's screen, she'd find little more than gobbledygook. Because she could tell Frances was ruffled and pretending not to be.

As if reading her mind, the PA glanced up and glowered. "I am actually working, you know? Perhaps you should try it instead of moping around sticking your nose in where it doesn't belong. I've seen you, bothering everyone with your creepy questions. And Claire and Queenie too. My God, do they think I'm an idiot? As if they suddenly care all about *Styled* and want to be part of it! Yeah, right." Then she sniggered and added, "Aren't you guys already in trouble with the cops for interfering where you're not wanted?"

Wow. Alicia really was impressed. Frances was more than just a willing lackey. She was like an omniscient know-it-all. A few more words Ginny could have circled. Oh and "liar". That's a good one too. Because Alicia might ask creepy questions, but Frances certainly didn't answer honestly.

As if she didn't know who cleared Ginny's desk out the morning after she died.

Frances ran that office, had just said as much. She knew what time the staff arrived and what time they all knocked off. Who had car spaces, who had to catch public transport. She knew secretive things, too, like the fact that Chloe was pilfering product. She'd said as much to Queenie.

And yet somehow, from her perch at the front of the room, she never noticed someone stroll in and box up all of Ginny's things—and there were a lot of things, it would have taken time—and simply walk out with them. In the middle of a working day? Not bloody likely. Chances are Frances did that herself, long before anyone arrived.

And it was also unlikely that Frances knew nothing of the circulation scam her boss was running with Ted and Austin. She read all Saffron's emails, had just confirmed that too. She would have seen the sales reports Austin emailed in, and she would have noticed the discrepancy between them. She had a head for maths, another thing she'd boasted to Queenie.

And what else had she told Queenie? That Ginny didn't try to win over Saffron, but instead, went *out of her way to do quite the opposite*. Chances are, Frances also knew Ginny had discovered the sales scam. That she was threatening her boss or at least mocking her with it, and that would not do.

Not on her watch!

And certainly not someone like Ginny, a subordinate who was never quite subordinate enough. Frances never thought Ginny was worthy of the magazine, had loathed her from the start. And for the same reason she loathed Alicia—because Ginny did not worship at the feet of Saffron and *Styled*. But Alicia wasn't threatening the viability of her precious magazine. Ginny was, and that alone was motive enough.

It would not have been hard for Frances to follow Ginny to the station that Monday and give her a gentle shove out of the way and into the path of an oncoming train. Hell, it would have been an honour to step in and protect the woman and the magazine she worshipped.

And that's what brought Alicia back to the word *stooge*.

"You know it's funny," she said, pulling a chair from a nearby desk and wheeling it across. "You get paid even less than I do, Frances, and yet you're totally devoted to Saffron. A true soldier, working your little guts out. Told me how you never leave here before Saffron, which often means working until very late. Except, you weren't working late the evening it happened, were you?"

Frances rolled her eyes and looked up briefly from her keyboard before continuing to tap. "What are you rambling on about now?"

"Sorry, am I rambling? Let me cut to the chase then. See, I'm talking about the evening Ginny was murdered." The tapping did not miss a beat. "I know for a fact Saffron left work at four for a Chanel launch. But of course, you knew that too. It left you free to knock off early, or early for you. I think you left the office just after five that evening. Just after Ginny did. And I think you followed her to Town Hall station."

Frances continued tapping. "Well, that didn't happen."

"Really? Because you were caught on CCTV that night."

Another glance up, then back to her tapping.

Alicia smiled. "Granted you'd covered your face with a hoodie. Hamish's hoodie as it happens. But you're the same size and shape as him, you wear black leggings which look a lot like his skinny jeans, so it was easy to disguise yourself as him in a baggie hoodie on a wet day on a crowded platform."

Her typing was annoyingly melodic. Tappity, tappity, tap. She did not seem at all worried, so Alicia forged on.

"Did you come up with the idea when you saw the distinctive Oasis hoodie hanging on Hamish's chair that morning? I know you went into his office. Hamish told me, but I've also confirmed it with Blake. Rang him last night. He said you passed by reception with some aftershave samples that Saffron asked you to palm off to *Lout*. Did you spot the hoodie then and decide to take action against your nemesis?"

"Nemesis?"

"Ginny, of course. You couldn't stand her, let's not pretend."

She finally stopped typing and looked up. "Oh, I'm not pretending. You're right. She was an untalented little slut who didn't deserve to work for us, but I didn't kill her if this is where you're heading. It's laughable."

Alicia recoiled at her words and her tone—so casual, so breezy—and tried to reflect that back at her as she said, "Is it *laughable* though? Because I can see it all clearly. In fact, I can describe how it went down if you like?"

Frances snorted, then sat back, arms folded. "Sure, go ahead, Miss Marple. Amuse me."

So Alicia cleared her throat and sat forward. "I think you knew all about Saffron's circulation scam. And you knew that Ginny knew, and you wanted to shut her up. It was that simple. Your boss had left early, so you had the perfect opportunity and the perfect patsy in Hamish. You're smart, a quick thinker. You probably came up with it all on the spot, the second you saw that distinctive hoodie hanging from his chair. You pilfered it, then later faked a note from Ginny, asking Hamish to meet her at a laneway close enough to Town Hall to put him in the vicinity but with no CCTV coverage so he'd have no solid alibi."

She snorted. "And how would I know that?"

"You probably did a walk-through at lunchtime. Because you did take your lunch break that day. Another thing Blake told me. See he's as switched on as you are. Sees everything from the reception desk. And he remembers that day well because he said you never take lunch breaks. Says he nearly fell off his chair. My guess is you found the perfect laneway, then scribbled that fake message luring Hamish there. That way you destroyed any chance he had of an alibi while you slipped into his hoodie, trailed Ginny to the station and shoved her in front of that train."

The words were shocking when said aloud, and Alicia nearly choked on them, but Frances looked unperturbed, and that was most shocking of all.

She'd just been accused of the worst of crimes—

murder—and she seemed... bored.

Alicia took a moment then, to catch her breath, to swallow the lump in her throat, to try to calm the waves of fury threatening to break, while Frances watched her, expressionless.

Eventually Alicia said, "My guess is, you casually slipped out of the station during all the commotion and quietly binned the hoodie somewhere before heading home like nothing had happened. Were you disappointed when the cops said it was suicide? Were you hoping to stitch up Hamish? Were you thrilled when they finally put it all together? Was that a fringe benefit for you—him getting arrested?"

Frances didn't answer, her gaze still eerily detached.

Alicia said, "Poor innocent Hamish, he didn't deserve that."

"Oh, what a load of rubbish," Frances replied, more annoyed than rattled. "There's nothing innocent about that slimeball. He was as embarrassing as Ginny. Sleeping his way around the building, the dirty old man. He's a waste of space and so is his filthy magazine. I can't believe it even sells. He'll get no sympathy from me."

Then she tightened her ponytail and said, "But that's neither here nor there. Because this is all lies and you have no evidence of anything."

Alicia nodded. "You may be right." Then she sat forward and added, "But there is evidence that will link you to the murder of Isla-Mae Cavendish."

Finally, after twenty gruelling minutes, Frances showed her first real flicker of concern. Her eyebrows knitted together, her lips tightened.

"You should have stopped with Ginny," Alicia told her. "If you had, you might've got away with it. Everyone would have let it drop, including me. Despite my reservations, I let everyone convince me Ginny killed herself, even when I knew deep in my heart that she would never do such a thing. Even her poor mother—"

"Oh, she's as embarrassing as Ginny," she spat out,

cutting in. "You know she's been stealing from the magazine?"

"So she deserved to lose her daughter over that?" Alicia shook her head. "What about Isla? Did she deserve to die too?"

Now the concern was back, except it wasn't concern, it was regret. Yes, there was the tiniest morsel of regret, deep in her stony facade. Frances had the good grace to look sheepish, and she glanced away and back to her screen.

Alicia felt her anger rising, rippling out. "Poor innocent Isla-Mae. Like I said, you should have stopped at Ginny, not tried to keep cleaning up Saffron's mess. You see, I know you own a car, Frances, although I didn't at first. You lied to me about that—"

"I never lied."

"No, you're right, you were just tricky with your words. You told me Chloe and Kora had parking spaces but not you, you had to slum it on the bus, I think you said. I took that to mean you didn't drive, but you do drive, don't you? A white car as it happens. The same make and model as the one used in the hit-and-run."

"A popular make and model I think you'll find."

"That is true. But I think the police will find, when they check your address, that it's parked under a tree where flying foxes hang—a paperbark? Casuarina? Fig tree maybe? Worse, it's missing part of its front head light."

Frances rolled her eyes flippantly. "I don't even have the car anymore, Alicia, so that won't work. Sorry. Not sorry."

She sang the words, like this was amusing, and Alicia was running out of patience.

"I don't know how you live with yourself, Frances. How you can justify any of this. How you could possibly sit in waiting for an innocent young woman, then apply the accelerator and ram your car straight into her."

There was that flicker again. A flicker of guilt. So there is a heart under there, Alicia realised, and Isla-Mae might be Frances's Achilles heel.

So she decided to keep going, to lay it on thick.

"Poor, innocent Isla-Mae," Alicia said, "all alone out here from England. Just trying to find her place in the world. Just trying to be her *best self*, the kind of girl who loves your magazine. Would lap up every word. All she was doing that day was trying to be fit and healthy like *Styled* tells her to. Just going for a morning jog, minding her own business—"

"Bullshit."

Alicia blinked. "Sorry?"

Frances folded her arms tighter, looked away.

"You think she *deserved* it? Isla-Mae? That you had every right to sit in waiting for her? Like she was vermin? Then slam on the accelerator and barrel down towards her? Bowl her over like she was *nothing*? Like her life didn't—"

"Oh it was the tiniest of taps! Not my fault she's anorex—"

Frances stopped. She gulped. She smudged her lips shut. But it was too late. The words could not be unsaid.

Frances had inadvertently confessed to murder, and they both knew it.

CHAPTER 36
Getting to the Crunch

Despite her confession, Frances was now frantically back-pedalling. Of course she was.

"I'm just saying, it would have been a tiny tap, knowing the size of Isla-Mae. She's a twig. But I had nothing to do with that. Nope. Not a thing."

"Oh Jesus, Frances," said Alicia, patience now at zero. "You heard what I said about the flying foxes? They have evidence they can trace back to your address. And do you really expect me to believe the police aren't going to find a paper trail to a local mechanic who fixed a busted front light for you?"

Frances paled a little then; it was almost heartening to see. Perhaps she wasn't quite as clever as she thought she was. Then she sat back and glanced around the room. When she finally spoke, she sounded almost weary, like she was unloading a burden and glad of it.

"Everything I say in here is off the record, right? Means you can't use any of it?"

"Of course."

She sat forward. "No, I mean this literally, Alicia. It's in your Code of Ethics. I know all about that, so you cannot repeat a single word. Yes or no?"

"Yes," Alicia said. "I can assure you, Frances, I won't repeat a thing. I will honour the code." And she wasn't lying about that.

Frances watched her closely for a bit more, then said, "Show me your phone."

"What?"

"Just do it."

Alicia pulled her mobile out and placed it on the desk. Frances tapped it, clearly checking it wasn't on and recording, then leaned back in her chair and sighed.

"If I did hit Isla—and I'm not saying I did—but *if* I did, speaking hypothetically, it would have been a terrible accident, one I never meant to happen. But you have no proof I had anything to do with that or Ginny's death. Nothing! If you did, I would have been arrested five minutes after she hit the tracks."

Alicia nodded. "Fair enough, but let's get back to Isla, shall we? Because I want to know why that poor innocent girl had to die."

"She didn't!" Frances was growing angrier, more indignant. It was clear she did not like this line of inquiry. Ginny's death had amused her. Isla's death not so much. "Look… off the record again, yeah? I just wanted her to fall, be hurt enough so I could help her inside and find that stupid report Ginny never should have stolen in the first place. *She's* the one who started all this. She's the one with blood on her hands."

Unbelievable, thought Alicia, but she let it slide as Frances continued.

"I tried to get in without hurting Isla. I did. I tried the day before, when she was on that shoot with Kora. But the stupid place was locked up tight. I tried again that night, after the shoot, but sleazy Austin was over, trying his luck, even though he's sleeping with Chloe, the cretin."

"How did you know he and Chloe—?"

Alicia stopped. Of course Frances knew about Hamish and Chloe's secret affair. And of course Austin was trying his luck with Isla. That had nothing to do with sex and everything to do with getting into her apartment and finding that missing report for Ted.

Alicia amended her question. "How did you even know to look for the report at Ginny's place? I only worked it out because of what Isla said to me at the memorial, and you weren't at the memorial. You were back here, manning the phones."

"Where else was Ginny going to hide it? I couldn't find it in the junk on her desk." A smarmy smile. Yes, of course she'd been the one to clear Ginny's things away. "But also, Tiani blabbed about it."

"Tiani?"

She shrugged. "If you think about it, it's her fault too. She gave me all the goss, after the memorial when they all filed back in. Said she'd overheard Isla speaking to you. Said she sounded hopeful, like the truth was going to come out about Ginny. The fool."

"So you had to act before I visited Isla on Sunday?"

Another shrug. "Tiani also said Arabella was forcing Kora to hire Isla-Mae for Saturday's shoot. Said it was good PR or something even though Isla's way too scrawny for yoga wear. You need a bit of shape, like me. Hips. Some boobs would help."

She blinked, seemed suddenly irritable. "Look, if Isla had just stuck to what she does best—strutting about on the catwalk—none of it would have happened. But how dare she try to interfere in all of this? The sales figures are none of her business, and they're certainly none of yours!"

"Except they absolutely are," Alicia snapped back. "Saffron pretending her magazine is doing better means the rest of us get less from the budget. It means advertisers are being hoodwinked. It's fraud!"

"It's called gumption, Alicia. It's what you do to keep your magazine going. Keep it alive."

"What are you talking about?" Alicia scoffed. "The magazine was still selling fine, even with its fall. You didn't need to—"

"I know that! Everyone knows that, except stupid bloody Ginny. Making such a big fuss about it. If she had blabbed, it would have become a big deal. Saffron might have lost her job over it. Can you imagine *Styled* without Saffron?" She looked horrified at the thought. "I did it to save Saffron."

"You did it to save yourself!"

"No!"

"Yes, Frances. Yes! Because this is all you have, isn't it?" Alicia flung a hand around the office. "You say this magazine helps readers live their best life? Well what about you? Is this your best life? Sitting in here, trawling through Saffron's junk mail? You have no life outside of these four walls. I know you live with your dad, still. Blake tells me you're estranged from your mum. Saffron's clearly a mother figure to you. Your only purpose in life. And that's why you killed two perfectly innocent women."

"There was nothing innocent about Ginny!" she screamed back, no longer caring who heard her. Or perhaps she thought Alicia's code was going to save her. "You need to stop calling her innocent! She was a slutty little troublemaker, and she deserved everything she got!"

Then she slapped Alicia with a defiant look and added, "But like I said, nothing to do with me. Your cop husband might link me to Isla's unfortunate accident, but you have no proof I had anything to do with Ginny. *Nothing.* Not a shred."

Again, Alicia nodded, conceding the point, and it emboldened her.

Frances leaned forward and said, "You know it's quite easy to make someone look like they're stepping in front of a train. You just slip in behind them and place your knee behind theirs. And they buckle. Super easy. I'm surprised it doesn't happen more often."

Alicia gasped now, unable to hide the horror in her eyes.

Frances just smirked and added, "But you never heard that from me. And no one will believe you, Alicia, because you're like the boy who cried wolf. Is there anyone left in this building you haven't accused? I know you spoke to Chloe and Saffron and Austin, even Mr Johnson. How rude you were, Dionne said. How brazen! You have all the subtlety of… of *Ginny* now I think of it. I heard her bitching about Saffron every chance she got. Then freaking her out at the Opera House on her special night. A night she should have been celebrating Saffron, not whispering in her ear about the sales figures. Wasn't brave enough to come out with it, but I knew she knew. She was as subtle as a sledgehammer."

"She was more subtle than you give her credit for, Frances, because Ginny left some clues about all of this on my desk before she died."

Now Frances was frowning and Alicia was the one feeling smarmy.

"That's right, you never spotted her dropping those clues did you? Probably too busy planning her murder. But Ginny knew I loved a good mystery, and she left a bunch of clues that led me to you. If it wasn't for Ginny, I'd be none the wiser."

Frances looked annoyed by that, vexed even, and so Alicia added, "And you never did find that circulation report. She outsmarted you there too. Even though you tore the place apart when you finally got in. See that was another red flag for me. If you'd done it carefully, I might've let that one slide too. Did you know it was hidden in a champagne bottle? You should've looked above the fridge."

The PA's eyes widened with surprise, and Alicia was rolling hers now.

"See, if you had bothered to get to know Ginny, really know her, you might have worked it out for yourself. If you had bothered to ask her about the report, you might have learned she wasn't going to use it to bring down Saffron or your precious magazine. She was just being mischievous. She wasn't malicious like you. She didn't willingly mow down an innocent woman to get access—"

"It was just a gentle bump!" she railed now. "How many times do I have to tell you? And I did stop! I parked down the road and went back and checked on her, but it was too late."

"Bullshit!" Alicia boomed, her anger now rolling out. "You weren't checking on her, you were searching for her keys, stealing her phone, letting yourself into her apartment so you could find that report. And you weren't doing it for Saffron or even for *Styled*. You did it to clean up the mess *you* left when you murdered Ginny. Because that report would lead back to the magazine and ultimately to you."

Frances was shaking her head now as if she wanted it all to go away or, more specifically, Alicia. She slowly got to her feet, stepped out from her desk.

"You know what? I'm done. This is getting us nowhere, and I have so much work to do. Like, serious amounts before Saffron gets back on Monday."

And Alicia gasped again, because after everything she'd just said, after confessing to two murders, her biggest concern was pleasing her boss?

My God, Frances really was a devoted stooge.

"None of this matters anyway," Frances continued, picking up Alicia's phone and handing it to her, "because I'll deny everything and no one will believe you. Like I said, you have form, Alicia. And I have work to do, so if you don't mind, I want to get on with it."

"Actually, Frances, I don't think you'll be doing any more work today. In fact..."

She also stood up, then strode across the room, to one side, where a camera was resting on a tripod. It was the same camera used to record Claire's vlog the previous week. It was switched on and it *was* recording.

"I think your job is now complete," Alicia told her. "And happily so is mine."

Then she tapped the camera gently and Frances just frowned. She stared at the machine for a full minute, then across to Alicia, looking disappointed.

"You *recorded* this? You really are an incompetent journalist! I said this was off the record. I said that clearly, several times. You can't use anything, Alicia. It was obtained illegally. You never got my permission. You might as well delete it now."

Alicia held her palms out. "This isn't journalism, this is police business. A warrant to record was issued first thing this morning, and nothing is off the record." Then she clapped her hands three times and said, "Sorry. Not sorry."

Frances frowned harder and turned full circle as Detective Inspector Jackson appeared in the doorway, followed closely by two uniformed officers. Shockingly, despite the frown, Frances did not look nearly as worried as she should. She just folded her arms and leaned against her desk and raised her chin defiantly, like she hadn't a care in the world.

And then a third person walked in.

She was wearing designer jeans and a Burberry trenchcoat, her hair in a topknot, deep disappointment breaking through her heavily Botoxed brow.

"Saffron?" Frances said, like she couldn't believe her eyes. "Oh, hey! I didn't realise you were here." Her tone had turned girlish, sickly sweet. "I… I don't know what you think you heard but—"

"Shut up, you stupid girl!" Saffron bellowed, striding towards her. "How could you? What were you thinking?"

Frances blinked back at her, eyes wide, lashes batting. "I… I don't know what you mean."

Saffron snarled. "Oh for God's sake! I heard everything. How could you possibly do something so monstrous?"

"But… but…"

"*But, but…*" Saffron mimicked her, cruelly mocking.

Frances gulped, her eyes now soggy. "I did it for you, Saffron. Ginny was trying to destroy the magazine. I… I did it to protect you."

"Did I *ask* you to do that for me? To kill the poor woman?"

"But you hated her! You kept saying how lazy she was and hopeless and—"

"*Human!*" roared Saffron now. "She was a human being, you fool! And one I could handle. I was shifting her to Sales. You didn't have to push her into a train!"

"But… but it wasn't just that. She was going to tell everyone about the report, the one she stole from Austin. She was going to take down the magazine. She was going to destroy your career."

Saffron looked more outraged by that comment than anything else. Her eyes were wide with fury. "Don't be so absurd! You think *that* would destroy me? Something so trivial?"

"But if they found out—"

"So what? Who cares? I would survive it! I don't need you to protect me. I've survived a lot worse. But oh my God, nothing is going to save you now, you evil little monster! You are finished. Gone. I can't even *look* at you!"

And that's when Frances finally crumbled, Saffron's disappointment like kryptonite to the young stooge, and she dropped to her knees, gasping into her hands, unable to show her face now while Saffron tsked and turned and stormed away.

And Alicia dragged her eyes from Frances to Saffron and watched her exit the room, wondering if the *Styled* editor understood that she was probably finished too. She sounded confident, but it was highly unlikely she'd survive this scandal. *Styled* too.

And if that happened, there was only one woman responsible.

Alicia stared back at Frances, now shrunken on the carpet, and sighed. After everything the devoted minion had done, she would go to prison knowing she was the one who had destroyed her beloved editor and magazine.

She hadn't helped them fly at all.

She had made them crash and burn…

EPILOGUE

Styled magazine did survive but only just. It was hanging on by its bootstraps or as Chloe might say, its Jimmy Choos. And despite everything that happened, Alicia was glad. If only for the remaining staff who did work hard and didn't deserve any of this.

Because when the news hit, soon after Frances's arrest, there was nothing Arabella could do to gloss over this one. The optics were woeful, and the advertisers fled in droves.

However, despite her confidence, Saffron did not survive. She had been unceremoniously "let go". Currently "travelling abroad", according to Arabella's media release, "enjoying a much-needed rest". And when she read that, Alicia realised that perhaps Saffron had survived after all. It wasn't a bad way to retire.

Chloe had also been sacked over the "Pilfered Product Scandal", as it was dubbed in the tabloids, and was last seen hocking her designer accessories at a seconds store.

Ted and Austin had been dismissed too, no golden parachute to soften their fall, and the new CEO was a haughty Englishwoman who scared the bejesus out of all of them but who seemed straight as an arrow, and Alicia liked that. She looked incorruptible. The advertisers liked that too and were returning, slowly, and mostly because *Styled* magazine had never looked so good.

As Alicia pored over the latest issue now, she hoped Frances could somehow see a copy in prison and realise that *Styled* was never just down to her and Saffron alone. It was always a team effort, and they had all pulled together to keep the magazine afloat. And no one more than Tiani.

That was biggest surprise of all. Despite Saffron's lack of

faith in her, the deputy editor was proving to be a dynamo, and while ad revenue had slumped, sales were booming. Tiani knew her reader and it showed. She also brought a softness to the magazine, the heart that had been missing, and they were gaining thousands of new readers every day.

And nothing illustrated this better than the double-page spread Alicia was now staring at, eyes welling with tears. It was a tribute to Virginia DeRossc and Isla-Mae Cavendish. There were behind-the-scenes photos of Ginny working with Isla on beauty and fashion shoots and plenty more of Ginny at glossy lunches and launches and product reveals. One of her assisting at a Margot Robbie cover shoot, another holding up Victoria Beckham's "Posh Gloss" and pretending to gasp. But there was no joy in her eyes, Alicia could see that clearly. Not like the image of Ginny seated behind the Arial reception desk, birthday cake in front of her, flowers just behind. She had a genuine glint in her eyes and a massive smile on her lips.

Alicia smiled along. She remembered that day. The moment that photo was taken.

It was Ginny's twenty-fifth birthday, and Alicia had done a whip-around and got her the flowers and cake, then snuck up and sang happy birthday, Hamish joining in, booming from behind. That was back when Ginny worked reception, where she probably should have stayed. She was happy out there, front of house, flirting with the couriers and keeping an eye across all the gossip coming in and out of the building. She was never suited to *Styled*, should never have been moved. Was always a square peg in a round hole in there.

Not everyone had grand ambitions, and it should have been okay.

Here at the reception desk, Ginny looked just as Alicia remembered her, or wanted to remember her at least. Happy and carefree and full of life.

"Looks so young there," said Hamish, staring over her shoulder.

Alicia glanced up. "She was. And always too young for you."

He sniggered. Their banter hadn't changed.

"You did good," he told her. "Saved my arse, thank you." It wasn't the first time he'd said those words.

"I did it for Ginny as much as you," she replied, also not for the first time.

Ginny didn't deserve what happened to her, and she certainly didn't ask for it. She was just a mischievous young woman with a mystery she wanted to share. Until Frances intervened.

"Heard any more about the court case?" he asked.

She shook her head. "It's progressing." But slowly.

Soon after Saffron stormed out, the day of the grand reveal, Jackson had stepped forward, cuffs in hand, and read Frances her rights, including the right to remain silent. Which she did, later retracting her confession and hiring a top barrister. But it wasn't going to save her. Not when there was bat faeces and a mechanic's report to explain away.

As suspected, there were large Eucalypts outside Frances's father's house, their colony of flying foxes splattering helpful evidence all over her white 2008 Toyota Corolla. And while she'd driven the car straight to her estranged mother's place in the Blue Mountains, pretending to offer it as a gift, a "palm branch", the truth was Frances was just palming off the problem. Because if her mum got that headlight fixed, it would be under *her* name, a different surname, a hundred kilometres away.

Clever, really, but not too clever for Jackson who managed to track it down. Another person she'd underestimated.

That alone should see her convicted of the vehicular manslaughter of Isla-Mae Cavendish. Alicia had been disappointed by the downgraded charge but knew it didn't really matter. It didn't bring Isla back, just as the murder charge did not bring back Ginny.

Alicia rubbed a finger gently across her dear friend's cheek as she grinned wickedly from the page. She was so much more than a receptionist or a beauty assistant or a girl who liked to flirt. Unlike Frances, Ginny had a full and happy life, was a devoted daughter and friend, flatmate and colleague.

And Alicia might not have been so devoted at the end there, but she'd made up for it now, and then some.

"She was my friend," Alicia told Hamish now. "Our friend. I did it for her." Then she dropped her head to the side and added, "Besides, she would've haunted me if I let you go down for something Frances did. Urgh."

He laughed. "Too right!" Then he said, "You nickin' off now?"

She nodded, and he drew her into a hug this time. When he pulled back, she noticed tears in his eyes, and he coughed and pretended it was nothing and left her to it.

Checking the time, she powered down her computer, scooped up her things and made her way out. Because she had a full and happy life too, not to mention great family and friends. She was meeting with the book club now. She had something she needed to show them.

It was long overdue.

~

"Ready?" asked Jackson, hearing the first knock on the freshly painted door.

She glanced around the room, admiring the small sofa and cushions she'd found on eBay, the desk, the computers, then nodded.

"Oh, I've been ready for a long while."

He stepped across and pulled her close. "Don't I know it." Then he kissed her gently, leaned back and nodded towards the door as the knocking got louder. "How do you think they'll take it?"

She shrugged. "Happy? Proud? Curious why we're standing in here while they're all outside?"

He laughed and let her go, then strode across and swept the door open.

The entire book club were standing out on the stairwell, some perusing the exterior sign confused, others glancing around curiously, one wielding a bottle of Australian sparkling wine.

That was Lynette and she offered Alicia a sly wink as they all filed inside.

"She won't tell us what's going on," pouted Perry. "Don't tell me you've left your lovely little apartment to reside in this…" He swung around. "Office?"

After kissing them hello, Alicia said, *"Private Investigator's* office actually." Then she stepped back to stand beside Jackson at the reception desk.

"I've left Arial," she told them, "and I'm hanging out my shingle. I'm now officially a PI."

"What?" This was Missy, squealing and swallowing her in a hug. "Oh my *God!* That's the best. You will be so *amazing.*"

Alicia laughed as she was swallowed again, then Jackson produced a second bottle of bubbly and a tray of empty flutes.

"Why didn't you tell us?" asked Ronnie, taking a glass. "Why didn't *you?* You clearly knew." She was staring at Lynette, who looked suitably shamefaced.

"She swore me to secrecy," said Lynette, also taking a glass and now plonking down on the guest sofa in front of reception.

"I wanted to make sure it was real first," Alicia explained. "I'm not sure I believed it was even happening myself until now."

As the sparkling wine began flowing, Alicia propped herself on the empty reception desk and explained.

Ginny's death had been a wake-up call for Alicia. She didn't need evil Frances to tell her she was unhappy at Arial. Blind Freddy could see she hadn't been happy for a long time. And it wasn't just Ginny's absence from the building. Alicia realised she was no longer satisfied producing the kind of content that sold magazines.

"Nothing wrong with Tay Tay," said Perry, clasping a hand to his heart.

"You're right," she said, laughing. "But I was the wrong person for the job. Ginny's death helped me realise life is short and I need to do what gets me out of bed in the mornings and puts a skip in my step."

"Murder!" said Missy.

"Mystery," she said, correcting her. "It doesn't have to be so extreme." Although solving a murder was the most imperative mystery of all and one she was good at. "I realised I could use my dark imagination for good—I'm always thinking the worst, right? So why not put it to use and help people solve real mysteries for a living? Seems like a win-win. Plus I couldn't keep interfering in Jackson's cases to satisfy my appetite. It wasn't fair on him. Or Singh."

Jackson sighed heavily, propping up beside her. "Poor Indira, she never could get used to you guys interfering."

"Tough!" called out Ronnie, but Alicia shook her head.

"Not fair on Jackson though, being caught in the cross fire. He's the one who came up with all of this."

She swept her hand around the room, and now he explained.

While Alicia was pretending not to investigate the two murders, he started working on a solution that would suit everybody. It's the reason he stayed late at work and got up early—he was doing what he does best and getting all his ducks in place, checking their bank balance, doing the research.

One night, soon after he'd locked Frances away, Jackson presented Alicia with a solution—why didn't she hand in her resignation and train to be a private investigator? While PIs operate independently from the police force, they often cooperate, especially in complex criminal cases. She wouldn't have law enforcement powers, but she'd have every right to ask her questions and probe for answers. There'd be a lot less acrimony.

Alicia loved the idea immediately. Couldn't believe she hadn't thought of it herself. They both had plenty of savings, enough to open her own practice.

As a trained PI, Alicia could still set her mind to solving crime—her true skill set—while no longer being a "meddling amateur". She would now be a professional. She'd be on the right side of the law and get paid for it.

"I'll toast to that!" said Ronnie, holding up her glass. "You deserve to be paid for your skills, young woman. Long overdue."

They all agreed and raised their glasses to Alicia.

"So it's that simple?" asked Missy. "You just open an agency and go for it?"

"Oh no, it wasn't simple," Alicia replied. She turned and pointed to a framed certificate on the wall. "I've been studying at night. Just completed my certificate three in Investigative Services."

There was another round of gasping and toasting, and several jumped up to study the qualification while others, well, Missy, swamped Alicia with hugs again.

Alicia then explained how she'd handed in her resignation at Arial soon after Frances's arrest and how they'd begged her to stay on to help. The company was now in chaos with their CEO gone, not to mention their Sales and Circulation manager and half the *Styled* team.

So she agreed to hang around on a part-time basis for the next six months, mentoring Tiani in the way Saffron never had, and pumping out a few specials while studying for her licence, learning things like surveillance and evidence collection and report writing.

"Oh, you can do all that in your sleep," said Claire. "You've already been doing it."

Perry said, "No wonder you've gone so quiet on us. I figured you were just lost in Loveland."

"Like *you* can talk," said Alicia, who knew Tag had now officially moved in with Perry. Then she glanced lovingly at Jackson, who smiled back.

He also had some news, telling them how he was no longer working with DI Singh on the Homicide Squad.

"I'm so sorry about you two," said Claire. "I know you were close."

He shrugged. "We're still close but not like we were. And it's better this way. I don't keep infuriating her—"

"And by 'I' he means me," said Alicia, pointing to herself.

Jackson laughed. "Well, if you meddle in a homicide now, it's not my problem."

"I pity Singh," said Perry, and they laughed again.

"So where are you moving to?" Queenie asked Jackson.

He gulped from his glass and said, "I've transferred to the Missing Persons Registry. I'm heading a team of analysts and detectives, investigating fresh disappearances as well as cold cases. I'm really looking forward to making a difference and, if I do my job right, finding people long before they reach Singh's desk."

They drank to that, then Missy said, "And we can always help you. We're good at finding people, aren't we, folks? We found a missing person in our very first case."

Jackson nearly choked on his wine. "Whoa, maybe let me settle in first." Then he cocked his head sideways and added, "I've just helped Alicia get qualified, do I need to sign you up for a Cert three too?"

Missy giggled. "Well… maybe…"

Alicia locked eyes with her. "I would love a partner, Missy, if you ever get bored at the library."

She was being serious, and Missy looked like she just might take her up on it, eyes twinkling behind her cat-eye glasses.

Jackson said, "Okay, one PI at a time please." He retrieved a bottle, topping up their sparkling wine, then added a drop to Alicia's saying, "Drink up, woman. We're celebrating."

Raising his flute, he called them back to attention. "I want to toast my brilliant wife, who is going to make one incredible detective—"

"*Going* to?" said Ronnie, one eyebrow now cocked.

He quickly corrected himself. "To Alicia, who is *already* an incredible detective but will soon make it official. Here's to the sharpest, most intuitive, *sexiest* gumshoe in the biz!"

They all cheered again, then Queenie said, "You don't need a PA do you?"

"Don't you *dare*," Claire gasped out. "My Simon would

be lost without you."

And Perry said, "I could come in and add some pizazz to these furnishings, Alicia. Honestly, darls, I'm not sure where you got those woeful cushions from."

And Lynette said, "I can bring you lovely packed lunches."

And Ronnie said, "And I can drop in and help you eat them while we chew over your cases."

And Alicia laughed and thanked them all because she knew she would still need them and call on them and there would always be their fortnightly book club to do some more chewing. For now, despite her untouched bubbly, she was drunk on happiness, and it was long overdue.

And so, as they settled in and caught up on each other's lives, she sat back watching. Filled with joy. It had been a long and sometimes turbulent road, but finally Alicia felt like she was doing what she was born to do, what her vivid imagination had been signalling to her all along. Now she could use it for good. Against evil.

She had found her true calling.

Smiling wider, she glanced down at her untouched champagne and then across to her husband who, for all his smarts, hadn't yet unravelled the latest exciting mystery in his life. But he'd know soon. She couldn't wait to deliver the happy news!

Then she patted her still-flat belly and made a silent toast to Ginny.

Thank you, my dear friend.
Farewell and thank you.

~~ the end ~~

ACKNOWLEDGEMENTS

First a correction. While I did once work in the dazzling world of women's magazines, please let me stress—none were as vacuous as the fictitious *Styled*, nor was anyone as nefarious as Saffron. In fact, I had a terrific time and my first editor, Lisa Wilkinson at *Cleo*, was a gem. The best mentor a young writer could ask for. Thank you for your kindness and encouragement, Lisa. It is not forgotten.

Might I also point out that my time in magazines was many moons ago, and the industry has no doubt changed significantly since then, so please forgive any inaccuracies and remember, it's a work of fiction, folks.

Or as Austin might say, "Just a bit of fun."

Speaking of fun, the Murder Mystery Book Club first started as a light bulb moment in the dead of night, fifteen years ago. I jumped up, googled the idea and held my breath, hoping it hadn't been done before. And it hadn't!

That's when my *fiction* career really kicked off.

Today, this is my bestselling mystery series with fans right across the globe and it's YOU I want to thank most of all. If you hadn't joined the Club, we would never have got to Book 2, let alone this eighth instalment. And I never would have moved beyond magazines to a world I am so much better suited to, crazed killers notwithstanding.

Thanks also to my agents and publishers in Japan and Europe, especially Marie Misandeau at Le Cherche Midi for being such a believer in this series, and to my French translator, Tania Capron, for querying my strange Aussie slang with good humour and warmth.

Thanks also to my agent, Gregory Messina, for being both a shoulder to cry on and a kick up the proverbial. I look forward to plotting more murders with you!

Thanks, as always, to my family, especially Christian, Nimo and Felix, and my editing team Annie Sarac and Elaine Rivers. Thank you to Nimo for another stunning cover and Kasper for walking me daily so I can keep the "leetle grey cells" firing.

Which brings me to my greatest inspiration, the Queen of Crime herself, the incomparable Agatha Christie. Without her magnificent mysteries this Book Club might not exist. And how sad would that be?

xo Christina

ALSO BY C.A. LARMER

Blind Men Don't Dial Zero
(Sleuths of Last Resort 1)

POLICE say the case is open-and-shut: The heir to a massive fortune slaughters his parents, confesses to the crimes, then turns the gun on himself. His grandfather says, "Not so fast."
With the case now closed, Sir George assembles his own crack team of detectives—five amateur sleuths with a nose for mystery and a need to prove themselves—then pits them against each other to solve it.

"Will have even the most seasoned sleuth baffled as these amateurs tackle a wealthy family, loyal employees, and unsavoury boyfriends. You will find this action-filled journey unforgettable and hard to put down"
Peggy Jo Wipf for Readers' Favorite

Killer Twist (Ghostwriter Mystery 1)

KILLER TWIST is the first stand-alone mystery in the popular 'amateur sleuths' series featuring gutsy ghostwriter Roxy Parker and her motley mates.

"Roxy is a compelling character and I couldn't help but adore her. She's 30, hip and fiercely independent. A great cozy."
Rhonda @ Amazon

"A fun read ... an easy style ... Lots of local flavour."
Parents' Little Black Book @ Amazon

calarmer.com